**She wanted to flee from the haggard, gray-faced** stranger in front of her, but she couldn't move.

"Aggie told me you were upstairs packing. You should've gone last week instead of coming to school like nothing was wrong."

"I didn't…" Her voice died away.

"I told you to go, and you didn't listen." His eyes—colder than they'd been the day he tore up her contract—repelled her now, where before they'd drawn her into his heart.

"I'm sorry. I didn't think…"

"It doesn't matter what you thought," he interrupted her. "All that matters is that you and your pupils almost died."

She stepped aside as he started laboriously for the door, his leg dragging.

"I didn't ask you to love me, either," she managed to whisper as he came even with her.

He stopped, but this time he didn't look at her. "It was a fling, that's all. A fling, like Gwen said. Go home, Miss Cooper. I want you out of Camden permanently."

When the outside door opened and closed, Ruthann raced to the window and watched him struggle down the walk toward his car. At one point, she thought he was going to fall, but he managed to stay upright.

*Was I really just a fling? All those talks we shared, all those sweet, sweet kisses…were they all lies? Am I really such a fool, believing anyone could love me the way I thought you did? Oh, Drew, why did you let me love you?*

**Other books by this author**
**and available from The Wild Rose Press, Inc.**
*Where Is Papa's Shining Star?*
*Finding Papa's Shining Star*
*Dancing With Velvet*
*The Showboat Affair* (writing as Gwyneth Greer)

# Ruthann's War

by

Judy Nickles

**Ruthann's War**

Cover Art by *Tina Lynn Stout*

The Wild Rose Press, Inc.
PO Box 708
Adams Basin, NY 14410-0708
Visit us at www.thewildrosepress.com

Publishing History
First Vintage Rose Edition, 2017
Print ISBN 978-1-5092-1140-1
Digital ISBN 978-1-5092-1141-8


Published in the United States of America

## Dedication

To all the men who fought in two world wars
and the women who kept the home fires burning

Chapter One

A hot wind whipped Ruthann's new red-and-gray-plaid fall skirt around her legs as she turned to wave to the young men hanging out the windows of the train now gathering steam. Half a dozen of them, still in uniform, had kept her laughing and sometimes almost weeping on the two-hour trip from San Antonio to Camden. "I've had me a bellyful of war," one freckle-faced private told her as he described the hell of the Huertgen Forest. "I'm going home to my daddy's farm and never leave till they carry me down to the churchyard."

She blew kisses with black-gloved fingertips as the train began to move. "Goodbye! Be good," she called. "Have a happy life!" They were going home for good. Home from every corner of the world, where they'd fought to stay alive for just such a day as this. Her arm drifted to her side as Jack's face replaced all those filling the windows of the train. His laughing eyes, just the way she'd seen them for the last time three years earlier, brought tears. She thought she'd shed them all and had no more, but they were back, blurring her vision and dimming the joy of the moment.

She'd seen him off at the depot in Denton on another too-warm September day much like this one. The small diamond he'd given her only the night before had sparkled in the midmorning sun as she ran along the platform with the moving train, waving and mouthing silently, "I love you! See you soon!" But today her finger beneath the cotton glove was bare. She'd returned the ring to his parents despite their protests.

She hadn't thought of him in months, though she'd kept his framed picture on her dressing table. In fact, she'd slipped it into her trunk at the last minute, more out of habit than need.

"Miss Cooper?"

For a moment she felt disoriented, as if she inhabited two spheres. Then she turned toward the voice. "I'm Ruthann Cooper."

The older of the two women, both wearing summer dresses in deference to the heat, extended her hand. "I'm Kay Clifton. My husband is the school principal."

"Oh, yes," Ruthann responded. "I interviewed with him. How kind of you to meet my train."

"I'm Rena Gilbert," the other spoke up. "You'll be taking my third grade this year. I got promoted." She tossed back straight, dark hair which fell to her slender shoulders. "At least, I think I did."

"We'll get your bags and take you to the boarding house to meet Aggie," Kay said.

"Aggie's the mother superior." Rena tossed her hair again. Ruthann noticed how the sun glanced off the thick silky strands and illuminated the young woman's smooth olive complexion. *Another beauty, just like Rose Ellen. It looks like I'll be the ugly duckling here, too.*

"Aggie Pollard," Kay said, moving toward the baggage claim area. "She and her husband Harry own the boarding house where some of the single teachers

2

live. You'll like them."

"And she's a wonderful cook," added Rena. "She caters community affairs all over town. You'll gain ten pounds the first month."

The short ride to the boarding house on a shady corner only a few blocks from the depot provided little time to talk. "You'll meet everyone tomorrow at the teachers' meeting," Kay said as she leaned out the window of the pre-war Packard. "And between now and then, I'm sure Rena will tell you more about the Camden schools than you want to know." She winked, waved, and shifted gears. "See you in the morning."

Model-tall and stylish in a sky-blue voile dress, a fiftyish Aggie Pollard looked anything but cloistered as Rena made the introductions. "Your room's ready," Aggie said. "You're right next door to this one, and she'll talk your ears off if you're not careful."

Rena stuck out her bottom lip. "Now, Aggie, that's not nice."

The older woman flicked her fingers in dismissal. "I'm doing dinner for the first DAR meeting of the year," she said. "Harry's going to set out a buffet at six. You might give him a hand cleaning up."

Rena saluted. "I'll volunteer for KP, General." Upstairs, she threw open the door to a large room where sheer white curtains billowed inward from the open windows, and a wooden ceiling fan whined in protest as it circulated the warm air. "Bath's at the end of the hall. Actually, both ends. Mr. Wolfe, who's the lone male, has a room with a private bath, for which all the ladies are extremely grateful. Of course, he's been here the longest, too."

Ruthann set down her bag and looked around. "Oh,

good, my trunk's been delivered." She crossed the patterned carpet to touch it. "That was fast. The man in San Antonio told me it might be a week or ten days because of everything they're shipping from the bases that are closing to those staying open."

"It came yesterday. What do you have in there? It took both delivery men to haul it up the stairs, and they were huffing and puffing like the big bad wolf. I gave them a good tip for their trouble."

"What do I owe you?" Ruthann opened her purse.

"Two dollars." Rena pocketed the bills. "It was probably too much, but the weather was hotter than Hades yesterday. I'll leave you to get settled, unless you'd like some company while you unpack."

"Please stay," Ruthann said and wished immediately she hadn't felt the need to be polite. She stripped off her gloves and the fitted red jacket which her mother had warned would be too warm for the journey. She'd worn it anyway because she wanted to look professional for her first teaching position. From a matching red leather handbag, she produced a key and unlocked the trunk. "Tell me about the school. About Camden."

Rena curled herself in the faded corner armchair. "It's a good place to live. A good place to work. Mostly."

Ruthann didn't like the way Rena said *mostly* but decided not to pursue it. "Why are you going up to fourth grade this year?" she asked instead.

"Because we're getting a student from Mexico who doesn't speak English, and I'm fluent in Spanish."

"Did you learn in high school or college?"

"Neither." Something about the curt reply triggered

Ruthann's curiosity, but she didn't pursue that topic either.

"I grew up with a neighbor who spoke only Polish, but the best we ever managed was a combination of pidgin English and signs." Ruthann laid a stack of folded blouses on the bed and went to the old-fashioned wardrobe for hangers.

"Being bilingual has been an advantage in a lot of ways. Miguel's father is an American who has a business in Mexico and plans to convert the ball-bearing factory to peacetime production. It brought Camden out of an economic slump during the war, and we'd hate to lose it now. So Mr. Mallory told John Clifton to do whatever it took to make the man happy."

Ruthann consigned a half dozen blouses to the wardrobe and went back to the trunk. "So they're not migrant workers."

"Oh, no, although there's a school for the children of migrant workers, but it only operates a few months a year." Rena uncurled her legs and stretched them in front of her. "You said you interviewed with Mr. Clifton."

"He seemed very nice. So does his wife."

"They are. They lost their oldest son at Iwo Jima, by the way. David. He was pre-med at the University of Texas when he enlisted."

The blouse in Ruthann's hands slipped from her fingers back onto the bed. "Oh. Oh, that's too bad. I'm very sorry." *We just thought the war was over, but it's not. We'll live with it the rest of our lives.*

"They've soldiered on. Their younger son, Daniel, teaches phys ed at the elementary school and helps the high school coach. He's nice enough, but he does seem to think a lot of himself. Did you happen to meet the superintendent when you came to interview? Drew Mallory?"

"I believe Mr. Clifton said he was out of town."

"Well, you'll meet him tomorrow. He's a good man. He looks after his teachers." She hesitated. "Two years ago I met someone, a second lieutenant stationed at Foster Field, and I really liked him. Then one day Mr. Mallory called me into his office and told me Edwin was married. He wouldn't tell me how he got his information, but he said he'd confirmed it with Edwin's commanding officer."

Ruthann straightened from the dresser drawer where she'd been arranging lingerie. "You had a narrow escape, then."

"Yes, I did. When I broke it off, Ed just laughed and said he'd never said he *wasn't* married."

A heaviness settled over Ruthann. "A lot of things happened during the war. A lot of things that shouldn't have happened."

Rena regarded her for a minute. "Look, I talk too much, and I know you're tired and need to settle in. I'll see you at dinner. Harry will ring a bell."

"Thanks for everything, Rena." When she was alone, Ruthann removed the framed picture of Jack from the tray of the trunk and set it on the lamp table beside the bed. He'd scrawled *All my love forever, Jack,* just under the new wings his mother had pinned on his uniform when he finished his training at Sheppard Field in Wichita Falls. His cap with the first lieutenant's insignia sat at a jaunty angle above his handsome—and so very young—face.

*If things had been different, I wouldn't be here.*

*We'd probably be married and living in our own home. You'd be a practicing attorney, if the war hadn't interrupted your plans. But it did, and you had to go off and get yourself killed and spoil it all.* Ruthann pushed away the anger which at some point had replaced stark grief. *Stop it, Ruthann. The Nazis killed Jack. It wasn't his fault. And why am I thinking about all this now, when I haven't thought of him in months?*

When she'd emptied the trunk, she shoved it against the wall on the other side of the bed and arranged a few books on top: a well-worn copy of Helen Hunt Jackson's *Ramona,* a volume of Elizabeth Barrett Browning's poetry, Edgar Lee Masters' *Spoon River Anthology,* and Thoreau's *Walden.*

In a spotless white-tiled bathroom a few steps down the hall, she splashed cool water on her face and arms and paused to take in the vista of a still-green backyard below the single high window. Back in her room, she powdered her nose and refreshed her lipstick just as a bell from somewhere below jarred the still air.

"Supper!" Rena called, tapping on her door.

The names and faces at the dinner table blurred in Ruthann's mind, but Rena went over them a second time as Ruthann helped her clean the kitchen afterwards. "Lillian Buford sat on your right. She teaches English at the high school. Rumor has it she lost a husband or fiancé in the first war."

Ruthann tried not to react beyond a simple, "Yes."

"Kitty Litton, who sat across from you, is the school librarian. Divorced, no children. Bernadette Clifton—Bernie—is the principal's sister-in-law. Her husband died the year before I came, so that must have been 1941. She teaches music. She and Kitty split their time between the high school and the grammar school. And Nathan Wolfe, the rather dour presence at the end of the table, teaches biology, chemistry, and physics at the high school. Keeps to himself, announces every year in March he's going to retire in May but never does. The kids like him because he makes learning fun for them. He's a perfect gentleman, so you don't have to worry. Oh, and Harry—that's Aggie's husband—is vice-president of the bank where most of us do business."

"I'm sure they're all very nice, and I'll get to know them," Ruthann murmured as she closed the silverware drawer.

"Everyone gets along. Mr. Clifton and Mr. Mallory run a tight ship." Rena hung the dishcloth on the service porch. "Ready to go up?" Without waiting for a reply, she led the way to the back stairs.

Just outside the door of her room, Ruthann hesitated. "You've been very kind to fill me in on everyone. I know I must seem a little standoffish."

"A little, but you're new, and everything's strange."

"My father has his own construction business, my mother volunteers all over San Antonio, my older sister is married with one child, and…and my fiancé died on a bombing raid over Germany in 1943."

Rena put a hand on Ruthann's arm. "I'm very sorry."

Ruthann nodded. "I finished college, came home, and went to work in a munitions factory instead of looking for a teaching position. Then when the war ended, I decided to try teaching since that's what I'd gone to school for."

"It'll be a good life here. I can say that after four years. My family lives in far west Texas, so I went to Sul Ross."

Ruthann chewed her lip. "You said it was *mostly* a good place."

"There are problems everywhere. Ours is named Merle Fulton, one of those rich women with too much time on their hands. Unfortunately, she's also a member of the school board. But just steer clear of her as much as you can. You'll be fine."

"She sounds like a lot of women I know."

Rena patted Ruthann's arm. "Breakfast at seven, and then we'll head to school for teachers' meetings. They're boring, but you'll meet the rest of the staff, and Mr. Mallory always finds the money to have Aggie cater lunch." She gave Ruthann's arm another pat and stepped through her own door.

Ruthann undressed in the moonlight streaming through the window sheers and got into bed. What she'd told Rena had been only half true. She didn't want to admit she'd long ago accepted Jack's death, even the fact his body had never been found. That's what hurt his family the most, that they couldn't bring him home. But they'd all accepted he was dead. He wasn't coming home, and she was already forgetting him. When she confessed to her mother how guilty she felt, Mary Ruth said, "Well, Ruthie, remember you didn't know him very long, only a few months. Now it's been two years since you saw him. Almost that long since he died. You shouldn't feel guilty."

Her older sister Rose Ellen was, as usual, more blunt. "You didn't have a boyfriend in high school, you chose a girls' school for college, and then there was the war. You were in love with love."

Ruthann didn't argue the point, but she mourned Jack as long as she was able. Then it was over. Grief turned to anger and then to regret as she did her bit for the war effort at home. But today the boys on the train had brought back the waste of his death and so many more, like the Cliftons' son David. *The war's over, so why do I feel like I'm still fighting? Maybe I'm only fighting myself, and I don't even know what I'm fighting for.*

Chapter Two

The principal introduced Ruthann before the meeting began. She endured a polite round of applause, but during the midmorning coffee break each teacher made it a point to welcome her personally. She gave up trying to keep names and faces straight. The voice of experience said they'd all fall into place eventually. As the lone new teacher, she found all the information almost overwhelming. She stayed too busy scribbling notes to be bored as Rena had predicted. She'd just jotted down the new attendance guidelines when John Clifton turned the meeting over to the superintendent, Drew Mallory.

Only slightly taller than Ruthann's five feet six inches without heels, and wearing a suit like the other men but with an open collar rather than a tie, he spoke so softly Ruthann strained to hear him from the back of the room. Given the cessation of all movement, she could tell he commanded everyone's attention. His barely lined face didn't match the age suggested by more than a few white strands threading his dark hair. But his blue eyes, bright like water reflecting the sun and sky, compelled more than her attention.

He finished the standard remarks—a combination of *welcome back, we're going to have a great year, I know each one of you will do his/her job*—with the announcement Aggie had arrived and only needed a

11

few more minutes to work her magic. As the teachers began to leave the library, he sought out Ruthann. Only then did she notice he walked haltingly with the aid of a cane.

"I'm sorry I wasn't here to meet you when you interviewed in June, but John Clifton gave you a glowing report."

Unaccustomed warmth suffused her cheeks. "I appreciate the opportunity to work here," she said politely. This time she felt certain those blue, blue eyes sought the depths of her soul. She looked away, but the scent of his shaving cream circled her like a lasso and pulled her in.

"I'm sure you'll like us, and we'll all like you. If you ever have a problem, my door's always open. I understand you're already installed at the boarding house. I hope you'll be comfortable. We've had a housing shortage since the war began, and I expect, with the factory conversion, more people will be looking for a place." His words, unhurried and matter of fact but with some underlying emotion Ruthann couldn't define, left her feeling like one of her soon-to-be third graders.

"I'm quite happy at the boarding house," she said.

"Excellent. Well, don't let yourself get overwhelmed with new faces and places. Miss Gilbert will give you a great deal of help, since she had the third grade for several years."

Ruthann nodded.

"I'll see you again today, I'm sure." He shook her hand, setting it on fire in a way Jack's touch had never done. As he moved away, Ruthann realized her gaze was following him and dropped her eyes.

At lunch, orchestrated at long tables set up in the main corridor, she found herself seated between Kay Clifton and a woman who introduced herself as Merle Fulton, a member of the school board and offspring of the town's founding family—emphasis on the latter. Attractive in a hard sort of way, and definitely overdressed for the occasion, she seemed almost too confident.

*Just my luck to run into her on the first day. She looks like trouble, too.* Ruthann tried to appear interested in what the woman was saying.

"I understand you finished college several years ago but this is your first teaching position."

Defensiveness took possession of Ruthann, but she managed to keep her voice neutral. "That's right. I wanted to contribute to the war effort, so I went to work in a munitions factory and also volunteered with my mother at the USO and the Red Cross."

"It seems strange to me you wouldn't want to get on with your teaching career."

"It doesn't seem strange to me," Kay interrupted. "I think it's very commendable."

Merle stabbed at a piece of tomato in her salad. "The skills you learned in college must have become rusty after being unused for so long."

"I don't think so," Ruthann said. "I hope not, anyway." She nodded at the bowl beyond Kay. "Will you pass me the salad dressing, please?"

In the afternoon, the teachers worked in their classrooms. Kay showed Ruthann to hers at the far end of the grammar school corridor. "Don't let Merle Fulton bother you," she said after closing the door behind them. "She's a nasty piece sometimes. She doesn't let anyone forget the Fultons founded this town. She thinks she's privy to everyone's business. Unfortunately, since she manages to get herself reappointed to the school board every three years, she's privy to ours, as well."

"I wondered how she knew I didn't teach during the war."

"I'm sure John mentioned it during the meeting when the board approved your contract. Listen, you can't avoid Merle altogether, but do your best not to get in her way. She doesn't like John because he stands up to her. He's crossed her more than once in the twenty years we've been here. When our older son died in the spring, she saw a chance to get rid of him by suggesting to the board he might not be emotionally capable of doing his job." Kay's voice rose slightly. "And she had the gall to do it in front of him!"

"Rena told me about your son," Ruthann said. "I'm very sorry. I lost my fiancé early in the war, though I realize it's not the same."

"It's very much the same. You don't ever completely recover from the loss of someone you love, but you go on. You don't have any choice." Kay chewed her lip for a brief moment. "Now, I'll leave you to get on with things. I'm sure Rena left everything well organized. Just explore all the cabinets and drawers. I see all your textbooks are on the floor under the windows."

"Thank you for coming to my rescue at lunch."

"It was my pleasure. But as I said, don't get in Merle's way if you can help it." She stopped short of the door. "I'm sure you're curious about Drew Mallory but too polite to ask."

"He's none of my business."

Kay lifted both hands. "But you wonder anyway, don't you? He had his leg almost blown off in the first war. When he came here a year after we arrived, he limped some, but he didn't use a cane. Now he can't do without it."

"I see."

"He's responsible for the good school system we have here. John was ready to resign, but when Drew replaced the former superintendent, John decided to give him a chance. As you can see, we're still here."

Ruthann nodded. "Thank you for telling me."

"I just thought you ought to know."

****

Hunkered down in a position her mother would call "unladylike" as she unpacked a variety of art supplies onto a low shelf, Ruthann almost didn't hear a familiar voice say, "Hello there. Hard at work already, I see." She felt her face flame as she tried to rise with some dignity but ended up scrambling to her feet and tugging at her dress like a schoolgirl. She hoped the man standing in the door smiling at her didn't notice she'd removed her hose to keep from snagging them.

"Yes," she said, tasting dust on her tongue. "Rena left things in order, but I wanted to put the new art supplies lower. I mean, for the children." She gritted her teeth. *I'm babbling. Why is he here already on my first day? Couldn't he give me time to get settled before he checked up on me?*

Drew Mallory's rubber-tipped cane made a surprisingly delicate sound on the polished wooden floor, but she heard his left foot dragging clumsily as he crossed the room and eased himself into a chair.

"You're the first new teacher since Miss Gilbert came, just before the war."

Ruthann wiped her hands on the back of her skirt. "Am I?"

"We don't have much turnover in Camden. John Clifton and I try to keep our teachers and staff happy."

"I'm sure you do." Feeling panic creep in, she took refuge behind the teacher's desk, which sat on an old-fashioned raised platform. She thought his eyes laughed, though his face remained pleasantly passive.

"I saw you had the misfortune to be seated next to Merle Fulton at lunch. I'm quite sure she engineered that arrangement. She wanted to get in her bluff, you see."

"Her bluff?"

"She considers herself more important than she really is and wants all the new teachers to think so, too." He watched her face for a reaction.

"Oh, well, there are always people like that."

"Absolutely. You mustn't let her bother you."

"No, I won't." *If he doesn't leave soon, I'm going to have to hide from those eyes somewhere. I've never seen eyes quite so blue and so deep. I think I'm drowning in them.*

He braced himself with his cane as he rose. "Well, I'll let you get on with it, Miss Cooper. As I said, if you have any problem, my door is always open."

"Thank you," she said. "I'll remember."

When he'd gone, she put her head down on the desk. *I can live without seeing him again the rest of the year.* She patted her perspiring face with a clean handkerchief from her purse and went back to the box of art supplies. But she kept seeing Drew Mallory's face reflected in every piece of cellophane she tore from the new packages of colored construction paper.

\*\*\*\*

At four-thirty, Rena knocked on the open door. "I hope you've found what you need. I tried to leave everything organized. Unfortunately, the fourth grade teacher who left us in May didn't do the same for me. I've been up to my elbows in a mess, or I'd have been in here sooner."

"You did a brilliant job, Rena. Look—I have one of the bulletin boards up and the books sorted on the desks."

"Which is more than I've done. But we have the rest of the week to work." She studied the colorful welcome-to-third-grade board by the door. "By the way, I heard you met Madame Fulton."

"Oh, yes. Kay gave me the same story you did."

"Avoid her like the plague."

"Believe me, I'll try."

"Unfortunately, she thinks she has to make an inspection of all the classrooms two or three times a year. She comes unannounced and manages to disrupt lessons—then wants to know why the children are squirming when you have to leave them and listen to her point out the error of your ways."

"Why doesn't Mr. Clifton put a stop to all that?"

"He's tried, believe me. So has Mr. Mallory. But in a sense she's their boss. Oh, the board wouldn't fire either of them. I've heard Mr. Mallory has done wonders with the Camden schools since he came. Bernie said the teachers were ready to mutiny against the other man.

"Anyway, she'll visit you first because you're new,

17

and then Mr. Mallory will come by the next day with candy for the kids and tell you what a good job you're doing. Like I said, he takes care of his teachers."

"That's reassuring," Ruthann made herself say. *Not in my classroom. Please, not in my classroom. Not either of them. Especially him.*

"It's the best I've got. So, now we can either go back to the boarding house and eat leftovers from today's lunch, or we can grab a sandwich and a milkshake at Troy's, downtown."

"As good as lunch was, I'm up for something light and cold."

"I'm filthy from all the dust I stirred up in that classroom, but if you can stand me, we'll walk from here."

"I feel rather dusty myself."

"Excuse me, I spent an hour with the feather duster in here before I left last May." Rena narrowed her eyes, but the corners crinkled with good humor.

Ruthann laughed. "You do realize that's been three months ago."

"Oh. So it has." Rena switched off the light. "Let's go."

Chapter Three

Ruthann's spirits soared as the first week of classes ended. She'd fallen in love with the children who, Rena said when she stopped for Ruthann on Friday afternoon, seemed somehow more like children now that the war was over. Their fathers, brothers, and other relatives—most of them anyway—had come home. "We were lucky not to lose more…" Her voice trailed off. "Ruthann, I'm sorry."

Ruthann slid a stack of papers into the leather case her father had given her. "No, don't apologize, Rena. It's like Kay Clifton said last week when she mentioned her oldest son—you don't get over the loss, but you have to go on."

"She's right, but I'm sure it's not easy."

Ruthann hoped the smile she flashed didn't look as pasted on as it felt. The dishonesty of accepting sympathy nibbled at her conscience, because the pain of Jack's loss had faded into nothing more than a wistful twinge. "Is it back to the boarding house, or downtown for a milkshake to celebrate a successful week?"

"Troy's, of course. Got everything?"

Ruthann glanced around. "All but Ronnie Peters' paper airplane." She plucked it from the top of the trash and placed it on his desk in the first row. "It's a work of art. I can't make myself throw it away, but I'll remind him again on Monday about not flying it while I'm in reading circle." She laughed. "He said his brother flew P-47s."

"Yes, and earned a few medals you can expect to see at Show and Tell if you institute that on Fridays. You're just a softie at heart, aren't you?"

"Maybe, but he's such a sweet child. They all are."

Ruthann flipped the light switch and stepped out into the hall directly onto Drew Mallory's left foot. "Oh, I'm sorry! Please excuse me!"

"No, no, I wasn't looking," he replied. "No damage done." He nodded at Rena. "Gathering your troops for an evening of revelry, Miss Gilbert?"

"It's Friday, Mr. Mallory. Don't you ever go home?"

Ruthann wondered at Rena's familiar tone even though the superintendent chuckled. "I occasionally find my way there. I just wanted to check on our new teacher and be sure she's going to show up again on Monday."

Ruthann's cheeks stung. "Of course I am. The children are wonderful."

"Good, very good. Always glad to hear things are going well."

"The school board hasn't met," Rena said. "Not yet anyway."

The man's smile disappeared as if someone had wiped his face. "The year's young yet."

Rena nodded toward Ruthann. "She's been warned."

Drew cleared his throat. "More than once, I expect. Well, you two go along now. Have a pleasant weekend."

Ruthann watched him limp down the empty

corridor until he turned the corner leading to the high school. "Weren't you a little free with him?"

"He knows how much respect I have for him, especially after he saved me from a potentially disastrous situation with my erstwhile knight of the sky. We all respect him."

"I just thought…"

"And don't think I'm flirting, either. He's old enough to be my father, and that's how I think of him. I don't remember my own, but I often think he'd have been like Mr. Mallory in the way he looks after all of us."

"I'm sorry, and I didn't think you were flirting. He's very nice, and I'm sure he has a lovely wife and family."

Rena frowned. "You don't know?"

"Know what?"

"His wife died years ago, before he came here. He only has a daughter, Gwen, who works as a buyer for Bond's Department Store on the square, and a sister, who keeps house for him."

Ruthann's stomach churned. "No, I didn't know." She shifted the leather case to her other hand. "I'm ready for that milkshake, aren't you?"

****

Wearing a hat which looked ready to take flight in a swirl of fall flowers, Merle Fulton sailed into the third grade classroom just after lunch on the following Wednesday. The children sat on the floor around Ruthann while she read aloud from *The Bobbsey Twins*. For a moment, no one realized they'd been invaded, not until the visitor cleared her throat.

Ruthann hesitated a moment before setting aside

the book and rising with a respect she didn't really feel. "Good afternoon, Mrs. Fulton."

"Miss. Good afternoon. And this lesson hour is?"

"I read aloud to the children every day after lunch. The quiet time begins our afternoon on a nice note." She threaded her way through twenty-five small bodies to retrieve the only other adult-sized chair in the room. "Please sit down."

"I'd hoped to observe you teaching a lesson."

"Certainly. Social studies comes next. I'll just finish the chapter we're reading." Straining to conceal her irritation, Ruthann sat down again and reached for the book. "Now, where were we?"

"Freddie's locked in the basement of the department store," piped up Karen Perkins, tugging at one of her blonde braids. "And he hears something."

Ruthann nodded. "Yes, of course. *Freddie sat very still...*" From the corner of her eye, she saw Merle Fulton sit down, remove her gloves, and uncap her fountain pen.

At the end of the chapter, she closed the book. Without prompting, the children returned to their desks, on which she'd already placed mimeographed maps of the continents and major oceans. She pulled down the map over the blackboard and pointed out all the places the children were to label and color with the art pencils she'd asked them to buy over the weekend. "Now I have several extra sets of pencils here for anyone who wasn't able to get to the store," she said, knowing full well Bobby Kinser couldn't afford them. "Just raise your hand if you need to borrow."

Bobby Kinser raised his hand. Not a single child appeared to notice as Ruthann placed a new box of art pencils on the boy's desk. Though clean, his overalls sported an obvious patch on one knee, and the shirt underneath had faded long ago from a rich plaid to a dingy blue-green. "Here you are, Bobby. Just keep them in your desk until you go to the store."

His eager freckled face glowed. "Yes, ma'am."

Merle muttered something under her breath, something which sounded suspiciously like *trash*. Ruthann's hand tingled with the urge to smack the woman for her blatant unkindness.

While the children labeled and colored, Ruthann moved up and down the aisles with compliments, suggestions, and trivia about the subject at hand. She could feel Merle's disapproval radiating around her. Finally, when the children had pinned their completed maps to the prepared bulletin board, Ruthann sat down at her desk and instructed them to take out their social studies books. "We'll read today about North America, since that's where we live," she announced. "Page forty-three, please." She had to steady her trembling hands as she opened her own book.

Halfway through the paragraph listing the countries comprising the North American continent, the unwelcome visitor pulled on her gloves and rose, letting the chair scrape noisily. Her large purse connected with the table holding a small globe as she swept out of the room, and only the quick reaction of a boy in the far front row kept it from toppling to the floor.

"Thank you for saving our globe, Sandy," Ruthann said without thinking how it might sound. The communal sigh which swept the room startled her.

Ronnie Peters raised his hand. "Now can I ask a question, Miss Cooper?"

"You *may* ask all the questions you like, Ronnie," Ruthann said, biting her cheeks to keep from laughing.

\*\*\*\*

The next afternoon at almost exactly the same time, Drew Mallory knocked on the classroom door. "May I come in?"

Ruthann started to get up.

"No, no, keep on with what you're doing. I just brought a little treat for the boys and girls." His announcement brought enthusiastic cheers. From a paper bag, he produced peppermint sticks, which he handed around. Then he moved to the bulletin board and remarked admiringly on the maps before he said, "You know, I had a teacher who read to us every afternoon after lunch. It was my favorite time of the day—except for recess, of course." The children giggled as they sucked greedily on the candy.

"Now I'll leave you to get on with things, Miss Cooper." The way his blue eyes lingered on her face made Ruthann feel he was searching for more than any discomfort about the previous day's invasion.

"Mr. Mallory's leg hurts a lot today," Karen piped up as soon as he'd gone. "I can tell. He didn't even try to pull a nickel out of Bobby's ear."

Bobby wrinkled his nose. "Aw, he doesn't get the nickel out of my ear."

Ruthann swallowed the sudden lump in her throat. "Well, we're glad he came to see us anyway." She picked up the book and began to read again, but the restful moment had fled with Drew Mallory.

\*\*\*\*

"The children know what happens after the Fulton invades," Rena said when Ruthann recounted the

24

incident. "So they're especially well-behaved when she comes."

"How do they know?"

"Well, this is their third year to endure her, you know."

Ruthann grimaced. "I hope Bobby Kinser didn't hear what she said."

"He's heard it before, and no one else is mean to him."

"Still..."

"It won't bother you so much the next time."

*Oh, yes, it will. It will bother me even more, because now I know what she's capable of. And...and then Mr. Mallory will come again and look at me and...what is he looking at? Or for?* She shook off her thoughts. "I suppose I'll learn to live with it. I won't like it, though."

## Chapter Four

John Clifton hand-delivered September's paychecks just before the final bell on the last Friday of the month. When Ruthann opened hers to endorse it, she realized the space for her retirement contribution was blank. "Take it to Mrs. Leland in the main office next week," Rena advised after dinner that night. "She'll fix it."

"Maybe I forgot to sign something. There were so many papers."

"Just go see her. She's a lot like Mr. Mallory when it comes to taking care of the teachers."

As Rena had predicted, Sarah Leland took care of things in short order when Ruthann stopped by the following Monday. "I'll take double out of your check next month, but you'll still come out even. Just sign this form, and it shouldn't happen again. Maybe you missed it, or maybe I didn't put it in your employment packet. Who knows? But it's not a problem. Go on and deposit this check, and remember how much it's over your net so you don't run short. The good Lord knows a teacher's check is small enough."

Ruthann had just thanked the woman when Drew Mallory came out of the inner office. "Problem, Miss Cooper?" The way his eyes lit up told Ruthann he was both surprised and glad to see her.

The secretary explained and added, "It's fixed now,

Mr. Mallory."

"All right. Very good. I'm just leaving, Mrs. Leland. My daughter borrowed the car for today, so she's picking me up." He held the door for Ruthann. "Do you need a lift anywhere?"

"No, thank you. I'm only going up the street to the bank."

"I'm sorry for the unpleasantness last week. You'll learn to live with it as the other teachers have." He lifted one shoulder in a gesture of surrender.

"I'm sure I will."

She tried not to notice how slowly and deliberately he maneuvered down the stairs, concentrating on each step as if it might be his last. At the bottom he paused to catch his breath with a glance in her direction which seemed to say, *Thank goodness that's over*. But when Ruthann missed the curb and pitched forward, he caught her arm immediately and with surprising strength. "Careful!"

Her arm burned where his fingers had touched it. "That was clumsy of me."

"All right?"

Ruthann squared her shoulders. "All right."

He paused beside a dark blue car waiting at the curb. "Here's my ride." Opening the door, he leaned down. "Gwen, this is Miss Cooper, the new third grade teacher. Miss Cooper, my daughter Gwen."

The young woman, about Ruthann's age, wore her hair in a smooth blonde chignon. Ruthann recognized the stylish cut of her dark green twill dress. "Hello, Gwen."

Gwen Mallory inclined her head. "Hello. Get in, Daddy. We're meeting Aunt Julia at that new restaurant outside of town. She made reservations."

Drew slid into the car. "I'm glad your problem is resolved, Miss Cooper. Goodbye now."

The car slid away from the curb, leaving a thin film of dust on Ruthann's new brown shoes.

\*\*\*\*

The following afternoon, noticing she had a run in one of her stockings, Ruthann stopped at the department store for another pair. She'd just paid the clerk when she heard someone call her name. Gwen Mallory's dark brown eyes presented an unspoken challenge. "Don't get any ideas about my father, Miss Cooper. He was devoted to my mother."

Ruthann's mouth went dry, but she managed to cobble a reply. "I'm sure he was, Miss Mallory. I was also devoted to my fiancé, who was a casualty of war. It's very difficult to let go of those attachments."

Gwen didn't back down. "Just so you understand you can't use my father to help you let go."

Ruthann's knees weakened. "I'm sorry you feel I would do that," she replied. "Excuse me." She sidestepped the other woman and made herself walk slowly toward the store entrance. She could feel Gwen—and the other customers who couldn't have helped overhearing—watching her.

\*\*\*\*

"She's usually very nice," Rena said when Ruthann mentioned the encounter. "She's dating the Cliftons' younger son, Daniel. I think they went to high school together and reconnected when he came back to work at the school."

"How long has Mr. Mallory been a widower?"

"Years and years. I heard his wife died when Gwen

was very young. Maybe even too young to remember her mother. I've also heard they were divorced, but that's just rumor. Mr. Mallory's sister came here with the two of them to help raise Gwen. Julia Schaeffer."

"I'm not familiar with the name."

"You haven't met her yet. She works in the county clerk's office and formed the community choir a few years back after her husband died. He worked in the accounting department of the Camden National Bank. They didn't have children." She seemed to consider her next words. "Which was probably a good thing, considering."

Ruthann didn't ask the obvious question. "Apparently Camden's a hotbed of gossip."

"Any town is, whether it's large or small. Even San Antonio, I'll bet. And the Fulton keeps things stirred up here."

"I suppose so. I made the mistake of calling her 'Mrs.' and she corrected me."

"She took back her name after she divorced her husband, who proceeded to hang himself."

"He did what?"

"He was Nathan Wolfe's brother, believe it or not, and Nathan was never convinced it was suicide, in spite of how the coroner's jury ruled. He still blames Merle for his brother's death, no matter how it happened. Anyway, the Fulton and Leonard Schaeffer had a thing after her divorce."

"A thing?"

"An affair, dear child. Oh, it was very hush-hush, but my source is reliable."

"Your source? Wait, never mind. I don't think I want to know."

"I won't tell you, then, but I heard Mr. Mallory told his brother-in-law to straighten up and fly right or get out. He didn't get out, so I assume he straightened up. However, he died a short time later. A very short time." Rena leaned in closer. "Officially, it was a heart attack, but unofficially…" She snickered. "At least it was in his own bed, or so they say, but I always wondered."

Ruthann suppressed a laugh and held up her hand. "Just stop."

Rena shrugged. "I don't know what got into Gwen, but don't let it bother you. After Julia's husband *died*, Merle Fulton made a play for Mr. Mallory by cozying up to Gwen, who was in high school by then. Showered her with attention and expensive gifts, the whole lot."

"You can't tell me she wanted that woman for a stepmother."

"I doubt it, and Mr. Mallory had no intention of getting involved with Merle anyway. Gwen graduated and went off to college, and that was the end of it."

"How long has she been back here?"

"She worked in Dallas for a year, I think, and then Bond's bought this store and some others in smaller towns. She came back here as a buyer and liaison between Bond's and Clyde's until the sale was completed. That was after I came here in forty-one."

"So she's around my age."

"Right around."

Ruthann rose from the end of the bed and walked to the window. "Maybe coming here wasn't such a good idea."

"Why? Because of Merle Fulton? Gwen? You'll find people like them everywhere. So unless you're really after our superintendent…you're not, are you?"

"Of course not! Why would you think something like that?"

"He'd be a catch, though. He reminds me a little of Paul Henreid. You know, the other man in *Casablanca*." Rena uncurled herself from the chair. "Listen, don't worry about it. Now I've got a stack of math papers to mark, so I'm going to do it."

"I've got spelling sentences." Ruthann turned around. "Thanks for the visit. I feel like I'm back in the dorm at college."

"Don't mention it. I was drowning in a middle-aged mire before you moved in. They're all very nice, but I needed a peer. Sleep tight. I'll see you at breakfast."

Ruthann stared out the window for another full minute after Rena left. *Rena's right. Merle Fulton is everywhere, and I suppose I can live with her. But being accused of pursuing a man old enough to be my father—especially someone I work for—I'm not sure I could live with any gossip like that if it got started.* She took a sheaf of papers and a red pencil from her leather case. *I hadn't made the connection between Mr. Mallory and Paul Henreid until now, but Rena's right about that, too. Mr. Mallory resembles him. I wonder if he never remarried because of his disability or because he never got over losing his wife?* She propped herself against the pillows on the bed. *And that is definitely none of my business. None at all.*

****

The first weekend in October, Rena accepted an invitation to visit a college friend near Floresville. "I've been to Fall Fest four years in a row," she told Ruthann as she packed. "It will go on without me. But you'll enjoy it. Be sure you get a barbeque plate and see the quilts."

At mid-afternoon on Saturday at the park, Lillian sought out Ruthann to tell her she, Kitty, and Bernie had found a fourth for bridge and were returning to the boarding house. "But you stay, dear," she said. "This is your first Fall Fest."

Kay Clifton stumbled on Ruthann later, watching the children's puppet show with several of her third-graders pressed around her. "Have you eaten yet?"

"I'm trying to decide between the barbeque and the chicken. Rena says the barbeque."

"Definitely. John and I are just going to get our plates now. Join us?"

"Thank you, I will."

Ruthann followed Kay and the smell of smoked meat to a stand on the other side of the park and then to a table near the fountain. When Drew Mallory, heaped plate in hand, joined them within a few minutes, Ruthann found herself possessed with a strong urge to flee.

"Julia and her musical minions have tossed me aside, and Gwen is eating with Daniel, of course. So may I join you?"

"Only if you're having barbeque," John Clifton said. "I helped fry chicken all afternoon, and I don't want to see or smell it."

"I had to pluck the poor man's feathers when he came home," Kay said. "Sit down, Drew." She glanced at Ruthann. "Move over a bit, Ruthann."

Keeping her eyes on her plate, Ruthann scooted over to make room.

"I don't take up too much space,"Drew joked.

Unfolding his paper napkin, he tucked it into the open neck of his shirt. "Not to offend anyone's sensibilities, but this is the only way I eat ribs."

Kay laughed. "No need to be stuffy among friends."

"How do you like our annual celebration?" Drew asked Ruthann.

She didn't look at him. "It's very nice."

"We have something in the spring, too. Everything scaled down a bit during the war with all the shortages, but now we're coming back." He turned to John. "Is the *school board* meeting?"

The principal's eyebrows came together over the bridge of his nose. "Not to my knowledge, but I'm sure *she's* around somewhere."

"Merle Fulton wants to be sure the faculty and staff support community affairs," Kay said by way of explanation to Ruthann.

The word *affair* struck Ruthann as both apt and also rather inappropriate, considering the company, but Drew Mallory seemed unaffected. "As if we wouldn't," he said. "Most of us, anyway."

Conversation flowed around a silent Ruthann until Drew collected all the paper plates and carried them to the trash barrel a few yards away.

"You haven't said two words," Kay said to Ruthann. "Look, I heard what Gwen said to you. My neighbor happened to be in the store."

A feeling close to nausea replaced the pleasant fullness in Ruthann's stomach.

Kay leaned across the table. "She's a nice girl, but she's been a little possessive of her father since she came back to Camden. His leg's gotten worse, and it worries her. And I don't think she ever quite got over Merle's attempt to…" She stopped speaking abruptly as Drew returned and stopped so close to Ruthann she could smell his shaving cream again.

"Have you seen the quilt exhibit?" he asked Ruthann. "We might have a look before time for the city choir to perform. Julia's in charge, and the music is always outstanding."

Ruthann kept her eyes down. "I should go home. I have some letters to write, and…"

Drew chuckled. "And a few things to wash out? Come now, Miss Cooper, it's Saturday evening."

Kay's foot made contact with Ruthann's under the table. "You mustn't miss the quilts," she said. "And John and I will save you a seat near the stage."

Panic, like she'd felt all her life when unwanted attention came her way, set her heart pounding. *There's no way I can get out of this without being rude, and he's my boss, after all. Just please don't let me run into Gwen or the Fulton.* "All right," she said finally. She slid off the picnic bench. "My grandmother used to quilt. I have one she made for me."

"Do you?" Drew asked as he fell into step beside her.

She noticed he didn't seem to be leaning so heavily on his cane tonight. "I didn't bring it with me, but it's across the foot of my bed at home."

"A true family heirloom, then. I don't have any of those to pass down to Gwen. My parents died of diphtheria within weeks of each other when I was ten. I have no idea what happened to any of their things. A welfare worker took my younger brother and me to an orphanage right after the funeral."

"Oh, I see. I'm sorry."

"Yes, so am I, but that's just the way things happened."

"How…how did you get into education?"

"Not easily. I ran away from the orphanage when I was sixteen, lied about my age, and joined the army. It was a good life, but then there was the war. I soon found myself in France, in a trench, with mud up to my ears." He tapped his leg with the cane. "That's how I got this, which I'm sure you've already heard."

Ruthann didn't reply.

"What I really wanted to do was stay in the army. Make a career of it, you know. But they didn't want me, so I mustered out. I took odd jobs along, but I wasn't going anywhere with those." He stopped walking and faced her. "Sorry. I'm sure you're not interested in my life history."

"Oh, yes, I…but I didn't mean to be nosy."

"Just making conversation?" He grinned at her.

"Not really, but…of course, I'm interested." She gritted her teeth at the words. Would he consider them impertinent—or worse, an attempt to flirt with him?

"Well, then, to make a long story short, someone I worked for encouraged me to go to college—or at least go for a teaching certificate—so I did. I liked teaching and kept going back to school during the summer terms until I'd gotten enough credentials to be an administrator. The future's in our young people, you know, more now than ever. We've lost too many of a generation during this last war, so it's doubly important to nurture the ones we have left." He stopped again. "I know your fiancé died in the war."

Ruthann nodded. "He flew B-17s out of England.

He didn't come back from his ninth mission."

She watched honest sorrow fill his blue eyes. "Daylight bombing. It was the only way to get the job done, but our losses were tremendous."

"Jack's whole crew was lost."

"I'm very sorry about that, Miss Cooper. After the first war, President Wilson said we'd set ourselves up for another one. I remember hearing him on the radio and hoping he was wrong, but it happened just as he said."

Ruthann couldn't speak past the lump in her throat, but she knew the memory of Jack didn't put it there. Rather, something in Drew Mallory's earnest words made her feel small and inadequate. It occurred to her he was passionate about his work. Education was his life, but she realized with a jolt she was only passing time no matter how much she enjoyed teaching.

He touched her elbow. "We can't change what happened," he said. "But we can't forget, either." A few more steps brought them to the quilt exhibit.

After the quilts, they spent a quarter of an hour admiring a large assortment of handcrafted linens. Ruthann couldn't resist a lace-edged dresser scarf embroidered in shades of lilac, deep purple, and green. "I don't need it," she said as she paid the seller, "but it's beautiful."

"Don't you remember what Sara Teasdale wrote about spending all you have for loveliness?" Drew asked as she completed the transaction.

"Oh, yes, the poem's one of my favorites." Ruthann smoothed the folds of the tissue paper in which the woman had wrapped the scarf and tucked it into her purse. "And I'm afraid I didn't count the cost."

Drew smiled and motioned her away from the booth. "Would it surprise you to know I own a large collection of poetry books? I've always loved poetry."

"Some of our most famous poets have been men."

"That's true, but when you're a boy of twelve caught reading poetry…" His smile crinkled the corners of his eyes. "Let's just say the other boys make you question whether or not you'll become a man in the long run."

She stared at him a moment, disarmed by his raw honesty. At the same time, a warning bell rang in her brain.

"But I kept reading anyway. Poetry has always touched something deep inside me. My books are dog-eared, and my daughter calls my library my folly. I see people heading toward the stage. You *are* staying for the music, aren't you? I can promise you a treat."

As they passed the next booth, her eye caught a display of watercolors and pen-and-ink sketches. "Oh, they're lovely," she said.

"A local artist," the woman in the booth said with a smile. "And they're all one of a kind."

Ruthann leaned in to see the signature *A.M.* on one sketch of two schoolchildren on the swings. "He or she lives in Camden?"

Before the woman could reply, Drew said, "Oh, yes, but he's quite the recluse." He touched her elbow and urged her forward. The electricity which shot through her body provoked another panicky urge to flee, and she thought she heard the woman laughing behind them.

"Do you also like art?" Drew asked.

"I don't know anything about it, really, not beyond

what I studied in a couple of required courses in college. But I appreciate it."

"Well, appreciation is the beginning of knowledge." He smiled, almost angelically Ruthann thought, and kept walking toward the sounds of the band tuning up in the stage area.

The city choir, a melodious blend of ages and talent, had just launched the patriotic section of their program when Gwen Mallory rushed to the end of the row where her father sat beside Ruthann. "Daddy, I need to go home." Though she'd lowered her voice, several people turned toward her and frowned.

Drew rose and walked out of earshot with his daughter. Ruthann forced herself to keep her eyes on the stage, but when Drew didn't return to his seat, an inexplicable sadness settled over her. Only with effort did she not smile when she saw him coming back as the concert ended. "I'm sorry," he said. "Family emergency. You'll let me drive you to the boarding house, won't you, Miss Cooper?"

A warm excitement flooded her at the eagerness in his voice, but this time the warning bell tolled sternly, and she said, "Oh, no, thank you, Mr. Mallory. I can walk. It's not far, you know."

"It's late," he insisted.

Beside her, Kay spoke up. "It's safe enough, but it *is* late."

In the car, Ruthann hoped Drew didn't notice how she hugged the passenger door. "I hope you enjoyed the festival," he said.

"Very much."

"My daughter quarreled with her boyfriend and wanted to go home."

"I'm sure they'll make it up."

"Yes, of course they will, but it was annoying to have to leave the concert before the grand finale."

"The choir is very good. Camden must be proud to have so much musical talent in town."

"Julia brought them together several years ago. She had thought of a musical career, but like so many other young women, she married instead."

Recalling the cheating husband, Ruthann didn't comment.

"The choir has won several competitions, and the school choirs, with Julia's assistance, have done the same over the years." He parked at the curb in front of the boarding house but made no move to get out. "I've enjoyed your company this evening."

Ruthann opened her mouth to reply, but no words came.

"But you were uncomfortable with me."

"It's just…well, I work for you."

"Actually, the school board employs us both. I'm a staff member just like you are."

"It's not really the same."

"Well, no, but we're not that different, either. And I think we have a great deal in common."

Ruthann's fingers closed around the door handle. "Poetry?"

"Don't forget an appreciation for art." He regarded her thoughtfully. "You're not like so many other young women. You don't flirt."

She felt her chest tighten.

"That's a compliment, though I'm out of practice in that department. You seemed genuinely interested in what I had to say, even if I did monopolize the conversation."

"You didn't…"

"It's just a feeling I have, Miss Cooper. Or may I call you Ruthann since we're not at school?"

She nodded.

"I've been alone since Gwen was very small. She was only four when her mother died. When she finally left home, even though she came back when she took the position with Bond's, I realized my life had become very dull." He turned toward her. "It was pleasant not to be odd man out this evening."

Ruthann looked away.

"I'd like to see you again."

She felt panic creeping up on her again. "Is that a good idea? I mean, there must be rules about…"

His soft laugh wrapped her in both anticipation and insecurity. "Fraternization?"

"Yes."

"Not to my knowledge. We've had a few faculty romances. One even ended in marriage."

"But you're not just another teacher. You're the superintendent."

"Just the man in the big office. Well, it's not so very big, but it's isolated, anyway. I visit the classrooms regularly just to keep from moldering away."

Ruthann couldn't help smiling. "Especially after a certain school board member has visited."

"Especially then. So, what do you say? Could we have dinner next Saturday? Gwen, Julia, and I tried a new place south of town recently. The roast beef practically melted in my mouth, and the lemon pie…" He licked his lips.

"I…would you let me think about it?"

"I understand. I'll call you tomorrow afternoon."

"Oh, don't do that! The telephone's in the lower hall, and…"

"Right, I'd forgotten. Then meet me at the hotel tomorow, and…"

"The hotel?" came out in a breathless gasp.

Drew slapped his forehead. "I really am out of touch. You don't know yet there's a coffee shop in the hotel, with a separate entrance on Second Street."

Ruthann squirmed. "I'm sorry."

"Don't be." He exited the car and came around to open her door. "Three o'clock?"

"All right. Three o'clock."

At the door, he shook her hand briefly but long enough to set her fingers burning despite the gentleness of his touch. "Goodnight, Ruthann."

She spoke her belated goodnight to his back and thought his limp seemed suddenly worse as he traversed the sidewalk to the street.

Chapter Five

Ruthann arrived at the coffee shop entrance with a detailed mental list of reasons to decline Drew Mallory's invitation to dinner. But over coffee, caught up in half a dozen rollicking stories of student peccadilloes over the years, the list eluded her.

"What brought you to a little place like Camden?" he asked over a second cup of coffee.

"I'm not really sure. A private school in San Antonio offered me a sixth-grade class, but after thinking it over, I felt I needed to get out on my own."

"Didn't your college years count as being on your own?"

"Not really. I went to a very strict girls' school. One of my Catholic friends described it as living in a convent."

"Did you like it?"

"Actually, I did. I'd always been protected at home, so it was just an extension. After I graduated and moved back home, I was just living a continuation of the life I'd always lived."

"So you thought you'd untie the apron strings by coming to Camden."

"Something like that, I suppose."

"There's not a lot to do here, and I know Aggie keeps a close eye on you and Miss Gilbert—being the youngest of her boarders and the most apt to get into trouble."

"I hardly think we'll get into trouble," she said, hoping she didn't sound as irritated as she felt at the suggestion.

"I'm teasing you. My daughter Gwen is close to your age. Her aunt and I protected her, too, and like you, she went to a girls' school. But she did live in Dallas for a year or so before moving back to Camden. Even though I'd miss her, I hope she doesn't stay at home too long. She needs more experience living on her own before settling down with a nice young man."

Ruthann smiled politely and hoped he didn't know his daughter had become a sore subject with her.

"What about you? Is teaching only a brief stop in your journey, or will it be a career?"

She shook her head. "I don't really know. I enjoy it, though. The rules about married teachers aren't as strict as they were even a few years ago, so I suppose I might keep teaching even if my circumstances changed."

"And so you should. I believe women can work and still successfully raise a family. Kay Clifton is a good example. She's worked in the school office since her boys were small, and both of them turned out well." He paused. "You know about their older son, I suppose. Losing David was a blow to all of us. A blow to the whole school community."

"I'm sure it was."

"I didn't start out to make a career in the field of education, but it's suited me very well. I can't imagine doing anything else."

"It's like you said last night—we've lost so many of a generation. Now we have to nurture what's left."

His eyes reflected pleasure that she remembered his words. "Exactly."

Ruthann didn't know where two hours had gone, but at five o'clock the owner of the Café came out of the kitchen and stood behind the lunch counter with his arms crossed and cleared his throat. Drew threw up his hands in mock surrender. "We're going, we're going." He laid a dollar bill on the table, slid to the end of the booth, and braced himself with his cane. "Thank you for sharing the afternoon with me," he said as he held the door for her. "And next Saturday night?"

"All right, if you're sure I won't be breaking any rules."

"Well, if you do, you'll be in good company."

\*\*\*\*

Though they went their separate ways, Drew's voice and face accompanied her back to the boarding house, where she found Rena unpacking her suitcase.

"Where've you been on a Sunday afternoon?"

Ruthann paused at the door. "Where I shouldn't have been, I'm afraid."

Rena pointed at the armchair covered in the same faded material as the one in Ruthann's room. "Sit down and tell all. Honestly, can't I leave for a weekend without you getting into trouble? I'm supposed to be looking out for you."

"Who told you to do that?"

"Mrs. Clifton. And Aggie. They're mother hens of the worst sort."

"Or the best."

"I adore both of them. So tell me what you've been up to." Rena closed her suitcase and shoved it under the bed before settling herself in the middle of the blue-

and-white chenille spread.

Ruthann bit her lip. "It's a long story."

"I want every dirty detail."

"There are no dirty details, Rena."

Rena tossed her dark hair out of her face. "Then why are you blushing? Just tell me, and I'll decide."

Ruthann summed up the previous evening, followed by the afternoon at the coffee shop.

"That's it?"

"Isn't that enough?"

"Look, I know you're honestly worried about all this, so I'm not going to tease you. You didn't go after Drew Mallory, but quite obviously he's gone after you."

"But why, Rena?"

"You're very attractive, and even though you're young—twenty-four, isn't it?—you look more mature. I expect a lot of that comes from losing your fiancé and doing war work."

"I'll admit I was less…well, less *stodgy* before the war."

"You're not stodgy, just mature. And Drew Mallory's older. He doesn't want someone who's still sowing her wild oats."

"I don't think I ever sowed any wild oats. Maybe I should have. Maybe then I'd be more equipped to deal with being asked out to dinner by an older man. A man who's my boss, by the way."

"You know what I mean." Rena regarded her friend for a moment. "So what are you going to do?"

"Probably the wrong thing. I told him I'd have dinner with him on Saturday night."

"Good for you. He's got to be lonely for

companionship, don't you think?"

"You know people will talk."

"Merle Fulton? Nobody listens to her anyway."

"Are you sure?"

"Pretty sure. Listen, Ruthann, are you attracted to the man? I mean, could it go somewhere? You're not just playing with him?"

"I've never played with anyone, as you put it, and I guess I'm attracted to him in some ways. He's different from anyone I've ever known."

"Is he anything like the man you were going to marry?"

"Not really—except for being a complete gentleman. I met Jack on a blind date arranged by my college roommate. He was already in uniform then. And he was a gentleman. He never tried anything."

"So it was a whirlwind wartime romance?"

"I guess so. The next year, Jack's younger sister came to TSCW as a freshman, and I'd go home with her for weekends sometimes. The Rowans lived in a small town about thirty-five miles from Denton. Jack had been sent to Sheppard Field in Wichita Falls, but we wrote letters, and he got leave a time or two. The last time he was home, before he went overseas, he asked me to marry him and gave me a ring."

"Would you have said yes if he hadn't been going off to war?"

Ruthann's head snapped back.

"So it *was* a wartime thing. I'm not saying you weren't in love, mind you."

"I did care for him, but if it hadn't been for the war maybe we wouldn't have gotten engaged so quickly."

"That's what I meant. You'd have dated. Spent

more time getting to know each other."

"Yes." Ruthann picked at a loose thread on the arm of the chair. "His parents came to Denton to tell Shirley and me about the telegram from the war department. Shirley went home with them. She adored Jack. I wasn't sure she'd come back, but she did. We were even closer after that. When I graduated and left, she cried because she'd have to finish the rest of her college course alone."

"So you went home, and then what?"

"I didn't want to teach. For a few months, I just wanted to hide and think about Jack. About the unfinished promise of his life. Of our lives together. But my mother wasn't having any of that. I got a job in a munitions factory, and when I wasn't working, she kept me busy at the local canteen and the Red Cross." Ruthann spread her hands. "And that's how I spent the war, and now it's over."

"That's true. It's over, and you have to go on."

"It's funny, Mr. Mallory said something about how he'd never gone on with his life after his wife died, but now he wanted to."

"Because of you."

"He didn't say that exactly. Jack's death did something to me, but sometime after I went home to San Antonio, I began to forget him. Mother said it was because I hadn't known him long. Still, I'm not sure I'm ready for another relationship. Not yet anyway."

"Death does something to you. Changes you, I guess. After the near disaster with Edwin, I swore off men, but I've reconnected with a high school friend at home. It's not serious at this point, but maybe it will be someday. I'm giving it a chance, and you should give

Drew Mallory a chance."

"I think I'm taking a big chance. Has he ever shown interest in another teacher? I mean, am I just another conquest?"

"I've never seen him show any interest at all in a woman. He's not like that."

"Would you know if he had?"

"Someone would, and you know how the grapevine tangles in the dining room."

"That's what I'm afraid of."

"You do realize how much older he is, don't you?"

"I'm going to have dinner with him, Rena, not marry him."

"Speaking of dinner, what are we going to do since Aggie doesn't cook on Sunday night?"

"I've got some canned tuna and crackers in my room."

"After eating Louise's mother's pot roast and mashed potatoes, excuse me if I don't get excited over canned tuna and crackers."

"What else is there?"

"Last year on the Sunday night after Fall Festival, Burt Exner opened up his place and served the leftover barbeque."

"I can't believe there was any left over. It was some of the best brisket and ribs I ever tasted."

"There'll be some if we get there early. And it's a long walk—all the way across downtown."

Ruthann picked up her purse. "We'd better get started, then."

\*\*\*\*

On Monday morning, Ruthann found a package filling most of her school mailbox. "Uh-huh," Rena said.

"What does that mean?"

"What's in the package?"

"I'll open it in my classroom."

Rena laughed. "I expect you have a not-so-secret admirer."

"Oh, stop it, Rena!" Annoyance replaced anticipation in Ruthann's soul. She edged past Rena and headed for her classroom, where she wasted no time untying the string and peeling away the brown paper. A miniature watercolor of the Camden School sprang out from a gold wood frame. Her eyes searched the lower corner for the initials: *A.M.*

"Quite the recluse!" Ruthann repeated the words Drew Mallory had spoken. "Why, that…" She stopped and laughed softly. Then she returned the painting to its protective wrappings and slipped it into a drawer in her desk.

****

Either intentionally or not so much, Drew Mallory made himself scarce at the elementary school during the following week. One minute Ruthann found herself stewing over agreeing to have dinner with him, and the next she mentally went through her closet for just the right dress to wear. She avoided the department store on the off chance she might run into Gwen, who couldn't have missed her sitting next to Drew at the concert. On Friday afternoon, she almost forgot the teachers' meeting in the high school library and slid in just as John Clifton rapped on the podium to quiet everyone down.

"Just a few things, and I'll let you start the weekend. First, the PTA is taking care of the Halloween carnival as usual, but they can use volunteers. Since it's a school night, we'll want to wrap up early, so the mayhem will commence right after school. The suggestion has been made we allow the children to bring their costumes to school and change into them before the last bell. Any problem with that? No? Okay, I'll pass it on. As for the high school, I'll give the kiddos the usual 'Feel free to come and spend some money, but don't get in little ones' way.' Mr. Wolfe, are you going to do your Wizard of Oz thing again?"

"If you like."

"It went over well last year. You can have the music room on the first floor, by the girls' entrance. Now, one more thing before we wrap up. Mr. Cabrera says the boys' bathroom has been left a mess for two days in a row. By grammar school, they should know how to flush. I need all of you to spend a few minutes talking to the kiddos about the school being their home away from home and treating it as such. Luís keeps this aging building in tiptop shape and gives us a pleasant place to work. He isn't here to clean up messes that shouldn't have been made in the first place." He glanced around the room. "I guess that's it. Any questions or comments?"

No one spoke.

"Then enjoy your weekend. See you all on Monday."

Nathan Wolfe fell into step with Ruthann as the teachers left the library. "Word of advice, Miss Cooper."

Ruthann glanced up at his deeply lined face. "What's that?"

"Merle Fulton has you on her radar."

"I guess I knew that. I'm about due for another visit."

"No, not your classroom. Your personal life."

"I don't understand."

The older man blew out a tired breath. "She had designs on Mr. Mallory a few years back. I'm sure Miss Gilbert has filled you in on all the sordid little details of our school community."

"It's a very nice community, as far as I can tell."

"We stick up for each other, if that's what you mean. And Mr. Clifton and Mr. Mallory have our backs. But Merle Fulton has the ears of some influential people in this town."

"Where are you going with all this, Mr. Wolfe?"

"You were with Mr. Mallory at the Fall Festival last weekend. I've heard by the grapevine she didn't like it."

"I wasn't *with* anyone. He joined the table where I was eating and then suggested we see the quilt exhibit and go to the concert."

"And he drove you home. There's nothing wrong with any of that. Not as far as I'm concerned. Or anyone else for that matter."

"Except for Miss Fulton."

"That's right. She's dangerous."

"That's a strong word."

"It's apt. I'm not minding your business, but you're young, and you're new, and I'd like to see you have a pleasant experience in Camden."

"I appreciate your concern, and I'll certainly keep in mind what you've said."

His thin lips turned up in what passed for a smile. "You do that, Miss Cooper." Leaving her standing in the corridor, he ambled on alone.

****

"So you're not going tomorrow night? Because of what Nathan Wolfe said?" Rena confronted her before supper that night.

"I don't know. I probably should have said no to begin with. I don't know why I didn't."

"If you ask me, it's tacky to break a date just the night before."

"Maybe tacky is the lesser of two evils."

"Listen, Nathan meant well. He's a good teacher and a supportive colleague. Everyone likes him. Everyone but Merle Fulton. I told you he's always blamed her for his brother's death."

"How does she keep getting elected to the school board?"

"She's appointed. Don't ask me to explain that, because nobody understands, unless it's the president of the school board."

"That's odd."

"Yes, it is. So what are you going to wear tomorrow night?"

"The navy blue linen with the eyelet collar... You're impossible, Rena. You knew I wouldn't break the date."

"I hoped you wouldn't." Rena's face wore an unmistakable look of triumph.

****

Lillian Buford passed Ruthann the peas. "I hear you have a date tomorrow night."

Ruthann helped herself before she replied. "Does everyone know everyone else's business around here?"

Lillian laughed. "In a small place like Camden? Of

course."

Ruthann accepted the platter of ham with unsteady hands. "I'm not…used to that."

Nathan Wolfe caught her eye. "It can be a good thing, you know. Other people having your back, so to speak."

Bernie Clifton laughed. "I overheard Mr. Mallory talking to John yesterday. He seemed quite pleased at having something to do on Saturday night other than sit at home with Julia and Gwen."

"I thought Gwen was seeing Daniel," Lillian said.

"I think they had what one calls a lover's quarrel."

"What about?"

Bernie shrugged. "Who knows? Daniel's my nephew, and I adore him, but he hasn't gotten past being the star in high school and later in college. Gwen, on the other hand, was very quiet, very studious. Kept to herself for the most part. He didn't know she was alive during their school days, but as soon as he came home, he gave her the rush."

Kitty Litton set down the gravy. "You're a young woman, Ruthann. I'd been married and divorced by the time I was your age, and I've always regretted never marrying again. When I say I had more than one opportunity, I'm not bragging, you understand."

"Why didn't you?" Ruthann asked. "I'm sorry. That's none of my business."

"No offense taken, my dear. It was fear, pure and simple. My husband was unfaithful, so I left him. I was afraid all men were the same. They're not, of course, but because I wasn't willing to risk another failed marriage, I've spent my life taking care of other people's children. I'd hate to see you do that."

"A dinner date isn't a marriage proposal, Kitty," Bernie admonished. "And you might have been more free if Merle hadn't started that despicable rumor about…"

"I don't want to bring *that* up," Kitty said, her face a shade paler than a moment before.

"Merle Fulton." Lillian spoke up. "She's gone after all of us at one time or another."

"But I'm a first-year teacher," Ruthann said. "My contract is only for a year."

"Oh, Merle's made sure all our contracts are only for a year," Kitty said. "She holds that over our heads like the sword of Damocles. I've never figured out how she has so much influence on the board."

"Dereliction of duty and moral turpitude," Lillian said. "Those are the only hard and fast reasons for non-renewal, and they have to be proven. None of us have given her any proof."

"Drew Mallory is a good man," Bernie said. "To my knowledge he's never before asked anyone to have dinner with him. He raised his daughter and did his job for the school district. Maybe he thinks it's time to do something for himself."

"I've heard Merle Fulton wanted to be his sweet-patootie," Rena said.

The others at the table seemed to freeze but only momentarily. "Well, it's true," Bernie said. "She went after him through Gwen when the girl was about thirteen or fourteen. Bought her expensive clothes, tried to take her on trips. Drew put a stop to it pretty quickly."

Rena nodded at Ruthann as if to say, *I was right*, and asked aloud, "Did she try to get him fired?"

"He'd done too much for Camden schools by then. Everyone respects him, and I like to think the faculty and staff do their outstanding jobs because of his leadership." Bernie took another roll and buttered it. "John's worked for other superintendents, and he says Drew Mallory is head and shoulders above all of them."

"Go and have a good time, Ruthann," Lillian said. "Forget about Merle Fulton."

But that night Ruthann dreamed the woman had backed her into a corner of the classroom and stood reading from a list of all the reasons Ruthann wouldn't be rehired the next year.

Chapter Six

Just before six o'clock on Saturday, Rena inspected Ruthann's appearance. "I suppose you'll have to do, but you need brighter colors."

"I don't have any. Not with me anyway."

Rena picked up the watercolor which Ruthann had propped on her dressing table. "This could be serious."

Ruthann grabbed the picture and returned it to its place. "It's just a picture."

"By a certain local artist."

"I couldn't throw it away."

"Of course not. For heaven's sake, have a good time tonight. The poor man deserves a little recreation." She winked and rushed out before Ruthann could reply.

In the deserted parlor, Ruthann reconsidered all the reasons she shouldn't be going out with the superintendent of schools. The list seemed endless. At the same time, she recognized a pleasant flutter in her chest like the one she'd felt whenever she waited at the dormitory for Jack. Maybe Kitty Litton was right. Maybe being afraid to take a risk didn't really keep one safe. A knock at the door propelled her out of the wing chair into the foyer.

"Hello," Drew Mallory greeted her. "I've wondered if you might change your mind about tonight."

"No, of course not."

He reached for the sweater she held and draped it across her shoulders. "Fall is in the air tonight."

As Drew edged the car away from the curb, she said, "The watercolor is lovely. It was quite a surprise."

"I'm glad you like it."

"I do. Very much."

"I donate most of my work to the Fall Fest booth. It's for a good cause, and I'd run out of room in my house if I kept everything I did."

"A.M. Andrew Mallory. Quite the recluse."

He chuckled. "Not tonight."

The lights of the Camden Inn blinked through a grove of trees well off the road. When Drew didn't take her arm, Ruthann felt relieved and disappointed at the same time. Her heart sank when the dimly lit dining room appeared full.

"I made reservations," Drew said. "Julia recommended them on a Saturday night."

A hostess wearing a swirling black dress and a single strand of pearls seated them at a secluded table by the wall of windows overlooking a patio. Ruthann smiled at the few hardy feathered latecomers splashing in a fountain pool made by a sculpted-stone woman pouring water from a pitcher.

Drew held Ruthann's chair, then skirted the table to his own and hung his cane over a third chair. "I'm a little rusty," he said, "so you'll have to tell me if I forget to do something, or if I do something I shouldn't."

Ruthann bit her lip. "Mr. Mallory…"

"Tonight I'm Drew."

"I can't help but wonder why you…"

"Decided to make the social scene again?"

She dropped her eyes. "I don't mean to be rude, but I'm sure there are dozens of more suitable… companions in Camden."

His eyebrows lifted. "If you want an honest answer, I've wondered that myself. How can I say I was attracted to you without casting myself as a predator?"

"I didn't mean that. I don't feel preyed on, just a little confused. I've been out of the social scene, as you call it, for a while, too."

"Then we're on somewhat equal footing. The truth is, I did find myself drawn to you. You're very attractive, you know, but not in a girlish way." He shook his head. "Now I've really put my foot in it."

"You mean I don't look *maidenly*."

"I think that's what I mean. There's a maturity about you." His eyes scanned her face. "And a sadness, too, I think. Because of losing your fiancé." She felt him watching her. "Would you like to tell me about him?"

"What do you want to know?"

He smiled. "Whatever you'd like to tell me. I'm a good listener."

"We'd only become engaged a week before he left to go overseas. I was still in college."

"Had you known him long?"

"Not even a year." She tried to call Jack's face to mind, but Drew Mallory's kept getting in the way. "When I graduated, I didn't want to teach, so I decided to do something to finish the fight Jack and so many others couldn't."

"That's admirable."

"And I wanted to believe it was all a terrible mistake, but as the war went on, he just faded away. I felt disloyal somehow. Maybe I still do." She spread her hands on the table. "I even returned my engagement ring to his mother."

His hand covered hers before she realized what was happening, sending unwanted yearning through her body, but she couldn't make herself pull away. "Your experience isn't so different from that of many young women, I expect. You were someone to come home to after the war. You were the symbol of hope that time would come. And your letters—because, of course, you wrote letters—cheered him up when being just one mission away from disaster threatened to overwhelm him."

"I guess I feel guilty because at some point I just stopped grieving for him."

"You shouldn't. Think of everything you did right, and then consider that life has many chapters, all of which have to end."

"That's very profound philosophy."

"Just the fruits of age and experience speaking."

Ruthann felt Merle's presence before she saw the woman looming beside her chair and staring pointedly at her hand lost beneath Drew's. "Good evening," she said with frost in her voice.

"Good evening, Merle," Drew replied. Ruthann wondered if he didn't rise because of the difficulty or because he didn't want to. He didn't move his hand, either.

The older man behind Merle urged her on. "Our table's ready."

"Just take a deep breath," Drew said as the woman moved away. "There's nothing in my contract—or yours either—that forbids *fraternization* between faculty members. I double-checked both of them, especially yours."

Ruthann's face burned. Reluctantly, she withdrew her hands into her lap. A waiter approached with two menus.

"Thank you," Drew said. "Breathe, Ruthann. I don't know what I'd do with you if I managed to pick you up off the floor—which I probably couldn't." He winked at her.

Ruthann bent her head over the menu and wondered where Merle Fulton had been seated and if she were watching. "You've been here before," she said. "Can you recommend something?"

"A serving of clear conscience and some spirited conversation. And perhaps the braised beef tips with asparagus and new potatoes." When he smiled at her over the menu, she couldn't help smiling back.

Despite Ruthann's misgivings and her feeling of being watched, the spirited conversation Drew suggested engaged her full attention. They found common ground in music, literature, a preference for being out of doors, and the desire to travel in England someday. "I've never wanted to go back to France," he said. "But England...I'd love to wander the Lake District reading poetry. Wordsworth, Coleridge, Southey..." His eyes responded to the recognition of the names in hers. "I see you know them."

"They're some of my favorites."

"Of course, I wouldn't admit that to just anyone, and London's still rebuilding after the bombing. But I won't be going either place anytime soon, I don't suppose."

Ruthann smiled. "I don't suppose I will, either."

They lingered over a second cup of coffee. Except for a few late diners, the room had almost emptied when they left. This time, he took her arm as they threaded their way through the empty tables. "This area is known as Sorrells Woods," he told her before he opened the car door. "It's very beautiful this time of year, and there's quite a history surrounding it."

"Local history?"

"And a ghostly one, too. Two lovers used to meet in a grove of trees, until the father of one killed them both. Now their spirits haunt the woods and protect other lovers who wander there."

"Is there any historical basis to the story?"

"Not to my knowledge, although I've heard more than one story of a sighting—usually by a fisherman who's had a little too much to drink after setting his trotlines. Sometimes the Boy Scouts pitch their tents by the lake and tell tales around the campfire at night. I was a scoutmaster for a while, until I had to rely on this cane and couldn't do the physical activities required. And the Methodist Church holds their annual picnic by the lake, too." He opened the car door for her. "There was a local tragedy here several years before I came. A high school student drowned at the lake, but..."

He closed the door and rounded the car to the driver's side. "I like to come here and paint," he said as he inserted the key.

"You really are an artist, then."

"Nothing so exalted. You've seen what I do. I started sketching in France."

"Paris?"

"The Eiffel Tower. Notre Dame. But more in the trenches."

"Did you donate those to the Fall Fest?"

"No, I've hung onto them. Maybe you'd like to see them sometime."

"Very much," Ruthann said, hoping she didn't sound too eager.

"I'll get them out sometime then."

"Art was my least favorite subject in grammar school. I couldn't fold and cut a snowflake or make a paper heart that wasn't lopsided. I use a very good book to plan projects for the third grade, and I come up with some excuse not to demonstrate the finished product."

"You cheat."

"You mustn't tell."

"I wouldn't think of it."

Ruthann found herself wishing the drive to the boarding house could be twice as long. When Drew did stop in front of the mostly dark house, he made no move to get out of the car.

"I enjoyed tonight," he said. "Thank you for going with me."

"I enjoyed it, too," she replied, "though I'm not sure I should have enjoyed it quite so much."

"Why not?"

"I don't have an answer for that."

"If you're thinking of Merle Fulton, don't."

"If looks could've killed, as my mother says…"

"I told you there aren't any rules about this."

"You're the superintendent of schools, and I'm a first-year teacher."

"It doesn't matter." He turned toward her. "I've been alone for a very long time, Ruthann, and I can't explain why it suddenly bothers me. Gwen is a grown woman, so I don't have a father's responsibility as I did when she was a child. Someday she'll marry and have a home of her own. I love my work with the children and the faculty at Camden Schools, but it's not enough anymore. Maybe it never was. Maybe I just thought it was, until a few weeks ago. But now I want more. I know I'm older than you, but you're older, too, in the ways that count. What I'm very clumsily trying to say is that I'd like for us to spend time getting to know each other better. How do you feel about that?"

"I wish I knew." She hesitated. "How much more about you is there to learn?"

"How much would you like to know?" His slightly lopsided smile made her stomach flutter.

"Would you think I'm a coward if I admit to being a little frightened by all this?"

"Not at all."

At the door, he took her hands between his. "Will you meet me at the coffee shop tomorrow afternoon?"

Ruthann started to say no but instead heard, "Three o'clock?"

He raised her hands to his lips and brushed them quickly. "Three o'clock. Goodnight, Ruthann."

"Goodnight."

As she had the night of the fall festival, she watched him down the walk to his car before she turned her key in the front door lock.

****

Just before the last bell on Monday afternoon, while Ruthann sat with the reading group needing a second daily session, Merle Fulton appeared at the door. Ruthann didn't acknowledge her presence, and the children, engrossed in their newly-acquired library books, didn't either. Ruthann dismissed the class at the bell but continued to stand behind her desk on the slightly-raised platform and waited for Merle Fulton to speak first.

"There's a rule against male and female faculty and staff having a relationship."

Ruthann sensed a challenge in the woman's voice. "Mr. Mallory said not. However, we don't have a *relationship*, as you put it. We had dinner on Saturday night. That's all."

Merle stepped closer. "And you met him at the hotel on Sunday afternoon."

Ruthann clenched her fists at her side and waited to speak until she felt in control of her voice. "In the coffee shop."

"You're a first-year teacher, Miss Cooper. If you want a second year…"

"If I don't give satisfaction in Camden, I'll go elsewhere."

"You just might find yourself unable to get a teaching position anywhere."

"Are you threatening me?"

"I'm warning you. Strongly."

"I see." Ruthann began to gather the papers she planned to take home for marking. "Good afternoon, Miss Fulton."

As soon as the woman had gone, Ruthann sank into her chair, thankful her knees hadn't buckled during the confrontation. *I can't do this. I fought my war. It's over, and I'm not going to fight another one.*

"Hey." Rena bustled in. "What's up? I saw *Madame* in the hall. Was she here?"

"Oh, yes, she was here."

"And?"

"She informed me there was a rule against men and women on the faculty having a relationship."

"Mr. Mallory ought to know."

"He said he double-checked our contracts, especially mine."

"I'd expect him to do that. I told you he was very protective of his teachers. What did she say to you?"

Ruthann shrugged. "It's not worth talking about."

"She threatened your job, didn't she?"

"I'm not going to fight her all year. She can make my life here miserable, and I don't have to put up with that." Ruthann stuffed the last paper into her briefcase. "Let's go home."

\*\*\*\*

"I saw Merle Fulton coming out of your classroom," Bernie said as soon as everyone had filled their plates at the buffet that evening.

"She came to tell me I broke the rules by having dinner with Mr. Mallory." Ruthann glanced up and literally felt the others closing ranks around her.

"Typical Merle," Kitty said. "But you know he'd never have asked you out if it were true."

"Don't let it bother you," Aggie said. "Though I know that's easier said than done."

"I taught her in high school, you know." Lillian said. "I was very young, and she tried to intimidate me by letting me know how prominent her family was in Camden. Then one day I caught her cheating on an examination and turned her in."

Ruthann looked up from her plate. "Did she get away with it?"

"Yes, she did. The principal at the time had close ties to the Fultons. He refused to let me give her a failing mark. Thankfully, she graduated within a few months, and I was well rid of her. And I still have my position, although I'll be retiring in a few years—but by choice."

"And the students will be poorer for it," Kitty spoke up. "Did you enjoy your dinner date, Ruthann?"

"Yes." Ruthann's voice came out barely above a whisper.

"And you'll see him again?"

"Is that a good idea?"

"It would be a worse idea if you want to and don't because of one woman's meanness," Bernie said.

"She's an old witch," Rena sputtered. "And if she ever came after me…" She tossed her hair out of her eyes.

Lillian glanced her way. "Rena dear, a barrette would solve that problem for you. Or a scarf fashioned as a headband. You remind me of that movie star—that Veronica Lake—when you do that."

Rena narrowed her eyes. "Is that a compliment?"

Lillian laughed. "Whatever you like. People should be able to see your pretty face. And while we're at it, it's been at least two years since your unfortunate experience with the perverse private. You should get out and meet young men who can appreciate you."

"Someday, maybe," Rena replied. "And he was a second lieutenant."

"Merle Fulton has a lot of answer for," Bernie said, taking up the previous subject again. "Lillian could tell you even more."

"Let it go, Bernie."

"Fine, I will. But Merle's gone after all of us at one time or another. Even Drew's sister Julia, though she's not with the school."

"I heard she had an affair with Julia's husband," Rena said.

Bernie nodded. "It's true. Leonard died of a heart attack soon after it all came out."

Kitty giggled. "Perhaps Merle was too much for him."

Harry cleared his throat, but Ruthann thought he looked hard pressed to keep from smiling.

"Enough of that," Aggie said. "Rena, help me clear, and Ruthann, you can dish up the peach cobbler and ice cream."

A tasty dessert held everyone at the table far past their usual time. The heaviness in Ruthann's chest dissolved as more pleasant gossip flowed around her. When Aggie went to answer the phone, she returned with the information Drew Mallory would meet Ruthann outside in five minutes. "He said it was a nice night for a walk."

"Run up and put on some lipstick," Rena said, giving Ruthann a nudge with her elbow. "We'll just sit here and talk about you."

The sage nods and friendly laughter of the others around the table warmed Ruthann as she hurried away.

Chapter Seven

"I thought we should discuss what happened this afternoon," Drew said when they reached the end of the sidewalk.

"I'd hoped you wouldn't hear about it."

"There's not much that happens in the school I don't hear about. Besides, Merle Fulton hit my office right after she left your classroom."

Ruthann sucked in her breath. "It happened, that's all. Maybe we shouldn't see each other again."

Drew stopped dead still. In the glow of a streetlight, his face mirrored confusion. "I hope you don't mean that. Why shouldn't we be friends?"

"Do you have to ask?"

"I think I do. We agreed we'd like to get better acquainted." When he touched the small of her back with the tips of his fingers, pleasure pulsed through her. He urged her farther down the sidewalk and out from under the streetlight. "I know I moved too fast. I can't explain it other than to say when I looked at you, I knew without a doubt I didn't want to be alone any longer."

She moved away from him as she searched for words to reply but found none.

"I can't walk far tonight, but I brought the car. Ride with me?"

He drove to the City Park by the back way, parked,

and gestured toward a bench near the fountain. "Our professional lives shouldn't dictate our personal ones."

"Maybe not, but I think in this instance they do."

"Merle Fulton has pursued almost every man in town, including me. The ones she caught, she tossed aside. The ones she didn't, she stalked with a vengeance. My sister Julia's husband found himself enmeshed in her web. When they came here to help with Gwen, Leonard found a position at the bank and advanced quickly. What he didn't realize was Merle had pulled strings for him, and eventually she wanted her payback."

"That sounds like something out of one of those magazines my mother wouldn't let me read."

"It's true. Julia offered him his freedom, but by then he understood Merle was only playing her dangerous game, with him as the pawn. Unfortunately, before things could be resolved completely, he died of a sudden heart attack. Julia held up her head and went on. She's done well in her work, but the wound Merle inflicted will never completely heal."

"I'm sorry."

"So am I. And I'm sorry I put you in this position, but for your sake, not mine. I know it's been only seven weeks, Ruthann, but knowing you has changed my life."

"We've just fought one war," she interrupted. "Maybe I'm still fighting mine. Fighting to find out who I am and what I want in life. That's enough battle for me."

"You'll fight many battles in your life unless, of course, you manage to live in complete isolation."

She sighed. "I did sound rather dramatic, didn't I?"

He took her cold hands between his warm ones. "No. Maybe just a tad bit sorry for yourself, and I can relate. The idea of not seeing you again makes me feel quite sorry for myself."

"After you brought me home on Saturday, I picked up Jack's picture from the table beside my bed and thought about what a short time I'd known him. I don't want to think it was one of those wartime romances, but whatever it was, it's over."

"He'll always be a good memory. He should be."

"That's the problem, isn't it? I hardly remember him at all."

"I don't want to be a soon-forgotten memory for you. I believe there's something between us worth pursuing." He turned her face toward his. "If you believe it, too, then a vindictive woman shouldn't make a difference."

"What about your daughter?"

"I'll admit she's given me the cold shoulder all week. I'm the only parent she has, so naturally she's concerned about losing me, too. But she'll come around, Julia says. Gwennie's a good girl. She wants me to be happy the same way I want happiness for her."

"Did she and Daniel Clifton quarrel over me?"

"Why do you ask?"

"That's the gossip at the boarding house."

Drew grimaced. "I think he teased her about you being her same age."

"I don't want to cause trouble for anyone."

"Don't you think a person makes his own trouble?"

"Not always."

"Gwennie's a grown woman. I don't really know how she feels about Daniel. They went to school together, so they've known each other a long time."

"I never had a high school sweetheart. Maybe that's why Jack swept me off my feet."

"We can be swept off our feet for many reasons. It happened to me, too, but that's another story. Right now I'd just like to hear you say you'll stand your ground."

"I don't know if I can."

"You'll never know unless you try." She felt the breath go out of her as he lifted her hands to his lips.

"I've never had to fight for anything, not really. I suppose I just expected I'd have everything I ever wanted just handed to me," she admitted.

"Life doesn't work that way."

"I'm finding that out."

He took her face between his hands. "It's been a long time since I looked at a woman. I like looking at you." Once again his eyes drew her and held her without the promise of escape.

For a moment she felt as if her breath had been cut off. "Why now?" she heard herself whisper. "Why me?"

"I don't know."

"You don't know."

"I do know I'd like to kiss you." When she didn't reply, he brushed her lips with his, gently at first, then with a depth of passion Ruthann couldn't ever remember feeling with Jack. "That was very nice," he murmured. "I'm not sure we can improve on it, but I think we should try." This time she could feel his heart beating against her, and his lips lingered until she knew she was losing all sense of reason.

He didn't kiss her again when he left her at the

door of the boarding house, but she couldn't wash away the taste of those hungry kisses, nor could she forget the reckless emotions they engendered in her.

****

On the last day of October, she waited for Rena before walking to the basketball court, where the PTA had set up the booths for the Halloween carnival. "I'm sure the Fulton will be here," Rena said, "but we can hope she leaves her resident ghost at home."

"Ghost? What ghost?"

"Did I forget to tell you?" A sly smile spread across Rena's delicate features.

"You know you did."

"Well, it's like this." Rena leaned into Ruthann's face. "It seems the Fulton had a younger sister who got into trouble at school and just up and disappeared. Maybe she's in the bell tower or the basement or even locked up in a secret room at the Fulton place on the end of Third Street. Who knows? But people claim they've seen her, especially when there's unexplained trouble in town."

Ruthann laughed. "I like the bell tower story best, because I've heard Mr. Cabrera has the scalps of everyone who's dared invade his basement."

"Hanging on the wall. He guards his territory like an old mother grizzly. But he also keeps the building healthy. It's almost eighty years old and beginning to show its age."

"I like old buildings, myself."

"So do I, especially if they're haunted."

Ruthann shook her head. "I don't do hauntings. We'd better get going. I see the little ghosts and goblins already gathering, and Kitty is supposed to show me how to run the popcorn machine."

By seven, as the festivities wound down, the unusually warm, humid night had straightened her carefully curled hair and bathed her face in a sheen of moisture. She lifted her apron to dry it. "You're in a steam bath," a middle-aged woman said with a smile. "I'm Julia Schaeffer. I've been wanting to meet the girl who's put a sparkle in Drew Mallory's eye."

A wave of heat which didn't come from the hot kettle engulfed Ruthann.

"You're blushing like a proper young lady, but you shouldn't feel embarrassed. Drew's a good man, and he doesn't do things impulsively. Well, not often anyway."

"I'm afraid it's stirred up a lot of talk."

"Not among the folks who really count. And speak of the devil…"

"Ah, Julia, you've met Ruthann." Drew appeared from the direction of the haunted house—in this instance an army surplus tent.

"I have, and I approve. Now I'm going home. Does Gwen need a ride, or is she with Daniel?"

"I have no idea."

"Well, I'll take a look around. Goodnight, Ruthann. Remember what I said."

"What did she say?" Drew asked.

"I'd rather not repeat it." Ruthann wiped her face again. "My face is red enough already."

"Have you been at this all evening?"

"Can't you tell?" With her forearm, she pushed her hair back from her damp forehead.

"You do look a bit flushed. Can I help you with anything?"

"I'm just shutting down." She noticed his knuckles

were white around the head of his cane and knew he'd been on his feet too long.

"Things went well," he said, taking the folding chair beside the brightly painted booth. "Mr. Wolfe has sent all the munchkins home to Kansas and is wiping greasepaint off his face. Miss Gilbert has led the last chorus of "La Cucaracha," the piñata has been successfully shattered, and we're all wondering why we do this sort of thing on a school night."

"Well, it's only once a year, and sometimes Halloween falls on a weekend." Ruthann wiped out the cooling kettle and handed Drew the last red-and-white-striped box of popcorn. "On the house."

"I'll be up all night after the mixture of food I've eaten."

"No one came to relieve me here, so I didn't get to eat."

"Let me see if I can find you a hot dog." He began to push himself to his feet.

"No, no, but thank you. I'll raid the refrigerator at the boarding house. Aggie always has something hidden away."

"We could stop at the coffee shop. I'll buy you a bowl of Buck's stew if there's any left over." The hopeful look on his face and the memory of his kisses in the park stirred a sudden longing to be with him away from the crowd.

"All right."

"Daddy." Gwen stood a few inches away. "I'm ready to go home."

"You'll have to hitch a ride with your aunt, Gwennie. Miss Cooper hasn't eaten, so we're going to have something at the coffee shop. At least, she is. I've overindulged."

Gwen's face darkened. "Well, fine," she retorted and strode away.

"Go on with her," Ruthann said.

"No. She's being intentionally rude to both of us. It's not like her, actually."

"She's very pretty. Does she look like her mother?"

"Somewhat. Marlene was fair."

Rena whirled up. "You about ready, Miss Popper?"

"We're going to stop for coffee," Drew said without giving Ruthann a chance to reply. "May I drop you at the boarding house, Miss Gilbert?"

"Yes, thanks. I'm dead on my feet."

"I think everyone is," Drew said. "I'm curious as to what tomorrow will be like in the various classrooms."

"Slow," Rena said. "Very slow."

Ruthann checked again to be sure she'd unplugged the kettle, then switched off the bulb hanging over it. "I understand a group of fathers will be dismantling everything later, so I guess I'm ready."

Drew got to his feet with more difficulty than Ruthann had seen before. Behind his back, Rena lifted her eyebrows. "This way, ladies," he said. "I'm parked in my usual spot."

After leaving Rena at the boarding house, Drew drove to the hotel coffee shop. "We're becoming regulars here," he said.

"I'm afraid so."

He stumbled a little on the curb.

"Your leg bothers you when you're tired, doesn't it?" Ruthann blurted and instantly regretted her words.

Drew grimaced as he stopped to regain his balance. "Yes, it does. It was pretty well shot up. More than one doctor has tried to take it off. The last one said there's less and less to patch, so it's inevitable I'll lose it eventually."

"I'm sorry. I shouldn't have said anything."

He smiled as he opened the door of the café. "Don't be embarrassed. It's part of me, and you've every right to know the facts."

"I'm just concerned," she said, sliding into their usual booth.

"Thank you for that. It looks like you're in luck. The stewpot is still steaming, and I see two slices of apple pie under the glass on the counter. How about some ice cream, too?"

"Why not?"

He reached for her hand across the table. "I'm sure you've seen *Casablanca*, but it's back at the Ritz for another run. Would you like to go on Saturday afternoon? Or we could drive out to Sorrells Woods, and you could watch me paint—though I think watching Humphrey Bogart might be more appealing to you."

"Actually, I always found Paul Henreid to be more suave and romantic."

"So an older man does appeal to you after all?"

Ruthann knew she was blushing again. "I don't know." She looked up from the bowl of stew. "But I'd like to watch you paint. I could pack a picnic lunch."

"I'll show you my favorite spot by the lake. It's very secluded."

"Do you think we need a chaperone?"

He frowned. "I hope you're joking."

"Only partly. Aren't we adding fuel to the fire by going off alone together?"

His blue eyes crinkled at the corners. "Well, the weather's getting cooler, so we need the warmth."

\*\*\*\*

A cold front came through on Friday. Ruthann woke in the night, chilled by the breeze blowing through the half-open window. She pulled up the quilt and turned so she could see Jack's picture. *Why can't I remember you?*

She did remember his mother's admonition the day she graduated: "Go home and start your life over, Ruthann. Jack's gone. We all have to accept that."

She knew it was true. Jack was gone, and Drew Mallory was quickly replacing him in her heart. *No, he's not replacing Jack. Jack left long ago. Drew's there in his own right. But he's old enough to be my father. If we have children, it's possible he won't live to see them grown. And his leg...what he said about eventually losing it. Can I cope with that? Then there's his daughter...there's Gwen. I have no right to come between them.* She turned over and watched the moonlight play across the ceiling. *He asked me to give things a chance. But is it a chance—or a terrible risk?*

\*\*\*\*

When she went down to breakfast the next morning, dressed in slacks and a long-sleeved plaid flannel shirt, she found the table empty except for Lillian. "Rena's sleeping in," Aggie said. "Nathan Wolfe has taken his eighth-graders on a nature trip to catch insects, Kitty went to visit a friend for the weekend, and who knows what Bernie's up to. Help yourself from the buffet. I already packed your picnic lunch."

"Oh, Aggie, you didn't have to do that."

"I wanted to. I'm fond of Drew Mallory, and I want to make sure he gets a good meal."

Ruthann wrinkled her nose. "You don't trust me?"

"Not as much as I trust myself." Aggie laughed and disappeared through the swinging door into the kitchen.

"So you're off with Mr. Mallory for the day," Lillian said. "Coffee?"

Ruthann held out her cup. "Thank you. He's going to paint in what he calls his favorite spot in Sorrells Woods. I'm taking a book to read."

"I'm glad you're going, Ruthann. The two of you are well suited."

"Why do you think so?" She filled her plate at the buffet and sat down again.

"You're quiet like he is. You seem comfortable together." Lillian paused with a biscuit halfway to her mouth. "The man I might have married died during the first war. He was the boy next door. We had an understanding."

"Oh, Lillian, I'm sorry."

"Unlike Kitty, I gave serious consideration to marrying another man I met after I came here."

"Why didn't you?"

"He moved away."

"Lillian…what Bernie said the other night about Merle Fulton…what she did to you…"

The older woman took a long breath and let it out slowly. "She never forgave me for turning her in."

"But she wasn't punished."

"No, she wasn't, but the very fact I'd had the audacity to turn her in was a mortal sin in her book. Her younger sister came along a few years later. Mona turned out to be worse than Merle. She almost managed to cause a mutiny of the entire freshman class that year. The principal told me if I couldn't keep order in my classroom, he'd find someone who would." She let the spoon drift around inside her coffee cup. "But that wasn't the worst."

"What was the worst?"

"A group of young people went out to the lake one night. Merle and Mona were there, too. One of the girls drowned. One of my students. It…it affected me very much."

"I'm so sorry."

Lillian leaned her head into her hands. "There were rumors the drowning wasn't accidental, but the investigation was swept under the rug. No one wanted to pursue anything connected with the Fultons. They were above anything like that. Mona was sent to boarding school in San Antonio."

"I shouldn't have asked."

"You should know what the Fultons are capable of. There's only Merle left now, but she's enough."

"How could you bear to stay in Camden?"

"I had to earn my living. After a while, I just didn't have the heart to start over somewhere else."

"What happened to Mona Fulton?"

"I don't know. After she left, it was as if she'd never been here at all. One story goes that she ran off with a young man just before graduation. Another says she died in a car accident. And she's also said to haunt the house and the school bell tower."

"Rena said that. She was joking, wasn't she?"

Lillian shrugged. "Over the years, people— credible people—have sworn they saw her in a third-floor window of the Fulton house or out in the garden late at night. Whenever there's a problem at school, some of the students joke it's the ghost in the bell tower. Some of their parents were Mona's classmates. A few were at the lake that night, but they don't talk about it."

Ruthann shivered. "As my grandmother used to say, I feel as if someone just walked over my grave."

"Don't let it bother you, dear. Enjoy today. Don't...don't guilt yourself into refusing the gift of Drew Mallory. He's a good man."

Chapter Eight

On the drive to the lake, Ruthann repeated Lillian's story to Drew. "That was the tragedy I mentioned occurring before I came in 1931, but there's more to it," he said. "Lillian had fallen in love with the local doctor, Simon Greene, a widower with one daughter, Elizabeth. Camden had been spared the worst of the flu pandemic, and he was asked to speak at a medical conference somewhere about how he'd handled the few cases we did have. He asked Lillian to stay at the house with Elizabeth, who was sixteen. One night she slipped out with her friends to go to the lake.

"Luís Cabrera found her body when he went to fish the next morning. Of course, some people tried to blame it on him. He was a Mexican and therefore an easy target. But he'd been driving Father Callaway's wagon when the priest was called to the country to see a dying parishioner."

"So the doctor blamed Lillian and moved away."

"That's what I understand."

"What about the other students? Did they…"

"They all told the same story—Elizabeth had slipped away from the campfire to meet someone and never came back. They decided she'd gone home."

"Who?"

Drew shook his head. "I could give you a lot of names connected with the unfortunate incident, but it might prejudice you toward all of them. They've all gone on to successful lives here in Camden."

"I don't really need to know. Lillian said Merle's sister was sent away to school after that and just sort of disappeared."

Drew laughed. "She's the ghost of the school bell tower—or hadn't you heard?"

"Twice. You don't believe that, do you?"

"She wasn't there the last time I looked."

Ruthann shivered. "The idea of her haunting either Fulton House or the bell tower is spooky."

"I don't believe in ghosts." Drew glanced at her as he slowed to negotiate a turn. "Do you?"

"No, but I can't help feeling there's something evil about all of this. Nathan Wolfe called Merle dangerous."

"The potential is there, but what happened to Elizabeth Greene is past history. When Merle tried to buy off Gwen in the days she was trying to arouse my interest in her, I took particular care not to let Gwen accept the gifts and offers of travel."

"Did she want to?"

"I think at first she did, but she believed what Julia and I told her—that getting mixed up with Merle Fulton wasn't in her best interest, no matter what the offer. But I don't want to talk about that woman today."

"What are you going to paint?"

"Whatever looks interesting." He glanced sideways at her and smiled. "I feel particularly inspired today." Then he reached for her hand, and she let him hold it tightly all the way to Sorrells Woods.

He parked off the road a little distance from the Camden Inn, closed until evening, and led her down a smooth path which ran through trees so thick they almost shut out the light. As they emerged, she caught her breath at the sunlight sparkling off the water. "It's beautiful."

"It is, isn't it? And peaceful. We'll have to step off the path for a few yards to reach my painting hideaway." He shifted the easel under one arm and took a firmer grasp on the fishing tackle box, which held his paints, before planting his cane firmly on the packed dirt trail. "I'm glad you wore slacks. Sometimes the chiggers in the grass are hungry. Are you managing the picnic basket all right? I can come back for it."

"You're talking to a girl who regularly hefted forty pounds of metal in the munitions factory," she said. "Let's go."

Near a triangular grove, he set up his easel close to the water while she spread a blanket under a tree and took out her book. "I'll be very quiet," she said.

"Only creativity requires concentration. I just dabble."

"But you said you were inspired today."

"So I did. All right then, be very quiet and let me get on with it." He winked at her before he opened his paints.

Just as the sun reached the center of the sky, he called Ruthann to join him. She gasped at the perfect replication of the small rowboat moored across the inlet with red and gold autumn leaves blanketing the bow and trailing into the water. "You're very talented," she said. "I mean that."

"I enjoy it, anyway. And I've worked up an appetite."

"Aggie insisted on packing the lunch. She said, and

I quote, 'I'm fond of Drew Mallory, and I want to make sure he gets a good meal.' "

"You can't cook?"

"Very well, thank you. My mother made sure my sister and I learned to cook and keep house. We had help with the laundry and ironing, but everything else we did on our own."

Drew eased himself down on the blanket, then toppled clumsily onto one elbow before righting himself. "If I can't get up, I hope you can find your way back to the car and go for help." He spoke lightly, but Ruthann discerned sadness in his eyes.

She filled a glass with lemonade from the jug, which she'd cooled in the lake while he painted, and handed it to him.

"I'm forty-six, Ruthann. Old enough to be your father."

"Daddy's fifty-three."

"Gwen suggested to me I'm refusing to accept my age. I believe she said I was having a middle-aged fling."

"A fling?"

"She said so." He peeled the waxed paper from around a thick ham sandwich. "The only thing I'll admit to is stepping out of character."

"If you're not happy outside, you can always step back in."

"And leave you behind?"

She made herself meet his eyes. "You've known me less than two months."

"Perhaps, at my age, that's long enough. Do you want to know what I thought the first time I laid eyes on you in the meeting before school began?"

"If you want to tell me."

"Well, that's the problem, you see, I didn't think. I felt."

The stirring low in her stomach unsettled her. "I see."

"Do you? I'd put myself on autopilot—you know, like the bomber pilots did when the bombardier took over for the bomb run. You know about that?" He didn't give her time to answer. "I sat in the cockpit and let the world skim by while I did nothing to make a difference."

"That's an odd comparison, isn't it? You're responsible for the whole school system in Camden, and I've heard you've made a big difference since you came."

"Ah, but that's professionally. I'm talking about my personal life. It was just up there in the clouds somewhere, with the world zipping past below. I was getting older and tireder. Then I saw you."

"My sister is the beauty in our family, and I'm not fishing for a compliment."

"If I had to use one word to describe what I saw when I looked at you, it would be *fresh*."

"Coming from you, I'm sure that's a compliment."

He cupped her chin in one hand. "You have a calm face."

"Calm?"

"It reflects your quiet spirit. And you have a sweet smile." He leaned closer. "Hazel eyes. They smile, too." He fingered her hair. The humidity from the water had straightened the curls a little, and he pulled one strand down along her cheek. "They say opposites attract, but you're very much like me, which is a comfortable feeling."

"My mother says I'm an old soul."

"Meaning I really am old?" He grinned.

"No," she stammered, "I didn't mean that…exactly."

"Well, it's true. I looked up your personnel records. You're twenty-four, and as I told you, I'm forty-six, soon to be forty-seven. I'm not doddering, but I'm not a young man any longer. Which brings me back to you. Some people might say I'm robbing the cradle."

"Are you?"

He let her question hang unanswered as he took another bite of his sandwich. "Aggie knows how to cook a ham." He chewed and swallowed. "But I didn't tell you how I felt when I first saw you." He seemed to be gauging her reaction to his words. "I felt like I should have put on a tie. Combed my hair better. Spruced up. I felt like a schoolboy who wanted to impress a pretty girl."

"I was impressed."

"You were? How?"

"I'm not sure I can explain it, but when you kept looking at me, I wondered what you saw. I thought how blue your eyes are."

"You like my blue eyes?"

"They're very nice. They're…mesmerizing."

"Mesmerizing. I like that. I never thought I presented a very dashing figure, even when I had two good legs." He finished his sandwich in silence and helped himself to a second watermelon rind pickle. "Tell Aggie I enjoyed her lunch. Mostly I enjoyed the company." He chewed his bottom lip. "I think it's time I told you about my wife. About Marlene."

He took a long swallow of lemonade. "I was twenty-two when I met her in New York just days before we shipped out to France. She worked in a club some of my buddies liked to visit. After she'd sung, she came to our table, and I couldn't believe she talked to me and ignored the others. I went back the next night and every night until we left. But I was rather backward with women, and we were never alone." Ruthann thought his eyes darkened a little as they gauged her reaction to his words.

"She came to the dock to see me off, and we wrote letters. I'd been over there six months when a German shell knocked me head over heels and left this leg barely hanging on. When I refused to let the doctors in the hospital in Paris take it off, they threw up their hands and shipped me home. Marlene came to see me."

He held out his glass for a refill and drank it slowly. "By the time I could manage a few steps, she said she thought we should get married so she could look after me. It had been a long time since anyone took care of me, and I couldn't believe my good luck." He sighed. "On our wedding night, she told me she was pregnant. Of course I knew it wasn't mine, but she begged me to stay with her until the baby was born. She promised she'd apply for an annulment then."

"We ended up in east Texas, and I found enough work to support us. I'd fancied myself in love with her, but when Gwen came along, I took one look and understood what love was really all about. I put down my name as the father on her birth certificate, and no one ever knew differently."

"Even your sister?"

He hesitated but only briefly. "Julia's not really my

sister. She and Leonard rented Marlene and me a garage apartment in east Texas. They didn't have children of their own and were besotted with Gwen. So when Marlene died, they offered to help me, and I let them because I had to work. Len had been in some trouble at the bank where he worked. Oh, he hadn't stolen anything, just temporarily covered up some irregular transactions by a bank officer who repaid the money before the auditors found out. But the bank trustees knew, so he was glad to move on when I was hired as superintendent in Camden."

"Does Gwen know?"

"Absolutely not. There's no reason for her to know."

"Aren't you worried she might find out?"

"How?"

"What about Julia?"

"I don't know if Marlene told her, but I know I didn't. After Gwen came, there was no more talk of an annulment. Marlene was a good mother. She did a masterful job managing what I earned and supported my going to summer normal school and taking classes at the college in Commerce, where we lived. I have to give her credit for what I've been able to do professionally. And we had a good life together until she died. A good life except for..." He paused so long that Ruthann thought he wasn't going to go on.

Suddenly she had to know the rest. "Except for?"

"We cared for each other, but for the rest of her short life, Marlene carried the guilt for what she'd done. She was unable...that is, our marriage was never consummated."

For a brief moment, Ruthann thought she might

tumble onto the blanket in a dead faint. Through sheer force of will, she stayed upright, but she couldn't force words from her mouth.

"You're shocked a man and woman could live together for five years without having a physical relationship."

She nodded.

"But you're more shocked we're sitting here talking about something so intimate. A woman might confide in another woman, but a man doesn't say such things to a woman."

"I…yes."

"We have to talk about it, Ruthann. You have to know the man who wants to be something more than just your boss. You have to know who I was, because all of it made me who I am now."

She nodded again.

"I did my best to help Marlene get over her guilt. We got along well, and we had a beautiful little girl. I managed to convince myself the rest didn't matter."

"Did it?"

He smiled. "What do you think? I'm a man, after all. And I was a young man then." He touched her cheek. "You're blushing, but you shouldn't be embarrassed. The physical side of marriage is important, but sometimes I think too many people get married for only that reason—to be together physically. Then, when the excitement fizzles, they drift apart." His fingers stroked her burning cheek. "Intimacy is more important. Sharing the deepest parts of oneself with another person and trusting them to accept and understand and perhaps love in spite of those parts. Do you understand what I'm saying?"

89

Without thinking she covered his hand with hers. "I think so. I hope so. You're not like anyone I've ever met."

"Then you're not sorry you met me."

"No."

He patted her face and lowered his hand. "After Marlene died, I convinced myself I didn't need anything except my daughter and my work. Then there you were, standing in front of me, smelling of whatever scent it is you're wearing today, and your hand, when I shook it, was so soft and warm. I imagined the rest of you that way—your soul, not your body."

Ruthann lifted a box of cake slices from the basket and served Drew while she tried to find words to respond.

He savored a bite before he said, "You wondered what else there was to know about me. I've trusted you with my deepest secret." He seemed to be waiting.

"I'd never repeat anything you've told me. Not to anyone."

"I felt I could trust you. I also felt you had to know the truth if our acquaintance was going any further— and I hope it will." Again the expression in his eyes—a mixture of sadness and hope—stirred an unaccustomed feeling of unworthiness deep inside her.

"I appreciate your honesty." She glanced away from him, then back. "Not many men would've stayed the course."

"I think you give me too much credit. Besides, there was Gwen."

"All the more reason you shouldn't risk an estrangement from her because of me."

"She'll come around."

"You're sure of that?"

"I raised her. I know how she thinks."

"Are you sure you want to take the risk?"

"I care for you, Ruthann."

"How do you know? How can you be sure after only a few weeks?"

"I can't explain it, but I'm sure."

"What attracts one person to another, do you think? I knew Jack such a short time, and I've known you even less time."

"I think it depends on where one is in his journey through life. You're young, but you've experienced a great deal of life. And, of course, I've experienced even more."

"Sometimes I think I haven't learned anything. You make me feel very shallow."

"I don't mean to. I've told you things you've never thought of, much less encountered. It's up to you how—or even if—you accept them."

"I wonder if I have the depth of character to do that."

He extended his hand and waited for her to take it. "I took a risk telling you all this, but I think you just took a larger leap of faith, and the rest will follow if you want it to." He lay back with his hands clasped beneath his head and closed his eyes. "I love the feel of sunshine on my face, especially in the autumn. I remember how dark and damp those trenches in France were. It's been over twenty years since I saw the last of them, but I've never been able to get enough of the sun."

By the time Ruthann had repacked the picnic basket, he'd fallen asleep. She walked to the edge of the water and gazed out across the lake. A sudden slight breeze stirred the water until it lapped thirstily at the bank.

*What am I doing here today...with him...listening to his secrets...witnessing his vulnerability?* She wrapped her arms around herself protectively and closed her eyes as if to shut out her thoughts. *And the way he talked to me...it seemed so natural. I can't imagine talking to Jack like that.*

*The way I feel about him frightens me. I thought I loved Jack, but I didn't feel close to him the way I feel almost at one with Drew Mallory. He's nothing like Jack. I was so sure I was in love before, but Rose Ellen was right. Jack was a handsome face in a uniform. He made me laugh, and when he kissed me, I felt special in a way I never had before.*

*When Drew touches me...when he kisses me...I feel something else. Desire? He as much as admitted that's what he felt for me the moment he saw me. Is that what mature people do? Want each other?*

*I feel a kinship with him I never felt with Jack. He's comfortable like a familiar place. But he's exciting, too. He knows so much, thinks so deeply, and reflects so much hope. There's something else about him, though...a need of some kind. Is his daughter right? Is this a fling for him at his age?*

*And then there's Merle Fulton. What Lillian told me this morning made me feel afraid for the first time. She's a nuisance, but is she really dangerous, like Nathan Wolfe said? Someone said the war was about fighting bullies, but we didn't get rid of all of them. I don't suppose we ever will. But I'm done fighting. I've had a bellyful of it, just like that young soldier on the train said the day I arrived in Camden. I don't want to fight Merle Fulton or anyone else...especially myself.*

Her whole body felt heavy as she walked back to the grove of trees. Drew's blue eyes flew open. She read an invitation in them and folded herself to her knees beside him. "That wasn't much of a nap."

"Forty winks." He reached to touch her hair and let his fingers skim her cheek. "And I dreamed of you."

"Isn't that a little trite?"

"It's downright corny." Laughing, he pulled her face down to his and kissed her, a long, thorough kiss that begged for more.

Fire raced through her. "Drew, this isn't..."

"A good idea? I agree. But I can't seem to care." He pulled her closer until she uncurled her legs and stretched out beside him with their bodies almost touching.

She closed her eyes. "I can't even explain how you make me feel. I don't know how to sort out my feelings."

He cut her off with a second kiss, this one longer and full of yearning. His arms went to her shoulders and slipped down her back circumspectly enough, but his touch aroused a pulsing abandon in her. He turned on his side and gathered her against him, close enough for her to understand the moment had become fraught with real peril.

His kisses, though soft, demanded more. She heard him whisper, "Precious girl," as his breath came faster. Then, abruptly, he rolled away from her. "It gets dark early this time of year. We should think about packing up."

She sat up and straightened her blouse, which had

become partially untucked. "Yes. Yes, we should."

Neither of them spoke until they reached the car. "I didn't mean to frighten you," he said. "Though frankly, I frightened myself."

"It's all right. I suppose I just wasn't prepared for what you said…what you did."

"I wish I could tell you I'm sorry, but I'm not."

She regarded him for a long moment. "It's as if I walked down that path this morning as a little girl and came back as a woman."

"That's an intuitive analogy." The approval on his face pleased her.

"I was the baby, you see. I've told you my parents sheltered me. Jack treated me like a trophy he'd won. He petted me and showed me off to his family and his friends, and I got used to it."

"Now you're on your own for the first time, and along comes an older man who's not interested in trophies or baby girls but rather in a real live woman."

Ruthann leaned against the car. "You're right."

Drew opened the door for her. "Sometimes I am."

An air of peaceful resolution filled the car on the silent drive back to town. Something had been settled between them, though Ruthann wasn't quite sure exactly what it was. At the boarding house she asked, "What will you do with your painting?"

"Would you like to have it?"

"Very much."

"I'll have it framed for you."

"No, I want it now. I'll do something with it later."

He retrieved it from the back seat and set it just inside the door of the boarding house. "Tomorrow at the café? Three o'clock?"

"Three o'clock."

He kissed her cheek before leaving her at the door.

"Cashmere Bouquet," she called after him. "I'm wearing Cashmere Bouquet talcum powder."

He waved over his shoulder and kept walking.

Chapter Nine

In the three weeks remaining before Thanksgiving break, the weather allowed one more Saturday at the lake. Despite Ruthann's dread of encountering Merle Fulton, she and Drew went out to dinner twice, to a movie, and spent several hours together in the coffee shop on Sunday afternoons. With no one around but Buck, the owner who kept the shop open on Sundays as a courtesy to hotel guests, they enjoyed total anonymity. Often, when they were the only customers, Buck pulled down the shades so no one could see in from the street. At least once Ruthann saw him turn the Open sign to Closed.

On the last Sunday afternoon before the break, Drew remarked on how the dim quietness invited the intimacy he'd mentioned their first time at the lake. "Buck's in the back, and we're all alone in a silent place." He laid his open hand on the table and smiled when she placed hers in it. "Tell me your dreams, Ruthann."

"I don't know if I have any."

"When you were a child, what did you dream of doing when you grew up?"

The gentle pressure of his fingers as he caressed her hand roused emotions Ruthann didn't want to acknowledge, but she didn't withdraw her hand.

"Oh, I thought of being another Shirley Temple at

one time. That didn't last long. My sister said my hair wasn't curly enough, and I had two left feet."

Drew chuckled. "That wasn't very nice of her."

She sipped the soda she'd ordered instead of coffee. "So then I considered being a business woman, and my mother gave me an old leather shoulder purse to stuff with papers and pencils. I carried it around for months."

"What led you into teaching?"

"I don't really know that either. Women still don't have much choice about their professional lives."

"That's changing because of the war."

"I like teaching. I think I'm suited for it."

"I think so, too. I've had several parents tell me what a good job you're doing."

"Really? That's nice to hear."

"So you're a teacher now and doing well. What do you see yourself doing in ten years?"

"I'm not sure."

He smiled. "I know what I hope you're doing."

"What about you?" she asked quickly to deflect the path of the conversation. "What did you want when you were growing up?"

"Well, let's see. Mainly I wanted to have enough to eat and shoes to wear in the winter. And a good coat. My father had all of us to feed and couldn't even read or write more than his name on a pay stub."

"You said you were sent to an orphanage when your parents died. What happened to your brother?"

"Actually, there were five of us. Gordon—he was the oldest—left home at fifteen. I was eight. I remember a few letters coming from him, but then nothing. Caroline married at fourteen and had a baby the next year. They both died. I remember going to the cemetery with my parents and seeing just one casket. I heard a neighbor say the baby hadn't actually been born." He patted her hand when her face mirrored shock. "Laurene died between Pop and Ma. She was five. Samuel and I went to the orphanage together, but he was only two—a cute tow-headed little fellow—and he was adopted within six months. I've always wished I could find him someday, but he wouldn't remember me anyway."

Ruthann closed her eyes to shut out the images.

"It's all right, precious girl. I landed on my feet with a dream or two left in my pockets. I've told you I want to travel someday. Sometimes I dream about going to bed at night and waking up with this leg miraculously fixed." He tightened his grip on her hand. "These days I mostly dream about being with you."

Ruthann felt hot tears welling up and turned her face away.

"What else makes you cry besides an old man's sad stories?"

"Sad movies. Happy endings. Christmas lights. Violins." She met his eyes again. "I thought I had a rotten time because of a bossy older sister and being such a wallflower in school. If I'd been through everything you have, I think I'd be very bitter."

"There's no percentage in bitterness."

"I still don't understand how you can be the way you are—so kind and gentle and caring—after so many bad things."

"Well, time passes, and life changes. I was never one to pick a fight. I ran away from a lot, though. Oh, not during the war. That would've been desertion, which was frowned on and would've gotten me shot. Although we were actually falling back when I got hit. That shell had my name on it, so I guess it was bound to find me no matter what."

"The doctors wanted to take your leg immediately?"

"Two of them did. The third said maybe I could make it home and let a doc here do the deed."

"But he didn't."

"Oh, he tried. But I was only twenty-three. I just couldn't see myself getting old with a peg-leg." His mouth twisted. "So now I'll get older with one. Someday."

"Soon?"

"Someday. Let's move on."

"All right. Where shall we go?"

"Maybe back to those happy endings that make you cry."

"I've done enough of that, haven't I?"

He lifted her hands to his lips. "I'm trying not to rush you."

"You're making me question who I am. I thought I knew. I never thought of myself as being a shallow person before, but when I realize what you're offering me...what you've already given me of yourself...how can I be sure I won't be the reason for another disappointment in your life?"

"You couldn't do that."

"If I did, I'd hate myself forever."

He separated her fingers and kissed the tip of each one. Impulsively, she stretched out the other hand. "Two hands," he murmured. "Is that symbolic?"

"I don't know what you see in me," she whispered,

"but I hope you keep looking."

****

School dismissed on Wednesday at noon. Ruthann spent the afternoon packing, and Drew took her to dinner at the Camden Inn. Later, parked out of the light at the railroad depot, he produced a thermos of coffee. "A moonlight tryst," he teased her.

"A tryst always seemed synonymous with trouble to me."

"You could get into a lot of trouble in the dark when no one's around."

She smiled. "Could I?"

"You're safe as a baby in its cradle. Not that I'm not tempted, even in broad daylight." He leaned across the seat and kissed her cheek. "That's for starters. You're sure someone will meet you in San Antonio? It's going to be almost midnight when you get there."

"Dad said he'd be there. He did wonder why I wasn't taking an earlier train."

"Did you tell him you had a rendezvous with your secret lover?"

"That's indecent!" She tried not to laugh and failed.

"Well, isn't that what this is?"

"I said I had some school business to take care of first and didn't want to rush. But I'll tell my parents the truth while I'm home."

"What do you think they'll say?"

"If you mean will they disapprove, no, they won't. Mother tried for those two years I lived at home to get me to go out with a parade of young men."

"I'm not a young man."

"Well."

"You said your father is fifty-three, so there's only seven years difference in our ages. They'll certainly have reservations about that, don't you think?"

"A few, maybe."

"You know I want this to last, Ruthann." He put one finger under her chin. "I want it more than I've ever wanted anything."

"I think they'll have more to say about the fact you're my employer. That and only knowing you for three months."

"Are you going to tell them about Merle Fulton?"

"I don't think so. Not yet. They'd only worry."

He finished his coffee, set the cup on the dashboard, and held out his arms. She moved into them without hesitation.

"I'll miss you. Get an early train back on Sunday. I'll meet it and take you to dinner."

She shivered without knowing why. "What was that ad during the war...the night has eyes?"

"Or loose lips sink ships?" He kissed her. "Does that sink your ship?"

"Straight to the bottom of the ocean." She put up her face for another.

"That's good. That's very good." He covered her mouth again. "I do love you, precious girl."

The sound of the train whistle in the distance saved her from replying. *I love him, but if I say it aloud...if I say it...* She put her mouth close to his ear. "I love you," she whispered. "I can't explain it any better than you can, but I love you, Drew Mallory. You're my knight in shining armor."

"That wasn't so hard, was it?" he whispered back but didn't let her reply as he moved in for one last kiss.

"I'll wire you as soon as I know what train I'll be on," she said as they approached a stern-faced porter who took her bag from Drew and hefted it up ahead of her. "Late for a young lady traveling alone," he admonished. "You get in that car and sit down and don't talk to strangers."

Ruthann studied his face. "I remember you from the trip from San Antonio to Camden. You didn't approve of all the soldiers paying attention to me."

The man cocked his head. "No, ma'am. Have a daughter of my own."

Drew handed the man a bill. "I'm glad you'll be keeping an eye on her." He held Ruthann's hand tightly as she stepped up onto the train. "Do what the man says, precious girl."

Only as the train began to move did he loosen his fingers twined with hers.

****

Ruthann waited until her sister's family had left after dinner on Thursday before she told her parents about Drew.

"He's the school business you had to take care of," her father observed. "The reason you didn't take an earlier train yesterday. So is this serious, Ruthie?" Matt Cooper took his pipe from the stand beside his chair and opened his tobacco pouch.

"It could be. I suppose it already is."

"And he's forty-six?" her mother asked. "That's only seven years younger than your father."

"Dad's still a very handsome man," Ruthann parried. "I know you think so."

Matt pretended to leer at his wife. "You'd better give the right answer, Mary Ruth."

Their shared laughter mingled with the crackling of the fire on the hearth. *They're comfortable together, the way Drew and I are. I never thought about them as anyone but my parents, but they're a couple. They have a good marriage. I want that, too.*

"There's more, though. A German shell shattered his left leg during the first war, and he says it's gotten worse. He'll eventually lose it. He uses a cane now. I've learned to tell when it's bothering him."

Matt removed his glasses and closed his eyes. "How do you feel about that?"

"It's just part of who he is."

"But you can accept it? The loss of his leg, I mean."

"He isn't his disability, Dad."

"No, he's not, which is the answer I wanted from you. I was in service, though the war ended before I saw any fighting. But a lot of my buddies did, and too many came home with injuries which changed their whole lives. There were broken marriages, at least one suicide, and a lot more."

"You said his wife died of cancer when their daughter was only four," her mother said. "How does she feel about all this?"

"She doesn't like it," Ruthann replied. "Drew says she'll accept it eventually. But if she doesn't, I won't make him choose between us."

"He's not worth staying the course for?" her father said.

"That's not fair, Dad."

"Well, certainly not to him anyway."

Ruthann flushed. "It's a risk I have to take. I can't make him choose between us."

"You don't believe that." He slid his rimless glasses back on. "And neither do I. So you're going to have to decide what you *can* live with. What you can survive. You grieved for Jack, but you finished with that. Drew Mallory is twenty-two years older than you are, so the law of averages says you'll eventually lose him, too."

"That's not something I want to think about."

"Well, you have to think about it. When you're forty, he'll be sixty-two. When you're sixty-two, he'll be eighty-four if he lives that long."

"So what are you saying?"

"I'm not saying anything, baby girl. You just need to face facts and decide what's best for you—and for him."

"Ruthann, your father and I will support any decision you make. You know that. Just consider the decision carefully. Look at all sides of the thing."

"I will, Mother. You know I'm not flighty."

"You've always been very levelheaded. I just worry about you, that's all. You came along when we'd given up hope for another child, so you're especially precious."

The words *precious girl* chimed in Ruthann's ears. *Precious girl. Oh, Drew, you've complicated my life in ways I never imagined, and I wish…I wish…*

Just before she turned off her lamp that night, her mother tapped on the half-open door and came in. "Ruthie, I want to have a talk with you."

Ruthann patted the bed. "We haven't had a good talk in a while."

"I'm not sure this one will be good."

Her mother's words put Ruthann on full alert, like

an air raid drill in the munitions plant during the war.

"You want to talk about Drew."

"I do. He's so much older."

"And I could find myself a very young widow."

"You just thought you grieved for Jack, but it's different to grieve for a husband. Thank God, I haven't had to face that. To be honest, it's something I can't even bear to think about. You only shared a few months with Jack, and I'm sure they were…"

"We were never together, Mother. Not that way."

"I was sure of that. But if you marry Drew, you'll share so much more. When you become part of a man—which is what the physical part of marriage really is—losing him will be losing part of yourself. It will hurt so much more than a telegram from the war department."

"I'm trying to understand that."

"Do you want children? How will you feel if it doesn't happen? How will you feel when you're still a young woman with needs and desires he no longer shares?"

"Is it even possible to know how you're going to feel years down the line?"

"I'm not trying to discourage you, but you've known him a very short time, and I think perhaps he's overwhelmed you. All I'm asking you to do is think about what I've said."

"You know I will."

Her mother went to the dressing table for a brush and began to draw it through Ruthann's hair. "I used to do this when you were a little girl. It was the time we'd talk about your day, and you'd tell me things you didn't want to say in front of your father or Rose Ellen."

"I remember."

"But you're a grown woman now, Ruthie. I'd be very wrong to interfere with your life at this point. I just want you to be happy."

"Drew is the kindest, gentlest man I've ever known. He's forthright about himself, even about his failings. He's made me understand just how much more growing up I need to do." She reached for her mother's hand. "Jack kissed me and held my hand, but I never felt the way I do when Drew takes me in his arms."

"How exactly do you feel?"

Ruthann hid her face against her mother's shoulder as she'd done as a child when she had something important to tell. "Like I've come home," she whispered. "Really home, forever."

****

When Drew Mallory presented himself at the door of the Cooper home just after lunch on Sunday, Ruthann couldn't hide her pleasure. "I thought I'd save you the train trip," he said after the introductions.

"Camden is a hundred and fifty miles from San Antonio. That's a three-hundred-mile round trip for you in a single day," Matt Cooper said.

"I'll have good company on the way back." Drew winked at Ruthann. "Besides, I drove in late last night and got a good night's sleep at a hotel. I'm no spring chicken, you know." He winked again.

Ruthann's face grew hot. "I'm already packed."

"I'll put up some supper for you to take with you," her mother said. "Come help me, Ruthann. I'm sure your father and Mr. Mallory have things to talk about." The look that passed between her parents didn't escape Ruthann. She'd seen it before and recognized the unspoken message: *Handle this.*

****

"So what did you and my father talk about?" Ruthann asked later as she slid into the car.

"Man-type things."

"I know that, but what exactly?"

"My intentions toward you. Were they honorable or dishonorable? Of course, I admitted to the latter."

"You did not!" Ruthann swiped at Drew's arm. He caught her hand and held it tightly.

"Are you glad I came?"

"You know I am."

"I missed you. Gwennie and Julia and I spent Thanksgiving with the Cliftons, as usual, but I kept wishing you were sitting at the table, too."

"How is Gwen?"

"It's hard to tell, but she's speaking to me again anyway. I think her fit of pique is over."

"You're sure of that?"

"I *hope* it's over."

He pulled into the first rest area and held out his arms. "Your father said he didn't have any objections to my *courting you*, as he put it, outside of the obvious."

"Your age."

"Yes, and he asked me for an honest assessment of my medical situation."

"Oh, Drew, I'm sorry. I know he's concerned, but asking you about anything so personal went too far."

"No, it didn't, Ruthann. I'm a father, too, and I know what he's worried about."

"All right, you're older than I am and a lot more mature. My immaturity concerns me. But as far as losing your leg, I don't care about that."

107

"You might change your mind. I have to face that."

"But I—"

"At my age, I know what I want," he interrupted her. "You're still trying to figure it out, but I think you've made progress. Did you mean what you said the night you left?"

"That I love you? Yes. But I don't trust myself, I guess. How did it happen so quickly? And more…" Her voice trailed off.

"Marriage? It's what I have in mind. I'm not playing games."

"What if you found I wasn't the person you needed? Not wanted, but needed. There's a difference."

"A big difference, and I worry about you needing more than what I am. Someone younger and especially without what I'm facing down the line."

"My father asked me how I felt about that. I told him you weren't your disability."

"But it affects me now, and losing the leg will create a whole new set of circumstances. And still I'm selfish enough to want to sweep all that under the rug and keep you with me." He curled a strand of her hair around his finger. "If you have any doubts, any at all, now's the time to lay them out."

"I thought I'd committed to Jack, but now it's like he never existed. Sometimes, when I think about him, I feel guilty for not grieving longer. For forgetting him."

"Do you think you should've locked yourself in an ivory tower and grieved 'til you died? What good would that have done him or you or anyone else? But let's say he'd come home all shot up. Then what?"

"Maybe that's what worries me. Maybe I didn't love him enough." She leaned against him. "Maybe I didn't really love him at all."

"The question is, do you love me enough?" He took her face in his hands and made her look at him.

"I don't love you like I thought I loved Jack. I love you as if I'm already part of you. Trying to imagine my life or even just tomorrow or next week without you...I can't."

"Just being without you for a few days was almost more than I could stand. Which is why I got in the car and came after you." His lips moved from her forehead to her pulsing temple and finally to her mouth.

"If we'd met under different circumstances..." she began when she came up for air.

"But we didn't. Rule Number One in life is we have to live in our present circumstances until we can change them, and ours seem pretty unchangeable right now." He stopped the words forming on her lips with a another long, hungry kiss.

Later, in a rest area a few miles from Camden, they lingered over the food Ruthann's mother had sent along. It was past dusk when the lights of the town twinkled on the horizon. Drew stopped again to hold her one last time.

"I don't want to be the reason for trouble at school or between you and your daughter. Especially between you and Gwen."

"I appreciate that. Maybe..."

"Don't say maybe it will go away. You know Merle Fulton isn't going to go away."

"I don't want you to go away, either. What about next year? There's no rule against married teachers."

"Wouldn't we be rushing things a little?"

"Not for me."

"You sound like a little boy who can't have dessert before dinner." She leaned her forehead against his and inhaled his clean scent.

"I feel very much like that little boy," he said with a hint of petulance in his voice. He stroked her neck. "Perhaps I'm not as mature as you think."

"I think you'd better get me back to the boarding house before Aggie locks up. I'd hate to wake everyone by ringing the bell."

"Not to mention being seen with a suitcase and me on the front porch. It might shock someone's sensitivities."

"Sometimes you surprise me with things like that."

"When you've lived in a place like Camden for as long as I have, you know its dark side."

"I guess I don't want to know its dark side. Rena's told me almost more than I can process."

"No." He slid under the steering wheel again. "No, you don't want to know." The car coughed and whirred to life. "By the way, that story you heard about Mona Fulton…"

"Which one?"

"How she haunts the house."

"You said you didn't believe in ghosts."

Drew looked out the side window. "I don't. But there are those in town who do."

"How do you know?"

"I asked around over the holidays."

"What are you saying?"

He shrugged. "I'm not sure. Just…just be careful, Ruthann."

Chapter Ten

By the time Ruthann arrived at school the next morning, a few minutes before her usual time, she found the dark of which Drew had spoken had preceded her. In the teachers' lounge a large typed notice screamed from the cork board:

*It has come to our attention that the wartime activities of a certain member of the staff are not as presented to the school board at her hiring. Credible information about illegal activities such as prostitution and fraudulent marriages for the purpose of collecting military allotments has been obtained. Since moral turpitude is one of two criteria for terminating employment, the staff member will be terminated immediately.*

Rena snatched the sheet of paper and crumpled it into a ball. "Look, we know who's behind this," she said as Ruthann sank into the nearest chair. "Mr. Clifton will take care of it."

Ruthann dropped her head into her hands. "It's done," she said, her voice only a hoarse whisper. "You can't put feathers back into a pillow or take back words. Why is she doing this?"

"Drew Mallory. She wants him, you have him, and she's not going to stand for it. That and she's totally deranged."

"Nathan Wolfe told me she was dangerous, and

Drew agreed. I didn't really believe either of them."

"Look, just hold up your head. You haven't done anything wrong, and no one's going to believe any of this anyway. I never mentioned it, but I've heard several people say Mr. Mallory looks happier than they've ever seen him."

Ruthann shook her head. "I can't fight her."

"You're not fighting her. You're fighting for your right to be happy. Mr. Mallory has a right to be happy, too."

Ruthann pushed herself to her feet without real hope she could stay on them. "I've got to put today's writing lesson on the chalkboard."

Somehow she got through the day despite the children's post-holiday restlessness, a steady drizzle which began mid-morning, and several interruptions, while the children were at recess in the gym, from other teachers who stopped in to say hello and ask about her holiday. Ruthann recognized and tried to appreciate their show of unspoken support, but she couldn't shake the cold, leaden armor threatening to squeeze the very life from her body.

The terse note delivered by a high school office assistant left Ruthann no option but to present herself in John Clifton's office as soon as the final bell sent the children tumbling from the classroom. His secretary smiled at her, but the gesture failed to calm the wave of rage finally engulfing her. Drew sat in front of the principal's desk. The despair written on his face caused a knot of pain deep in her chest.

"Miss Cooper, sit down, please."

Ruthann took the chair farthest from Drew and kept her eyes on the floor.

"The anonymous note Miss Gilbert handed me this morning has breached all common decency. I won't insult you further by offering trite words of comfort or saying I know how you feel. But I don't take lightly underhanded schemes to discredit any one of my faculty, so I want you to hear from me the notice I'm posting on the board in the staff lounge tomorrow morning."

Ruthann sat in stony silence, but his quiet voice had blanketed enough of her emotions to make her aware that the weight she'd carried all day had all but crushed her.

John plucked a piece of paper from his desk and began to read:

*I will not comment on the cowardly notice placed in the faculty lounge over the holiday weekend. I will state the facts, which are these, received by me when I checked Miss Cooper's references before hiring her. She graduated from TSCW in Denton in the spring of 1943 and returned to San Antonio to live with her family. Wishing to contribute to the war effort, she went to work for Henderson Munitions, receiving two promotions due to her outstanding performance in that dangerous employment. At Henderson, she organized efforts to set aside a small chapel for use of the employees. A priest conducted Mass every morning, and Protestant employees could seek solace there during breaks. In her time away from Henderson, she worked with her mother at the Red Cross and at the USO Canteen for soldiers from Ft. Sam Houston. Because of her moral example, she was asked to supervise the younger girls who participated in the effort, making sure they did not leave the building in the company of a soldier nor engage in any behavior detrimental to the purpose of the canteen. When the war ended, she decided to embark on the teaching career for which she had been trained. Camden Schools was fortunate to acquire her services.*

*I am directing each staff member to place his/her initials in the proper place to signify you have read this notice. We have always stood together as professionals, and I fully expect we will do so now.*

He lowered the paper. "I'm not asking your permission to post this, Miss Cooper. I deem it necessary to address what is an attack not just on you but on us all. I can only assure you of my support and ask you to carry on as well as possible during the next few weeks before the Christmas holidays."

Ruthann heard herself speaking from a far-off place. "My letter of resignation effective at the end of the term will be on your desk tomorrow."

John took a deep breath. "I'm going to step out and let you and Mr. Mallory discuss this."

Drew stumbled to his feet. "Ruthann, I'd give my life to erase this horrible thing. I blame myself."

She drew back as he reached to touch her. "Don't. Please don't."

"We've all been bullied long enough. We need to stand together now and end it."

"And you want me to be your Joan of Arc?" She sprang from her chair and retreated across the room. "I've already been burned enough, don't you think?"

"Listen to me, precious girl." He followed her with his arms outstretched.

"I'm not your precious girl or your Joan of Arc. I'm just a silly first-year teacher who should've known better than to get herself in over her head!" She heard her voice rising as if it came from someone else.

He stared at her and let his arms fall to his sides. "That's what I should've done from the beginning, isn't it? Leave you alone."

She buried her face in her hands.

He had her in his arms before she could move again. "Please, please stay. I care so much." He put his lips against her hair. "When I went to war, I didn't hate the Germans. I didn't even hate them after they blew up my leg. I know I killed a few, but I only shot at them because they'd have shot me. But right now…today…I could take pleasure in killing the person who's hurt you like this."

She pulled away. "You shouldn't say that."

"It's how I feel." He brought her back against him. "I'm so sorry, Ruthann."

"Just let me go," she murmured. "Please. I don't want to fight this. I can't."

"I'll let you go if that's what you really want. I have to, because I love you. But we can fight this together."

She shook her head. "But can we win?"

"Even a general can't predict victory on the battlefield. We don't have to stay in Camden. Experienced superintendents are always in demand."

"I won't let you give up everything you've worked for here."

"If I lose you, I've lost everything anyway." He rocked her in his arms. "Go get your things. I'll drive you back to the boarding house."

Chapter Eleven

"I need some things downtown," Rena said after breakfast on Saturday. "Come with me."

Ruthann shook her head. "I'd feel like everyone's looking at me."

Rena stopped halfway up the stairs and turned to stare. "You think people in town know about the notice in the lounge?"

"How could thirty-five people keep something like that to themselves?"

"Not just any thirty-five people. What goes on in the school stays there. Not one parent ever knew about my brush with disaster. Oh, they'd seen me out with Eddie, but when that stopped, they just assumed he'd shipped out. Some of the faculty knew what happened. Lillian, Kitty, Bernie, Mr. Wolfe, and a few more. And all they ever said to me was how relieved they were I hadn't gotten myself in deeper and good riddance to bad rubbish. I did hear by the way of the grapevine that the Madame had tried to get the school board to fire me for going out with a married man, but Mr. Mallory quashed that with the facts."

"I guess I'm selling them short, huh?"

"I guess you are, but you're still learning the ropes. You'll find out just how tightly knit the school community is. We have to be for a lot of reasons, not the least of which is Merle Fulton. And understand,

Ruthann, the little tidbits of gossip I've passed on to you were only to help you get to know us and beware of that woman. I don't gossip over the back fence."

"I stand reproved, then. Where do you need to go in town?"

\*\*\*\*

On the way home, they stopped for a grilled cheese sandwich at Troy's. "Rena, did you ever hear anything about Merle Fulton's house?"

"You mean about it being haunted by her long-lost sister?"

"I know it's silly, but…"

"It's not silly. A lot of people believe it."

"Do you?"

"I don't know. The first…no, the second year I taught in Camden, Harry said something at dinner about Mona floating around the garden the night before. Aggie shushed him, and no one else said anything, but later Kitty told me she'd heard Mona came home from boarding school in San Antonio at Easter one year and never made it back to school."

"According to Lillian, she might've run off with someone."

"I suppose, but it was about that time—so Kitty said—that Merle told her husband she wanted a divorce."

"How were the two related?"

"I don't know if they were. I'm just telling you what Kitty said."

\*\*\*\*

At Aggie's invitation, Drew came for dinner on Saturday night. Ruthann noticed how the older teachers were on a first-name basis with their superintendent outside of school.

Nathan Wolfe entertained them with the saga of the freshmen's campaign to acquire a hundred different insects for classification. "It happens every year—the boys suddenly become aware of the girls, and the girls use it to their advantage Suddenly they're terrified of anything that flies or crawls. Their squeals drive me insane, but the boys love it."

Lillian shook her head. "They're a fickle bunch, because they laugh at their heroes whose voices are changing. The freshmen were reading aloud from *The Rime of the Ancient Mariner* this week, and I actually had to call a halt when Larry Farrell came close to throwing a book at one of the gigglers."

"He didn't do it, I hope," Drew said.

"Only because he couldn't identify the one who laughed, but I knew. I had a word with the young lady after class."

"Every day is an adventure," Kitty said. "One of the girls—who shall remain nameless but who wears a pep leader's uniform and gyrates a little more than necessary at every football game—asked me on Thursday if the library had a copy of Fitzgerald's *The Great Gatsby.*"

"Do you?" Drew asked.

"I do not, and I told her I wouldn't check it out to her if I did. She just laughed and walked out."

"These kids lived through a war," Bernie said. "They're going to be different now. Let's face it, their culture is much more free even than what we called *flaming youth* in the twenties."

"More's the pity," Kitty said.

After dinner, when everyone dispersed upstairs,

Drew suggested a drive. "You're looking brighter," he said as they walked out to his car.

"There are only two weeks until the Christmas holidays. I can survive."

"How am I going to survive with you away for so long?" Drew pecked her cheek and opened the door of the car.

"The best you can, I suppose."

\*\*\*\*

Merle Fulton paid another long but silent visit to Ruthann's classroom the following week. She sat scribbling in a notebook, then snapped it shut and sailed out without a word. Ronnie looked up from his geography book from which he was supposed to be copying the names of the forty-eight states and their capitals. "I hope Mr. Mallory brings licorice tomorrow."

Karen made a face. "Not licorice. Caramels."

Ruthann found it difficult to look stern. "You are avaricious children," she said.

"Huh?" Ronnie's eyes grew wide.

Ruthann printed the word on the chalkboard. "Go to the dictionary and look it up," she said. "Both of you."

She watched them scamper across the room to the large dictionary on a stand beneath a window and laughed when Ronnie, his eyes round with amazement, announced, "It means we're greedy!"

"Well, perhaps *if* Mr. Mallory visits tomorrow, he'll bring candy of both varieties. Now go back to work."

Ronnie slid into his desk again. "Yes, ma'am."

When he glanced up at her later, she winked at

him.

John Clifton came by the classroom after the last bell. "I understand you had another visit today."

Ruthann sighed. "I'm afraid I did. But at least the children are happy they'll get a treat tomorrow. And they really do deserve it. They were especially angelic while she was here."

The principal smiled. "I don't doubt it. Of course, now I've got to address her complaints with you. Do you have a few minutes?"

"Surely."

He pulled out a piece of paper Ruthann recognized as coming from Merle's notebook. "Let's see—too much seat work, not enough teaching."

"When she came in, they were finishing copy work in geography left over from the day before. It was a deal we made—they were to come in and start right away before arithmetic and I wouldn't assign homework."

"I'm sure they liked that."

"Then we switched to arithmetic. I reviewed yesterday's lesson and then walked up and down the aisles monitoring their work."

He nodded. "Which is the way it should be done. Let's see, the paper cover was coming off one student's book. The shades on the windows were open, which she felt was a distraction to the children since they stopped several times to watch a couple of squirrels on the ledge. And Bobby Kinser didn't have his shoes on." He tore the paper into four pieces and dropped it into the wastebasket beside Ruthann's desk. "Now I've done my duty."

"Bobby's shoes are more holes than leather, and

they're too small anyway. I spoke to one of the PTA members about it yesterday, and he should have some new ones this week."

"The situation is getting worse for him. His grandfather's dying by degrees, and the medicine is expensive. Troy has carried their account as much as possible. Kay's looking through our boys' outgrown clothes to see if she can find Bobby a coat, but she said Merle has already reported him to Child Welfare."

"Oh, no! I know his mother barely makes ends meet, but she loves him. She's come by twice to ask how he's doing and if he needs anything. Not that she can afford it."

"She cleans for George Baucom at home and also at the bank. He makes sure she gets extra at Christmas so Bobby will have a gift or two. But if Child Welfare comes in…" He shook his head. "I swear that woman gets worse by the year."

"Is there anything I can do? I make sure he has what he needs. His lunches are adequate but without any extras, so the other children share their treats with him unasked."

"I'd say you're managing his needs well." He walked to the door. "Oh, and don't mind me popping in. I can say if she asks—and she will—that I've addressed her list of concerns." He gestured toward the trashcan. "*In depth*. Keep up the good work, Miss Cooper. And however inappropriate it may be to speak of anything personal, I want you to know Drew Mallory is one of the finest men I've ever known, and he's been happy these last few months in a way I've never seen."

Ruthann felt the warmth rise to her cheeks.

"Now I'm really going to step over the line. You

aren't just playing with him?"

"No, sir, I'm not. I…he's…"

"That's all I wanted to hear." He walked to the door.

"And his leg's getting worse, isn't it?" she blurted without thinking.

The principal turned, his eyes icy. "Yes, it is." He closed the door softly behind him.

****

It sleeted on Saturday, and Drew accepted another invitation to dinner at the boarding house. Afterwards, he and Ruthann had the parlor to themselves. "You know about the faculty Christmas party next week."

"I'd gladly come down with the plague if I could skip it."

"You can count on Merle being there, but so will I."

"Which will only make things worse."

"Maybe." He took her hand and lifted it to his lips. "I'm trying to head off Child Welfare from picking up Bobby Kinser. Dr. Leeson doesn't give his grandfather more than another few days, and after that, there's a possibility for a live-in housekeeping job for Jessie."

"In Camden?"

"Unfortunately—or maybe not—it's in Kerrville. George Baucom has a friend there whose wife is in poor health and could use some help around the house, which has nice living quarters attached."

"I'd hate to lose Bobby, but it sounds like a much better situation."

"Kay was going to talk to Jessie about it this weekend."

Ruthann studied the faint frown lines between his

122

eyes. "Rena said you took care of your teachers. You take care of the students, too."

"When I can. And I don't do it alone. We all pull together."

"My life has been so insulated. Even the war didn't really expose me to some things."

"Poverty is a permanent human condition, I'm afraid. I grew up in something close to it. At least in the orphanage I got enough to eat. Most of the time, anyway."

Ruthann leaned her face against his shoulder. "How can I possibly live up to you?"

His free hand drifted to her hair and stroked it. "It starts with caring, and you do."

"Sometimes I think I've never really cared about anyone except my immediate family and myself."

"I liked your father, Ruthann. He's very direct, but he's not confrontational."

"So you did talk about more than you admitted to."

"He's your father, precious girl. Your natural advocate. As a father myself, I know exactly what his concerns are."

"Your age and…" Her mouth went dry. "Your leg."

"Actually, he's more concerned with my ability to be a father again at my age. Maybe not the actual siring of a child, but later."

Ruthann caught her breath.

"Oh, I'm not so old I couldn't give you a child. I'm not sure how old is too old for that. But being a father is entirely different. And he said you might've moved on from a wartime romance with Jack, but he's not sure you could move on from the end of a lifetime commitment. He wonders if you really understand the chance you're taking."

"Maybe I don't. Maybe I can't. But I want to take it anyway."

"I told him I'd talk to you plainly, so I'm doing it. I may do it again." He lifted her face from his shoulder and wiped away two tears with his thumbs. "I believe in love, precious girl. I believe it comes unexpectedly and in surprising ways sometimes, but it's nonetheless real. When I saw you, I had the feeling I could love you forever."

Ruthann felt herself caught up in the deep whirlpools of his blue eyes. "I believe in love, too," she whispered. "Mostly, I believe in you."

Chapter Twelve

With no legitimate excuse not to attend the faculty Christmas party at the home of the school board president, Ruthann pressed the new red wool-blend dress her mother had sent and put on her grandmother's pearls. "Mr. and Mrs. Baucom are wonderful hosts," Rena said. "Don't let Merle spoil it for you. Not that she won't try."

"That's what I'm afraid of."

"She's not important."

"She thinks she is."

Rena tossed back her hair. "She'll get what's coming to her one of these days, you mark my words."

Harry and Nathan drove the boarding house residents to the party, which Aggie had been hired to cater. Kay Clifton attached herself to Ruthann like a destroyer running interference for a battleship. Drew made the rounds of all the guests before finally gravitating to Ruthann. "You look lovely," he whispered as Kay relinquished her guard dog duties to him and moved on.

"When I wrote about the party, Mother went shopping."

"She made a good choice."

"I haven't seen Gwen and Daniel."

"Daniel's around somewhere, but Gwen refused to come."

"Because of me?"

"I don't know what's going on in her mind these days." He glanced over her shoulder. "Here comes trouble."

Merle Fulton, wearing a black cocktail dress which would have been at home in a city like San Antonio but was glaringly out of place in Camden, halted beside the two of them. "Well, Miss Cooper, you're dressed for the season. Or are you in costume as the scarlet woman?"

Everyone around them stopped talking.

Ruthann stared at the woman. "Pardon me?" She felt frozen to the spot.

Merle laughed nastily. "You heard me, Miss Cooper. You've caused a great deal of trouble since you came. Perhaps you should consider not returning after Christmas. It would save the board the embarrassment of terminating you." Malicious satisfaction gleamed in the woman's eyes.

"Find new prey, Merle," Drew said. His low voice held an unmistakable warning. "Leave my teachers alone."

"And I'm sure at least one of them belongs to you in a particular way."

"I have thirty-five faculty members whom I'd defend to the death," Drew replied. His words carried deliberate meaning—and the shadow of a threat.

The woman narrowed her eyes but didn't reply before slinking away like a cat on the prowl.

"I'd like to leave," Ruthann said in a barely audible voice.

"Indeed you won't," Kay Clifton said, slipping an arm around the younger woman's waist. "Let her leave.

No one wants her here anyway."

Drew led her to a chair in a corner away from the crowd. "Look," he said, nodding toward Merle's back, "she's leaving. You've won this round."

Ruthann had to swallow twice before she could reply. "I think you fired the decisive shot."

Barbara Baucom, the school board president's wife, approached them. "I haven't met this lovely young lady yet, Drew," she said.

He made the introductions.

"We're glad you're here and doubly glad she's gone," the woman said. "But watch your back, my dear. Please."

Daniel Clifton, looking irritable, left before the buffet. When the party broke up just after eight, Drew offered to drive Lillian, Rena, and Ruthann back to the boarding house while Harry stayed to help Aggie pack up. The younger women gave Lillian the front seat and climbed into the back. "There's a car behind us," Rena said after they'd gone a few blocks.

"Following us, you mean?" Drew asked.

"I don't know, but it's weaving a little."

"Someone had too much Christmas cheer," Lillian observed.

"Not at the Baucoms' party," Drew said. "They're teetotalers, as we all can attest by the unspiked eggnog with dessert."

Rena laughed. "I'm not sure who around here would spike it."

"Oh, it's been tried," Drew said. "Coach Billings' predecessor was very young, and he gave it a good try once. That must've been right after I came in '31 or..."

No one actually saw the car swerve around them

and cut in front of Drew as he attempted to go straight on Main. He came within an inch of broadsiding the newer model Plymouth, throwing out his arm to keep Lillian from pitching forward as the Plymouth picked up speed and disappeared down Third Street. In the back seat, Rena and Ruthann untangled themselves.

For a moment, Drew's car remained motionless halfway into the intersection. Lillian broke the shocked silence. "That was Merle Fulton's car."

"Are you sure?" Drew asked.

"I'm sure it's her car, but she wasn't driving."

"Then who was?"

Lillian took a deep breath and let it out. "Someone younger." The name *Mona* hung unspoken in the stillness.

"Lillian, I…"

She waved a gloved hand. "Don't say it, Drew. I'm not crazy, and you know it."

"I'm not suggesting that."

"I know. Just wishful thinking."

Ruthann heard Drew's sharp intake of breath.

"Just let it go, Drew."

He turned around then. "Are you ladies all right?"

"We're fine," Ruthann said, searching the floor for her purse.

"Speak for yourself," Rena said in a shaky voice. "You left claw marks in my arm."

"I did not. I have on gloves."

"Well, it felt like it."

He didn't wait for an invitation to come inside with them. "I'll be back in a few minutes," Ruthann said. She followed Lillian and Rena up the stairs. On the landing, she caught the older woman's arm. "Lillian,

128

who was driving that car?"

"Mona Fulton."

"You're sure of that?"

"I'll never forget her face."

Rena's face went chalk white. "Lillian, do you realize what you're saying?"

"I don't know if she's dead or alive, but I saw her face tonight. Now I'm going to bed."

Rena followed Ruthann to her room and stopped. "Your door's open."

"You followed me out. Maybe you didn't pull it to."

"I did. I remember hearing it click."

Ruthann pushed on the door and snaked her arm around the frame to switch on the light. Rena's shocked yelp brought all the occupants of the second floor from their respective rooms. Drew arrived seconds later, breathing hard from the effort of hauling himself up the stairs.

Ruthann sank down on the foot of her bed and stared at the large round mirror of the dressing table where someone had scrawled a single filthy epithet. The snapshots taped around it had been taken at a distance, but they were obviously of Drew and Ruthann at the lake. Jack's picture, the glass shattered, lay on the floor nearby. Rena crossed the room and picked it up.

"I'll get the carpet sweeper," Bernie said.

Rena tore the pictures from the mirror, ripped them into small pieces, and dropped them in the wastebasket. Then she bent to pick up the larger pieces of glass from the frame.

"She was watching us," Ruthann whispered.

"We weren't doing anything wrong," Drew said as

if the others couldn't hear.

Bernie returned with the carpet sweeper and a bottle of glass cleaner. "It's only lipstick," she said, scrubbing at the mirror.

Kitty began to push the sweeper over the rug. The smaller pieces of glass clicked as the brushes caught them. "Remember to wear slippers in here for a few days, and use the sweeper several more times."

Ruthann picked up Jack's picture and shook the remaining glass into the wastebasket. Then she slipped it into a drawer.

"Go downstairs with Mr. Mallory," Lillian said. "We'll take care of things in here."

"No, I…"

Drew took her arm and propelled her out of the room. "They want to help. Come down to the parlor." As soon as he'd closed the doors, he said, "Merle left the party early."

"Did she leave the party, come here, and then return to wait for us to leave and nearly run us over?"

"And so did Daniel, and Gwen didn't come," Drew went on as if he hadn't heard her.

"Gwen didn't do this, and you know it."

Drew leaned his head back on the sofa. "She's been distant for a while."

"I told you I wouldn't come between the two of you. I'm going home at the end of the term, and if we're meant to be together later, it will happen."

His eyes flew open then. "If you go…" He stopped and pressed his lips together tightly for a moment. "No, you're right. I can't ask you to stay here in light of everything that's happened." He drew her head down to his shoulder. "Tomorrow is the last day of school, and you'll be going home on Saturday. Are you going to tell your parents what's happened?"

"I've never lied to them, and not telling them would be the same as lying, wouldn't it?"

"They won't want you to come back to finish the term."

"I can't break my contract. I wouldn't anyway."

He held her gently. "I'm so sorry about tonight."

"So am I, but mostly for what I've done to you. I feel I'm tearing down everything you've built up."

He kissed her twice before he let her go.

\*\*\*\*

Rena came by as usual after school and found Ruthann sitting at her desk amid the disarray from the class Christmas party. "You're not ready."

"No, you go on." Ruthann pushed herself away from the desk.

"Are you all right?"

"Yes, of course. I'll see you at supper."

"Are you sure?"

"I'm fine, Rena, really. I've just been lazy, but it won't take me long to put things right." She began gathering up bits of tissue and ribbon which hadn't quite made it to the wastebasket when the children opened their gifts.

"Don't stay too late."

When she'd gone, Ruthann turned her attention to the tree. She'd just reached for the star at the top of the classroom tree and turned to put it in the box with the other decorations when Gwen Mallory stormed through the door.

"I hope you're satisfied! You nearly got my father killed last night!"

"He told you about the driver who cut in front of the car?"

"Yes. Merle Fulton, I'm sure. But she wouldn't have done it if you hadn't been in there with him."

"Rena and Miss Buford were also in the car."

"You told him I went into your room last night and wrote that awful thing on the mirror." The young woman's flushed face twisted into a mask of rage.

"No one even suggested that. I know you didn't do it." Ruthann gestured toward one of the desks. "Please, sit down, Gwen. I know you're angry with me, but you don't have any reason to be."

Gwen's shoulders twitched as she walked a few nervous steps away from the door. "He's a good man. Too good for you." Gwen opened her fashionable leather purse and fumbled with something inside for a few seconds before snapping the clasp again. "What was he even doing in your room last night?"

"Everyone came running when they heard Rena yell. It's not what you're thinking."

"What am I thinking?"

"Look, I don't know if it will make you feel any better, but I'm not coming back next year. Maybe not even next term, if Mr. Clifton can replace me."

"You're lying!"

"I'm not lying, Gwen. I'd never come between you and your father. I told him as much."

"You've already done it."

"Then I'm sorry. I didn't mean to."

Gwen stared at her for a long moment before whirling around. Ruthann flinched at the sound of the slamming door.

For a moment she stood very still, trying not to see

Gwen's face or to replay the tawdry scene. *What have I done? Drew's bared his soul to me and told me he loves me, and all I've done is make trouble for him. I can't hurt him any more.*

On unsteady legs she went around the room, closing the blinds against the early winter dusk. She put the boxes of Christmas decorations on the top shelf of the closet and thought with sadness how another teacher would take them out next year. At her desk, she slipped her planning book and two textbooks into the leather case, put on her coat, and paused to look around. She'd loved teaching, loved the children, loved being part of the school community. That kind of love she could manage. She could even live with Merle Fulton's vicious animosity, but she wouldn't make Drew choose between his daughter and someone he'd known only a few months.

Mr. Cabrera had already turned out the corridor lights, and the winter dusk which filtered in from the glass of the doors at the end of the hall threw shadows along the walls and into the corners. Hearing soft footsteps not her own, she stopped. "Mr. Cabrera?"

Silence. She began to walk toward the doors again, this time with growing alarm, and the footsteps resumed. "Who's there?" She turned and searched the emptiness without seeing anyone. "Who's there?"

Later she couldn't remember if she heard the sound of running first or if something came out of nowhere to strike at her before the feet fled. Instinctively she put up her arm to shield her face, and her ungloved hand caught fire. Dropping her case, she sprinted for the door, but the piercing pain engulfed her in nausea and weakness. Hitting the locked doors full force, she dropped to her knees, and blackness closed in around her.

She drifted up from somewhere soft and silent only to be met by the returning pain. "It hurts," she whimpered.

Luís Cabrera's lined face bent over her. "Get up, *niñita*. Quick."

He rushed her down the hall to a flight of stairs leading to the basement, where he held her burning hand under a steady stream of water at a concrete sink.

"What are you doing?" Ruthann's knees buckled.

He shoved a stool under her. "Sit. It's acid. Water will stop the burning."

"Acid? What do you mean?"

He shook his head. "Just keep your hand still under the water."

"Papa?" A younger man came down the stairs and approached the sink. "What's going on?"

Mr. Cabrera slathered Ruthann's hand in what she recognized as baking soda. "Muriatic acid. She's been burned with muriatic acid. "Get me a clean cloth out of the cabinet, Tomás."

The younger man obeyed. "I'm Tomás Cabrera," he introduced himself. "I came to drive my father home. How did it happen?"

"Somebody threw something on me in the hall," Ruthann said.

"Did you see who it was?"

She shook her head and looked more closely at the man. He wore slacks and a thick sweater, and towered over his father, but his face resembled the concerned one bent over her hand.

"Shouldn't we get her to Dr. Leeson, Papa?"

"No, I'm all right," Ruthann said. "I don't need…"

"It's a bad burn," Tomás said, inspecting her hand as his father unwrapped and rewrapped it more to his satisfaction.

"I'll see my family doctor after I get home tomorrow."

Tomás and his father exchanged glances. "All right. You live at the boarding house, don't you? I'll drive you there."

Ruthann's hand still throbbed as Tomás escorted her from his car into the foyer of the boarding house, where Aggie met them. "I was about to send out a search party. Did you forget we're having an early dinner tonight? Nathan, Lillian, and Kitty have already left. Hello, Tomás. I didn't know you were home already." Her eyes drifted to Ruthann's left hand, held close. "Your coat… What are all those holes?"

"Someone threw acid at Miss Cooper. Fortunately, my father knew what to do, but we both feel she should see a doctor."

"Oh, she will," Aggie said. "Get out of that coat, Ruthann. What a mess!"

"The high collar saved her neck. Apparently her hand caught the worst."

"Acid!" muttered Aggie, shaking the coat before she hung it on the rack by the door. "Who…"

Tomás set down Ruthann's case and purse, which he'd carried for her. "She didn't see anyone."

"I'm calling the police right after I phone Dr. Leeson."

"No, please don't," Ruthann begged. "I'm all right."

"You're not all right." Aggie reached for the

phone. "Go sit down and have your dinner. You go with her, Tomás. You'll need to talk to the police."

"My father's in the car. I'll come back."

"I've got enough for everyone," Aggie said. "Go get Luís."

Dr. Leeson arrived in the middle of dinner. "What kind of acid do you think it was, Luís?"

"Muriatic acid. I could tell from the odor," the man said. "I keep a little for cleaning drains if nothing else works. Jonas Edwards buys it for his photography studio and orders some extra for the school."

"You did the right thing for her. It's a bad burn, but with your quick thinking, she'll have minimal scarring."

"I've called Chief Edmondson," Aggie said. "He said he'd be here. Tomás said Ruthann didn't see anyone."

"I saw someone," Tomás said slowly, "but I'm sure it wasn't the person who did this."

"Who?" Rena demanded.

Tomás shook his head. "I'll tell the chief about it."

"It's unbelievable something like this could happen in the school. Anywhere in this town, for that matter," the doctor said with a shake of his head. "I've never seen an acid burn except for the time Billy Gee went nosing around in his daddy's garage. But that was battery acid, and he's still got a scar on his arm." He shook his head again. "But at least it's not as bad as it could've been," he said. He turned to Tomás. "How long do you have left in law school?"

"Two more years."

"Coming back here?"

"Camden's too small for me to get a good start on

my own. I'll do better in a city."

"Sounds like the ticket," the doctor said. He patted Ruthann's shoulder. "Keep the hand dry. Put petroleum jelly on it tonight, and keep it covered with gauze. I think I hear Edmondson in the foyer. He never knocks."

Chapter Thirteen

The police chief didn't try to disguise his irritation at being called out after hours. He talked to Ruthann first behind closed doors, then sent her out and called in Tomás. After a few minutes, he opened the door. "Aggie, get Drew Mallory and his daughter over here."

Ruthann felt dizzy. "No, please." She swayed and stumbled a little.

Rena pushed her down on the stairs. "Sit before I have to pick you up off the floor."

Ruthann buried her face on her knees. "This is horrible."

Within minutes Drew, followed by an openly hostile Gwen, burst through the door. Drew went immediately to Ruthann. "Are you all right?"

Gwen's "What are you doing here?" to Tomás set off a new shockwave in the tense atmosphere.

"I just drove in for the holidays," he replied.

Despite her unsettled state, Ruthann didn't miss the way their eyes locked before Gwen dropped hers.

"Are you all right?" Drew repeated.

"I just want to go home and forget all this ever happened," she murmured without looking at him.

"Gwen, I want to talk to you next." Chief Edmondson stepped to the door of the parlor.

Ruthann looked up at Drew. He wore an expression of mingled disbelief and defeat. "Drew, Gwen didn't do this."

His stricken face assaulted her with fresh guilt. *Why did I come here? Why did I let him into my life? I'm ruining his.*

Gwen's pale face mirrored her father's disbelief as she followed the chief into the parlor.

"Luís recognized the acid burn and knew what to do for Ruthann's hand," Aggie said, trying to deflect the discomfort of the moment. "Dr. Leeson said it might've been a lot worse."

Drew's eyes searched the crowded foyer until he found the custodian. "Luís, thank you."

The man waved his hand dismissively. "I thought the building was empty, so I'd turned off the lights and locked up. I was on my way out to meet Tomás when I heard Miss Cooper scream."

Drew winced.

An uneasy silence descended on the group. Finally Chief Edmondson came out alone. "I'm done," he said.

Drew took a step toward him. "Gwennie didn't do this. She couldn't. You know that."

"Nope. But she did tell me what nobody else bothered to mention. What happened last night is relevant, so you should've told me, Miss Cooper."

Ruthann looked away.

"I'm going to find out who did this. You can bet on that." The string of words which followed made Ruthann cringe. Then, "This isn't New York or Chicago in the thirties!" He slapped on his hat and strode to the door. "Meanwhile, I'd suggest you all stop this personal bickering, because it's just plain trashy, if you ask me."

"Nobody did," Aggie snapped.

The chief glared at her before slamming the door behind him.

Tomás approached Drew. "Mr. Mallory, I was sitting in my car outside the school and saw Gwen walking toward the school. She tried to get in, but Dad had already locked the doors. Then when she started running toward the street, I knew something had frightened her. That's when I got out of the car and went to the door and saw Dad helping Miss Cooper. I went around to his private entrance. Gwen didn't do anything. You and I both know she couldn't hurt anyone."

Drew's jaw tightened. "Yes, thank you, Tomás. I know she couldn't."

"I think I'd better take Dad home now. Tomorrow I'm going to help him clean and close up for the holidays." He smiled at Aggie. "Thanks for dinner. Dad's not much of a cook compared to Camden's queen of cuisine."

The older man narrowed his eyes. "You survived."

Tomás slapped his father's shoulder affectionately. "Yes, sir, I did, and pretty well at that. Let's go."

Ruthann and Drew found Gwen curled into a knot of misery on the sofa in the parlor. Ruthann deliberately headed for an armchair so Drew would have to sit beside his daughter. "Are you all right, Gwennie?"

"All you care about is her," Gwen mumbled.

"That's not true, but after so many years of being alone and telling myself I was content to be that way, I thought I'd been handed a second chance." He rubbed her back. "I'm sorry, Gwennie. I love you."

"You love her."

Drew breathed deeply. "Why can't I love both of

you? Is it because Ruthann's so close to your own age?"

Gwen shook her head.

"Then tell me. I'll listen to every word and try to understand."

"You can't."

"Try me."

Gwen sat up straight and met Ruthann's eyes. "I was coming back to apologize this afternoon."

"Apologize for what?" Drew asked.

"I went to Ruthann's classroom again and…"

"She came to talk," Ruthann interrupted. "We needed to talk."

Gwen kept looking at Ruthann. "I didn't come to talk. I came to be hateful, and I was. I came back, but the doors were locked. When I heard you screaming, I guess I just panicked and ran."

"I expect I'd have done the same thing."

"Don't patronize me," Gwen snapped.

The venom in her voice shook Ruthann. "I'm sorry, that's not what I meant to do."

"I wasn't upstairs in your room last night, and I wouldn't…couldn't do anything to physically hurt you. What I said was bad enough."

Ruthann felt a sudden unexpected connection with the other young woman. "Gwen, it's all right. Really it is."

The hard lines in Gwen's face dissolved. Ruthann thought she looked heartbreakingly vulnerable. "How…how's your hand?"

"Fortunately Mr. Cabrera recognized it was an acid burn and knew what to do. It hurts some, but I'm okay."

"It could've been your face or even your eyes,"

Gwen said.

"I was lucky." A sudden weariness swept over Ruthann, the kind which had become a permanent resident in her body and soul for at least a year after Jack died. Rose Ellen had said she was depressed and needed to snap out of it, so she'd thrown herself into war work and tried to regain some perspective. "Gwen, what I said about coming between you and your father—I meant it." She turned to Drew. "I told her I wasn't coming back next year. If Mr. Clifton can find a replacement for me, I'll leave after the term ends."

"Don't I get any say in this?" Drew pushed himself off the sofa and walked over to Ruthann. He reached for her uninjured hand, but she pulled away from him.

"Gwen is your daughter, and I'm…"

"I know who both of you are!" Drew said in a sharper voice than Ruthann had ever heard. Even Gwen appeared startled.

"I never considered how I might feel if my father began a relationship with someone, especially a woman young enough to be my sister."

"Your mother isn't dead, is she?" Gwen asked.

"No, but if she died, my father might not want to spend the rest of his life alone, and I have to wonder how I'd feel. Maybe I'd feel the way you do."

"It's not what you think," Gwen said. "It's…I'm really sorry, Ruthann. I can't believe I've been such a horrible person." She walked to the front window and looked out into the darkness. "I want you to be happy, Daddy. Can we go home now?"

Drew nodded. "I think we should." He turned to Ruthann, although this time he didn't try to touch her. "I'll be here tomorrow around two to drive you and

Miss Gilbert to the train."

"You don't have to do that. I'm sure Harry will take us."

"No, I said I would, and I will." He followed Gwen to the door, the stopped and turned around. "This isn't over, Ruthann. We'll talk tomorrow."

\*\*\*\*

Later, with her suitcase packed and waiting beside the door, Ruthann let Rena smooth petroleum jelly on her throbbing hand and wrap it with gauze. "It's like a nightmare I can't wake up from."

"And you believe Gwen Mallory?"

"Yes, I do. Besides, Tomás saw her outside after the fact. She couldn't have done it. And she apologized for everything. I felt sorry for her."

"Actually, I never thought she could do anything like someone did the night of the Christmas party. And certainly not the acid. She's Drew Mallory's daughter, after all. Do you remember seeing anyone? Anything?"

Ruthann hesitated. "A shadow. Just a shadow, but it was..."

"What?"

"White. Almost transparent."

"A ghost?" Rena's face went pale.

"No! I heard footsteps. Ghosts don't make noise, and I don't believe in them anyway."

"Did you tell the police chief?"

"No. I got the feeling he didn't believe anything I was saying."

"But your hand. He had to know that was real."

Ruthann shrugged. "Is the police chief often so angry with everyone?"

"He's mad because he knows he's not going to find

out who did this, and even if he does, he can't do anything about it."

"I don't understand that."

"I don't either, but he does." Rena gathered up the jar of petroleum jelly and box of gauze to return them to Aggie. "What are you going to tell your parents?"

"I don't know."

"You better figure it out. You can't hide your hand or your coat."

"I'm too tired to think tonight. I'll come up with something on the train."

"Good luck. We can sleep in tomorrow and grab some breakfast at the City Café on the square. Is Mr. Mallory still coming to drive us to the train?"

"I tried to tell him Harry would do it."

"But he didn't buy it."

"No, he said he'd come around two."

"Well, after I catch the two-forty, you'll have some time to talk."

Ruthann began to turn down her bed. "That's what I'm afraid of."

"You told me you loved him. Has all this changed your mind?"

"No. That's the problem, isn't it?"

Chapter Fourteen

Rena embraced Ruthann before she boarded the train. "Think hard," she whispered. "Don't do anything you'll regret for the rest of your life."

Ruthann and Drew took refuge in the car from the damp chill as soon as the train began to move.

"I talked to Gwen when we got home last night."

"She can't help how she feels."

"Maybe not. I think someone's manipulating her."

"How? Why?"

He grimaced as he tried to get comfortable. "It's just a feeling I have. Gwen was an easy child to raise. Sweet. Accepting of the late hours I had to put in at the beginning. Even in high school when some of the other girls were getting a little wild, she toed the mark. I wondered at the time if it was only out of respect for my position as superintendent, but she never seemed resentful of any rules Julia and I laid down. She and Tomás were good friends. We didn't have many Mexican students full time back then. I think I told you Luís came here with his parents when he was a baby, and the schools were segregated for Mexicans then, as they still are for colored people. He didn't have much chance at an education, but he was smart and learned on the job from several people he worked for here in town. We hired him to take charge of the school plant when Tomás was a little boy. His wife had died, and I knew from experience that school hours and holidays would work out well for him."

"Obviously they did. Now Tomás is in law school."

"He'll do well with his law degree. Oh, he'll face prejudice because of his Hispanic background, but he'll succeed."

"What does that have to do with Gwen?" Ruthann remembered the spark that had flashed between Tomás and Gwen the previous evening. Though the electricity had died quickly, she couldn't forget it.

"Like I said, he and Gwen were good friends, especially since neither one of them ran with the crowd, so to speak. I'm going to ask him to talk to her while he's home. Maybe she'll tell him what she's not telling me."

"I hope she will. I don't like to see either one of you hurting."

"What you said about not coming back…"

'I'll finish the term."

"Maybe that's best."

Cold dread knotted her chest and made it hard to breathe.

"How I feel about you hasn't changed, but what happened yesterday made me realize I'd acted foolishly and put you in danger."

"It's not your fault."

"I think it is. You're a young woman, Ruthann. You have your whole life in front of you. Maybe…maybe you were looking for something…for love…after losing your fiancé like you did."

"Do you really believe that?"

He covered his eyes with one hand. "I don't know

what I believe after everything that's happened. I want you to go home and think things through very carefully. Come back after the holidays and finish the term if you feel obligated. But we can always manage with a substitute while we look for a replacement."

She turned her face away.

"John will give you a glowing reference. He'll come up with a plausible reason for your leaving mid-year."

She nodded.

"This isn't how I wanted things. You have to believe that." He reached for her hand, but she pulled it away. "You'll meet someone else. Someone right for you. You'll look back on this the same way you look at your brief romance with Jack—as preparation for the real thing."

She fumbled with the door handle. "I'll wait inside," she choked. His deep sigh tore at her heart.

"All right." He got out and signaled a redcap. At the door of the waiting room, he touched her arm. "You were right, Ruthann. You don't need to fight any more battles, and neither do I." Then he kissed her wet cheek and limped away.

**** 

When the train arrived in San Antonio just after midnight, Ruthann fell sobbing into her mother's arms. Her father half-carried her to the car. At home, Mary Ruth tucked her into bed as she'd done during her childhood years. "Tomorrow," she whispered. "We'll talk tomorrow."

It was noon before Ruthann wandered downstairs. Her mother brought a tray into the sitting room where her father sat in front of a crackling fire. "Why aren't you at work?" Ruthann asked.

"Eat something, baby girl. Then we'll talk."

She didn't have an appetite, but urged on by her mother, she ate most of the poached eggs and toast and drank the coffee. When she'd finished, Matt folded the newspaper and set it aside. "Drew Mallory called last night."

Ruthann's head dropped. "So you know what happened."

"Everything. Including the note you didn't tell us about and how someone got into your room at the boarding house."

"He shouldn't have…"

"Were you going to tell us?"

"Maybe not all of it."

"He also said he didn't want you back after the holidays."

Ruthann moaned softly. "It's really over, isn't it?"

"Not unless you want it to be."

She scrubbed her eyes with the sash of her chenille robe. "What do you mean?"

"The man is in love with you, Ruthann. I knew that at Thanksgiving. He loves you the way every father wants his daughter to be loved. The way I love your mother."

Mary Ruth put her arms around her daughter. "Your father and I discussed everything thoroughly after you left in November—Drew's age, his disability, his daughter's disapproval—but we kept coming back to the same thing. He loves you. You love each other."

"Sometimes love isn't enough."

"Love is all there is," Matt said. "As your parents, we don't want you in danger. The note, the idea of someone having access to your room, and the possibility you could've been seriously injured by that acid makes us think you should stay home. But it has to be your decision."

"Your coat's beyond repair," Mary Ruth interrupted. "We'll shop for a new one tomorrow."

"The coat can be replaced," Matt went on. "You can't, and Drew knows that."

"It was all so final," Ruthann said, trying not to cry again.

"Not really. I remember I didn't want you to work in that munitions factory either, but you went ahead. Life's a risk any way you look at it."

"I don't understand what you're telling me, Dad."

"We just fought a war for what we believed in, Ruthie. Now you've got to fight for what you believe in…for what you want."

"For Drew?"

"If he's what you want."

"I do, but…"

"There can't be any *buts* or *ifs*. You either love him, or you don't. You'll either stand by him no matter what, or you won't."

"But he told you he doesn't want me back."

"He's willing to give up what he wants for your best."

"What…what did you tell him?"

"What could I tell him? I said we'd talk to you. He thanked me and hung up." Matt sat forward in his chair. "You only felt a passing sadness for Jack, Ruthie. You couldn't feel anything else, because what was between the two of you was superficial. He was a nice boy, and you were a nice, sheltered little girl. But Drew Mallory is a man, and you have, I believe, become a woman through your association with him. I heard real grief in Drew's voice. And you were already mourning him when you got off the train last night."

"You were our baby, Ruthann," her mother said. "We let you stay our baby too long. Now we're giving you permission to grow up and move on."

"Time passes, and life changes," Ruthann murmured. "Drew said that to me once."

"He was right," Matt said. "This war has changed a lot of things, not all of them for the better. And it's not really over. It won't be over for a generation or two. The wounded vets, the families who don't have their husbands and fathers back, our collective feelings of insecurity, world politics…the battles rage on."

"I've never heard you talk like that, Dad."

"Maybe because I never really spoke to you as an adult."

"After V-J Day, I just wanted to get back to the way things had been before."

"But it didn't happen. You walked straight into a brand-new war, didn't you?"

"I guess I did."

"Well, it's up to you now. You can go back to Camden and fight that war, risky as it is, or you can stay here. Get another job, find an apartment, make a new life. But you'll have battles to fight in a new life, too."

"Drew said something like that once. He said I'd always have battles to fight unless I lived in total isolation."

"He was right."

"Don't make a decision this minute," Mary Ruth

said. "You're home for Christmas, and you need the break. You've got time to think about what you really want to do."

Ruthann felt her mouth turn up in a smile. "What I really want to do." She leaned over and kissed her mother. "I've got time."

\*\*\*\*

Later Ruthann reflected how her twenty-fifth Christmas had been the strangest she could remember. Loneliness pervaded each day, but she felt free somehow, almost reborn. She thought of the gift she hadn't given Drew, a slim leather-bound volume of the Lake Poets with biographical notes. She'd even had his name stamped in gold on the cover. She wondered, too, what he'd meant to give her. Not an engagement ring, she hoped, but rather something personal—something uniquely a part of himself—would've been perfect.

She thought of the battles ahead if she went back, but the only one she determined not to fight was with Gwen. Both of them would lose, and Drew would be the real casualty. Her students' eager faces peppered her dreams. Would they feel she'd deserted them? She saw Drew in every corner, felt his arms and kisses, heard his gentle words echo in her heart.

She and Jack had shared so little, but her students, her colleagues, even the school building itself had become part of her—and Drew had become part of her most of all. A week before school started, she wired John Clifton: *Returning to finish term or the year at your convenience.*

On her last night home, she sat in the bay window of her room overlooking the front lawn and watched a million stars twinkle in the winter sky. When a bank of clouds obscured them, she wondered briefly if Drew had really meant what he said to her. But when the clouds moved on, revealing a pale distant moon, his face smiled at her. When she saw him from the window of the train the next afternoon, she couldn't get off and into his arms soon enough—and she didn't care if everyone on the platform was watching.

## Chapter Fifteen

"I met every southbound train yesterday and today," Drew told her as he bundled her into the car.

Ruthann moved across the seat until their shoulders were touching. "I hope you're glad I was on this one."

"You know I am. But I still think it's a bad idea."

"I couldn't give up. Couldn't give you up."

"What I said was for your own good."

"I know. But this is for my best."

Instead of driving to the boarding house, he turned on the road leading to the Camden Inn and parked near the woods. "I have to hold you, precious girl."

Wrapping her in his arms, he kissed her with a passion she found both pleasurable and disturbing. "Are you really sure about this?"

"Very sure."

"I'm sure I love you more than my life, but if anything else happens, you have to know I'll send you home to stay."

"Life is risky. War is worse."

"Do you think we're at war?"

"In a way. But I'm willing to do battle for you. For us. I won't fight Gwen, because all of us would lose. We'll have to negotiate a truce."

"I think she's leaning that direction. She's asked several times if I've heard from you and seemed upset that I hadn't."

Several long kisses later, he said, "Are you hungry?"

"Starved."

"I didn't make reservations, but being a week night, the Inn shouldn't be crowded."

She saw him wince as he got out of the car in the parking lot. "Your leg is bothering you tonight," she said when he came around to open the door for her. "It's getting worse, isn't it?"

"Just the cold weather," he said, not meeting her eyes. "I'll be fine in the spring."

"It's a long time until spring."

She wasn't really surprised when he didn't reply.

They'd ordered coffee and dessert when he said, "Luís locked up his acid supply."

"So someone did get it from him?"

"Not much, but enough to do you some damage."

"It wasn't his fault."

"He's put padlocks on all his cabinets. Until now, all he's felt necessary was to lock the basement door at the end of the day."

"Whoever's doing all this…"

"We know who."

Ruthann shook her head. "I'd think she could get whatever she wants."

"We don't have to make it easy for her. And I want you to promise you'll be careful."

"I thought I had."

He captured her hand as it reached for her cup. "Ruthann, I've been miserable without you, but it's because I love you so much I'll do whatever it takes to keep you safe. You have to understand, if there's another…incident…I'll send you home to stay."

"You'll have to fire me, then."

"I will."

Unaccustomed anger flared in her, then died as she met his eyes and recognized a mixture of longing and fear. "If you fire me, I'll just find a job in town," she said. "I won't leave you."

He shook his head. "What have I done?"

She leaned across the table. "You've taken a little girl and turned her into the woman who'll love you forever."

\*\*\*\*

Ruthann wasn't sure exactly what had changed between them, but their relationship had deepened in ways she couldn't describe. Her romantic fantasies had fled and been replaced with a fierce certainty that Drew Mallory was now and would forever be the sole focus of her life. His gentle consideration of her, the way he called her *precious girl* in their private moments, and the depth of passion in his kisses remained the same. But there was a new element in their relationship, too. She'd thought he'd shared the depths of his soul with her, but he'd only skimmed the surface.

They began to take long drives on Saturday afternoons and stop at scenic spots to picnic in the car. Sometimes Drew actually suggested she do part of the driving, which she saw as progress in several ways. Over the contents of Aggie's gourmet baskets, he opened up even more about the anguish caused by the setbacks in his life.

"There was a big age gap between Gordon and Caroline and the rest of us. No one ever said anything, but I had the feeling we were only half-siblings. I don't know if they were Pop's or Ma's. Laurene was two years younger than me, and Samuel came along later. I remember crying when the matron at the orphanage took Samuel away and gave him to his new parents. She told me I was too big to cry. I was ten, so maybe I was. But everyone else was gone, and now he was, too."

He looked out the front window of the car at the leaden skies threatening rain. "So after Gwen was born, I never brought up the annulment Marlene had promised. I didn't want it anyway, and I really thought we'd have a normal marriage once she got over the birth. But when we didn't, I knew I couldn't lose Gwennie like I'd lost everyone else."

"I'm sure that's what made you a good father. Some men take their children for granted, but you didn't."

"Did your father take you for granted?"

"No. He was always around. Mother lost two babies between Rose Ellen and me. I always knew how important I was to them."

He held out his cup for more hot chocolate from the thermos. "I remember Ma showing us affection, but Pop was beaten down from just trying to put food on the table. He left early and came home late six days a week. And if he could find an odd job on Sundays, he did that, too."

"He loved you, then. A lot of men would've walked away from the responsibility."

"When I ran off and joined the Army, I thought I might run across Gordon. I didn't remember a lot about him, but we'd shared a bed until he left home, and he used to talk to me at night."

"What did he talk about?"

"Mostly the fights he'd get into at school." Drew chuckled. "He was a tough kid. Ma would cry when he'd come home all bunged up, and he'd promise her he wouldn't do it again, but he always did. I guess I knew before anybody that he was thinking about leaving home. He'd already quit school and was working. At least, he said he was working. He brought Ma some money, anyway. Once she asked him how he got it, and he just said he earned it. Maybe he did earn it, just not the acceptable way. It could be that's why he left—things got too hot for him in New York."

"New York. That's the first time you've mentioned where you came from. I'd think about it later and then forget to ask the next time I saw you. Where in New York?"

"The Bronx. Not exactly Hell's Kitchen—that was in Manhattan. I guess it still is."

"Do you know where your people came from?"

"I looked up the name once. 'Mallory' comes from the French word *malheure*, which means unhappy or unlucky." He squeezed her hand. "But I don't think it means that for me now. Not since you showed up in my life."

"That's nice."

"I've thought a lot about what you said when you came back after Christmas, and you're right. I hovered over Gwen. Maybe I protected her too much."

"She's all you have."

"I have you now. I don't want to lose you by selling you short."

She leaned her head against his shoulder. "Then promise not to send me packing."

"I can't go quite that far. Not yet anyway." He put

his fingers across her lips when she started to protest. "I'll only promise to give careful consideration to whatever I do. You'll just have to live with that much for now."

****

Just after midnight on the last Saturday before the end of term, Rena burst through Ruthann's door without knocking and landed on the end of her bed. Jolted from a sound sleep, Ruthann became aware of sirens ripping through the fabric of the night's stillness. "What in the world?"

"They came right by here. I thought for sure we were on fire." Rena untucked the blanket from the bottom of the bed and wrapped it around her.

"Are we?"

"No, they went on."

From the hall came the sounds of opening doors and footsteps. Bernie stuck her head through the doorway of Ruthann's room. "Are you girls all right?"

"I think so," Ruthann said. "What's happening?"

"I don't know. Nathan's going downstairs to check."

It seemed a long time before he came back, accompanied by Harry and Aggie. "They went to the school," Nathan said.

"Fire?" Lillian asked, clutching her throat.

"I didn't see any smoke," Harry said.

A few minutes later, the phone rang in the downstairs hall, and Harry hurried to answer it. "It's not a fire," he called up, "but something's going on at the school. The police are there."

"Who's on the phone?" Aggie asked.

Harry returned to the second floor. "Luís Cabrera.

158

He drove up to the school." He chuckled. "It's an old building. He's always afraid something's going to happen to it, even though he tucks it in like a baby every night. But there's no catastrophe. Unless you want to count the report of a ghost in the bell tower and the bell ringing three times." He looked around at the ladies and snickered.

"That's ridiculous!" Bernie said.

Kitty yawned. "Frankly, I don't care. I'm going back to bed."

When the others had followed suit, Rena remained huddled in the blanket on Ruthann's bed. "Who would've been out this late in Camden? To see a ghost in the bell tower, I mean."

"They do tend to roll up the sidewalks here at dark."

"That's what I mean."

"I'm sure tongues will be wagging tomorrow."

Rena grinned and threw back the blanket. "They will indeed, and maybe we'll hear a gory story!"

"Oh, go on."

"I'm going. But tomorrow..."

Ruthann switched off the lamp and snuggled under the covers again, but she couldn't put her finger on the reason for the unsettled feeling in the pit of her stomach.

## Chapter Sixteen

Over Sunday morning breakfast, Harry Pollard enlightened everyone on the previous night's excitement. "*Bailarina de fantasma*," Harry said, mangling the phrase. "I got that from Luís this morning when I went out for a paper."

Rena paled. "Ghost dancer," she murmured.

"What?" Bernie asked.

Harry brought his plate to the table and poured maple syrup over a stack of pancakes. "It seems Carter Hodges worked late at the newspaper and was on his way home—he lives two blocks the other side of the school—and saw something white flitting around the bell tower. Then the bell started tolling. He drove home and called the police—and also Luís Cabrera, who beat the police there by three and a half minutes."

"I take it no one found the phantom of the tower," Nathan drawled over his lifted coffee cup.

"The door to the tower was unlocked, but it was empty."

"So that's that," Bernie said. "Until next time, anyway."

"It's happened before?" Ruthann asked.

"A time or two," Aggie said.

"Three times," Bernie said. "The first time was just before..." She glanced at Nathan.

"Just before my brother died," he said.

"Just before Mona…" Bernie began but stopped as the phone rang.

"I'll get it," Aggie said. She was back in under a minute. "Drew Mallory's on his way over," she said to Ruthann.

**** 

"You know what happened last night," he said as he held the car door for her.

"I heard the sirens, and Harry filled us in this morning."

"A student prank, I'd say."

"Bernie says it's happened before."

Drew blew out his breath. "It has."

"So it really wasn't a prank, was it?"

"It might've been. A copycat sort of thing."

"All right."

"Ruthann, maybe you should go home at the end of the term."

"Home! What does all this have to do with me?"

"I'm not sure, but I want you safe."

"I'm all right."

He reached for her hand. "I want you safe, and I want you here. I'm not sure one is the same as the other."

"No one came right out and said it, but I got the feeling at breakfast this has something to do with Mona Fulton."

"It might."

"Is she in Camden?"

"I'm not sure."

"It's Merle who has a grudge against me."

"Yes. Yes, it is. I brought some of my sketches. I thought you might like to look at them over a cup of coffee at the hotel."

She realized the topic of the previous night's events was closed. "I'd love to see them, Drew."

\*\*\*\*

At the end of the term, the students had a two-day break to allow high school teachers to grade exams and calculate term marks. John Clifton announced the grammar school would have a break also. Drew left on Wednesday for the regional superintendents' conference in Kerrville. The following morning Rena and Ruthann walked to school to work in their classrooms.

By midmorning, Ruthann had taken down the seasonal bulletin boards and washed the tops of all the student desks, making a mental note of which students needed to overhaul their supplies inside. Then she turned her attention to the closet and decided to rearrange the contents of two shelves.

A few minutes after entering the long narrow storage space, she heard the door close with a soft click. The light went out almost immediately, leaving her in total darkness. She felt her way to the door, but the knob wouldn't turn. Then she felt for the light cord put there as a backup but couldn't find it.

*Now what do I do? Pound on the door and yell for help, or wait until Rena comes to eat lunch? The last thing I want to do is make another scene. The other teachers have been supportive, but they're bound to be tired of the focus on a first-year faculty member.*

She groped her way to the step stool and sat down. *Okay, I'll wait. The door tends to swing on its hinges, and it's probably just a coincidence the light went out. Surely no one's out there. Or are they? I've had three weeks to stop looking over my shoulder—well, almost. But what Drew said about me going home...I have a feeling he's not telling me everything he knows, and I guess he's not obligated, but...*

The sound of soft laughter just outside the door made the hackles rise on her neck. "Who's out there?" In the darkness, she wondered if she'd imagined it.

She shivered. *Did I make the right decision to finish the year? I don't want to leave Drew, but the situation with Gwen isn't really resolved. And if I'm locked in here on purpose, someone else is still targeting me. I can't believe Merle Fulton would risk so much just to get me out of Camden.*

"Ruthann! Ruthann, where are you?"

She felt her way along the shelves back to the door. "In here."

Rena jerked the door open with such force it hit the wall. "What in the..."

"The door closed while I was working in here. I'll get Mr. Cabrera to check the latch."

"And the light just happened to go off, too?" Rena hit the button, and the darkness disappeared.

Ruthann looked for the cord which should have been hanging from the light. It had been cut off near the bulb, too high for her to reach. She leaned against the door. "I guess not."

"It's started again," Rena said. "I'm sick and tired of this!"

Ruthann's laugh sounded shaky. "*You're* tired of it?"

"I'm going to get Mr. Clifton and Mr. Cabrera right now."

Ruthann caught the other teacher's arm. "No,

don't. I'll speak to Mr. Cabrera after lunch. Let's sit down and eat what Aggie packed for us."

"You have to tell Mr. Clifton." Rena flounced to a desk and sat down. "If you don't, I will."

"Don't be dramatic."

"Me? Dramatic? I'm not the one who's the target here."

"Just hush." Ruthann brought the box from her desk and sat down across from Rena.

"What's next?"

"I don't know, Rena, but please, let's just keep this to ourselves for the time being."

"You're being an idiot, you know."

"I felt like one, getting trapped in that closet."

"Which didn't happen by accident."

"Maybe not. But I have to think."

Rena opened her mouth to retort, but Ruthann held up her hand. "Please, Rena. Let's talk about something else while we eat."

Ruthann refused to discuss the incident further, but the next day Rena brought her planning book and a stack of teachers' manuals to Ruthann's room and made herself at home. "I'll be quiet," she said. "Just go on with your housekeeping."

"What's next?" Ruthann said, trying to see humor in the situation. "Sleeping on a pallet at the foot of my bed?"

"I might. Do you snore?"

"I don't think so, but I could cultivate the habit if it would keep you out of my room."

"Ha, ha."

Ruthann began to rearrange the chairs in the reading circle corner to accommodate an extra in her highest group. Tiptoeing to retrieve a book from the top of the tall shelves where she kept the supplemental readers, she felt the bookcase move. Then without warning, it toppled, raining books around her. She put up her hands, but the piece of furniture weighed more than she did. Before she hit the floor, she heard someone scream and hoped it wasn't her.

She woke to a sea of faces bending over her. "Just lie still, Miss Cooper," John Clifton said. "Dr. Leeson's on his way."

"I don't need..." She struggled to sit up, but several hands pushed her back.

The concerned crowd of people began to move away when Dr. Leeson arrived. "What happened?"

"The shelves fell on top of her," Rena said.

Dr. Leeson hunkered down beside Ruthann. "I don't see any blood, anyway. Does anything hurt?"

"Just about everything. I'm sorry to be so much trouble."

"There's a knot forming on the side of your head. How many fingers am I holding up?"

"Four."

"And now?"

"Three."

He checked her arms and legs for possible fractures, then helped her sit up slowly. "Is there any ice?"

"I'll get some from the faculty lounge." Rena sprinted off.

Mr. Clifton dispersed everyone except Rena as Dr. Leeson held the ice wrapped in a towel to Ruthann's head. Ruthann saw the principal standing beside the fallen bookcase where Mr. Cabrera punctuated his words with flying hands, but she couldn't hear what he said. Whatever it was, John Clifton appeared to be in agreement.

Finally, Mr. Cabrera left, and the principal sat down beside Ruthann. "He's going to bolt the shelves to the wall. Had they seemed unstable before?"

"Not really. I'm just thankful there weren't any children present who might've been hurt."

Rena's eyes flashed. "I'm going to tell about yesterday whether you like it or not."

When she'd finished, the principal said, "You should have reported it, Miss Cooper."

"I didn't want to make a mountain out of a molehill. It might have been a joke."

"This was no joke," the doctor said, snapping his bag shut. "If those shelves had hit just right, you might be on your way to the hospital with a fractured skull. As it is, I don't think you have even a small concussion, but you're going to have a nasty bruise on that side of your face. I want you to go home and lie down for the rest of the day, and someone should be with you."

"I'll be right there," Rena said.

"If she dozes, make sure you can wake her easily. Otherwise, call me."

"Don't worry."

"Mr. Cabrera will need me to help lift the shelves and hold them while he does what needs to be done," John Clifton said. "So if you could drive these ladies home, Dr. Leeson?"

"I'll be glad to."

\*\*\*\*

Aggie came out of the kitchen when she heard the front door open. Julia Schaeffer followed close on her heels. "What are you two doing here before noon?" Then she saw Dr. Leeson and the ice pack Ruthann had pressed to her head. "Not again."

"What happened now?" Julia asked.

"A bookcase fell over on me, that's all. I'm all right."

"I told her to rest this afternoon. Miss Gilbert said she'd keep an eye on her."

Rena, with their boxed lunch under her arm, urged Ruthann toward the stairs. "I'll come down and get some tea to go with this."

Julia turned back to the kitchen. "I'll put on the kettle and bring it up."

Aggie followed the young women to Ruthann's room. "All right, now tell me what happened. All of it."

"The shelves just tipped over," Ruthann said. "I don't know why, and Mr. Cabrera didn't give any reason." She slipped off her shoes and stretched out on the bed.

Aggie's eyes narrowed. "I don't like this."

"Well, I'm not excited about it," Ruthann said, "but if Rena will turn loose of that box, I could eat something."

"I'll go see about your tea. Julia and I were going over the menu for the City Choir dinner concert in March."

Ruthann ate her portion of the box lunch, then dozed, only to be wakened twice by Rena shaking her and calling her name. "I'm not dead," she said the second time.

"Only through sheer luck."

"I still have some things to do in my classroom before Monday."

"They'll keep. We'll go in early, and I'll help you."

Just after five, Gwen Mallory put her head around the half-open door of Ruthann's room. "Aunt Julia came by the store and told me you had an accident."

"It wasn't an accident," Rena snapped.

Ruthann frowned. "Of course it was. I reached for a book on top of some bookshelves, and they fell over."

"You've been reaching for books since September, and it hasn't fallen over on you." Rena stood up. "Is it safe to leave you two alone in here?"

"Rena, that was uncalled for." Ruthann sat up and pushed a pillow behind her back.

Rena flushed. "You're right, it was. I'm sorry, Gwen."

Gwen's face paled. "I'm not the one trying to hurt you, Ruthann," she said softly. She stepped closer. "Oh, look at your face!"

"I'll just tell everyone Rena punched me because I took too long in the bathroom," Ruthann said, trying to lighten the moment.

The dinner bell rang. "I'll bring you a tray," Rena said.

"That's not…"

"I'll bring it." She gave Gwen a wide berth as she strode to the door.

"She saw the bookcase falling on me and couldn't stop it," Ruthann said. "She's upset. Sit down, won't you, Gwen? It was nice of you to come by."

Gwen hesitated before taking the chair just vacated by Rena. "Daddy's going to be furious."

"Your father won't be home from that superintendents' meeting in Kerrville until tomorrow, will he?"

"Around noon, I think." She knotted her fingers together. "After all that driving, his leg will be giving him fits."

"It's worse, isn't it? Just since September, I mean."

"Dr. Leeson told him to see the specialist in Dallas, but he says he doesn't have time to make the trip. I know he's afraid the doctor will want to…" She swallowed hard and looked away from Ruthann.

"Amputate," Ruthann finished for her. The word tasted bitter on her tongue.

Gwen nodded. After a moment she said, "How will you feel about that?"

"Sad for him. But it would be a relief, too. He's lived with it since before either one of us was born. I hate seeing him in pain."

"I meant…seeing it if…"

"If we get married."

Gwen chewed her lip. "You really love him, don't you? I know he loves you."

"Yes, I do. As to how I'd react to seeing him without his leg, I won't know until it happens. What worries me most is how I'd help him without doing too much. A man has his pride, after all."

Rena walked in with the tray, put it across Ruthann's lap, and left without a word.

"You're worried about him, aren't you? I mean, more than you ever were."

"Dr. Leeson told him there might be an infection starting up in the bone. It could kill him." Gwen's voice broke. "Daddy would be so mad if he knew I was here talking to you about this, but I don't have anyone else. Not here in Camden anyway."

"What about your aunt?"

Gwen shook her head. "I used to talk to her, but she's been different lately. It's like she doesn't want to hear anything…" She shrugged. "I can't explain it."

"I'm glad we're talking." Ruthann unfolded her napkin. "Gwen, we both love your father, though in different ways. We should be friends. Good friends."

Gwen looked away. "I'm so ashamed of all the things I said to you."

"You had your reasons."

"Not good ones. Not really."

A loud voice on the stairs interrupted the conversation.

"You can't go up there in her bedroom."

"Hang it all, Aggie, I'm a cop. I can go anywhere I want to."

Chief Edmondson loomed in the door almost before his words died away. "What are *you* doing here?" he asked Gwen.

"She heard what happened this afternoon and came to see how I was," Ruthann said, swallowing the food in her mouth almost whole in her haste to defend Gwen.

The police chief lifted his heavy brows in mock surprise. "Oh, she did, did she?"

"Yes, she did," Ruthann said, not bothering to hide her irritation at the man's rudeness. "And I appreciate it."

"Why did it take all afternoon for somebody to call me about the closet and the bookcase?" he demanded.

"Closet?" Gwen asked.

"I got locked in the closet yesterday," Ruthann said quickly. "Fortunately, Rena came in and let me out."

"And then the bookcase fell over on you after that?" The confusion in Gwen's voice turned the chief's attention back to her.

"You wouldn't know anything about either incident, I don't suppose."

Ruthann set down her glass with more force than necessary. "Of course, she wouldn't. Her aunt was here when Rena and I came home today, and she told Gwen. I don't understand why you're here. The closet might have been a joke, but what happened today was just an accident." Gwen took a step toward the door. "Please stay, Gwen. We haven't finished talking."

Chief Edmondson's face got red. "An accident? When Luís Cabrera moved that bookcase upright, he saw it had been shimmed from the back. That's why it fell."

"What does that mean—shimmed?" Ruthann looked at Gwen, who shrugged.

"It means, young lady, someone went in there and put some thin pieces of wood under the bookcase at the back to make it lean toward the front."

"I can't believe that."

"If Cabrera says the bookcases were shimmed, they were shimmed!"

"And you know who's responsible," Gwen snapped. "You know who's behind all this and why, but you're not going to do anything about it, because this town needs Merle Fulton's money."

"Watch your tongue, missy!"

"Just stop," Ruthann said. "Please."

The police chief turned to go. "Then try to stay out of trouble, will you? Cabrera's still going over your room with a fine-tooth comb. He says he's going to start locking it after you leave in the afternoons—which should be as soon as you can get away after the last bell. No more late evenings staying to do whatever it is you do. Walk home with Rena Gilbert or another teacher. Don't go out by yourself, especially after dark. And think hard about whether or not you want to stay in Camden."

Aggie, who'd stayed at the door, stood aside to let him leave. "I'll find out who's behind all this," he muttered. "See if I don't!"

"A lot of things have happened in this town that no one's found out about," Aggie said clearly. "But lies don't hang around unrecognized forever."

"What does she mean?" Ruthann asked Gwen.

"I don't know, but she does, or she wouldn't have said it." Gwen sank down on the end of the bed. "But even if he finds out, he won't do anything."

"Because of who Merle Fulton is?"

"I don't understand all of it, but she buys people. She tried to buy me when I was starting high school. I guess I liked the attention, but Daddy and Aunt Julia put a stop to it. Aunt Julia said she was really after Daddy. Chief Edmondson doesn't like me, you know."

"Why?"

"He caught me…I was out too late one night. I wasn't doing anything wrong, but he chewed me out and hauled me home and…" She shrugged. "Maybe I'll tell you about it sometime."

"When I came back after Christmas, your father said he'd terminate my contract and send me home if anything else happened, and now I guess it has."

"You can't let him do that!"

"I may not have any choice. Mr. Clifton will tell him, unless Chief Edmondson gets to him first."

Gwen covered her face with her hands just as Rena

burst through the connecting door. "I heard all the yelling," she said. "I was right, wasn't I? This morning was no accident."

Ruthann sighed. "I guess not."

As Gwen fished a tissue from her purse, a small photograph fell into her lap.

"That picture," Ruthann said. "That's what you opened your purse to take out when you were in my room that afternoon, isn't it?" She held out her hand. "May I see it?"

"Did you wonder later if I was reaching for something like acid?"

"Certainly not after Tomás said you weren't even inside the school."

Gwen handed over the black-and-white snapshot. "It's my mother. I don't know why I brought it with me. I don't really remember her. She was sick for a long time before she died."

Ruthann studied the picture. "You look like her."

"That's what Daddy says. He never talks about her, though. It makes me wonder..." She stopped. "But none of this was about her. That first day I met you, when you walked out of the school with Daddy..."

"There was a mistake on my paycheck, and I'd taken it to his secretary, who fixed it. We only walked out together because we were both leaving at the same time."

"He told me, but that night, Aunt Julia said something about the way he looked at you, and it bothered me. I don't know why. When you came into the store the next afternoon, I'd had a rotten day— merchandise listed on the invoices but not shipped, two telephone calls complaining about dresses sent out on approval…I took it out on you when you came into the store. Then when I saw you with Daddy at Fall Fest…"

"Another coincidence."

"I know, but Aunt Julia said it looked like I was going to have a stepmother who was my age." Gwen fumbled with her purse. "She just kept mentioning it. I don't know why."

"I don't either. She was friendly enough to me."

Gwen shook her head. "It doesn't matter." She stood up again. "Look, I really have to go, but maybe if you feel like it tomorrow you could come down to the store after lunch. I'm going to be unpacking a new shipment of dresses. You might see something you like. You come, too, Rena. I know you like new clothes. We had a hard time stocking really nice things during the war, but it's getting better."

"I think an afternoon of new clothes and good conversation would make me feel a lot better."

Gwen's face lit up. "I tell you what—meet me at the drugstore about eleven thirty. We'll grab a sandwich and a milkshake and go back to the store afterwards."

"I'll do that. Thank you for coming, Gwen. I'm sorry Chief Edmondson was so rude to you."

Gwen shrugged. "That's just the way it is. I'll see you both tomorrow, then." She chewed her lip. "And we'll figure out some way to keep Daddy from sending you home."

## Chapter Seventeen

Just at closing on Saturday afternoon, the three young women left the department store by the employee entrance and hurried down the damp alley to the street. Each one carried a white dress box tied with gold cord. "I'd have bought this dress even without your employee discount," Rena said. "It's gorgeous."

"I'd have bought mine anyway, too," Ruthann said, shifting the box a little, "but thank you for saving us some money."

"I knew you'd like them. I love unpacking new merchandise, even though I've seen everything modeled before I order. It's new all over again." Gwen glanced up as a streak of lightning, followed by thunder, came out of nowhere. Giant raindrops pelted them. "Just our luck," she grumbled. "I've got to get a car."

They hurried under the awning at the front of the store. "Now what?" Rena asked. "It's five blocks to the boarding house."

"And eight home for me." Gwen shook her head. "We can leave the dress boxes in the store and make a run for it, I suppose."

"Maybe not." Rena nodded at the car pulling up to the curb. "I think rescue is at hand." A blue sedan slid to a stop at the curb in front of them.

"It's Daddy!" Gwen jerked open the back door so

Ruthann and Rena could scramble in, then tossed her box after them and got into the front seat. "You're just in time, Daddy. You saved us."

"I come in handy sometimes," Drew said.

"We've had a wonderful afternoon watching Gwen unpack a new shipment," Ruthann said quickly. "And of course we couldn't resist a new dress apiece, especially after she offered us the use of her employee discount."

Drew glanced over his shoulder. "What happened to your face?" he asked Ruthann.

She put her hand to her cheek, which had caught the edge of the bookcase as it fell. "Just a little accident with the bookcase in my classroom," Ruthann said. "Nothing to worry about."

The young women fell silent.

"It goes without saying I'm surprised to see the three of you together." He made no effort to leave the curb.

When it appeared no one else was going to speak, Ruthann said, "Mrs. Schaeffer was at the boardinghouse when I came home from school yesterday, and she told Gwen what happened. Gwen came to see me after work and invited Rena and me to watch her unpack a new shipment of dresses today."

"I see."

"No, you don't see, Daddy. Ruthann has accepted my apology for everything. We're grown women. I know I acted like a bratty kid, but it's not the unforgiveable sin."

"Hear, hear," Rena said. Ruthann elbowed her into silence.

Drew seemed to be waiting.

Ruthann broke the silence. "It's a long story."

"And it goes without saying I want to hear all of it."

Gwen's shoulders twitched. "Excuse me, Daddy, but we're not some students who got sent to your office for misbehavior."

Her words seemed to startle him. "You're right, Gwennie. I apologize."

Gwen turned around to look at Ruthann. "She's all right. Aren't you, Ruthann?"

"Of course I'm all right."

Rena snorted, and Ruthann elbowed her again.

"Look, ladies, if you don't have plans, let me do penance and take you to dinner."

"I'm going to wash my hair," Rena said.

"And I didn't finish my paperwork because we were having too much fun trying on dresses," Gwen said.

"But Ruthann would love dinner," Rena added.

Drew dropped Gwen at home before he took Ruthann and Rena to the boardinghouse. "I'll just run upstairs a minute," Ruthann said. "I won't be long."

It took Drew two tries to rise from the sofa when she came back downstairs. "Where would you like to eat?"

"I'd like to tell you what happened before we go. If I don't, Mr. Clifton or Mr. Cabrera will."

"That might be a good idea." He sat down again and stretched his leg out in front of him. "Too much driving," he said.

"Maybe you shouldn't do any more of it today."

"No, I want to spend some time with you."

Ruthann took a deep breath and told him about the

closet and the bookcase, as well as Chief Edmondson's visit. "Gwen came to see me out of honest concern, and like she said, we're starting over. I'm glad, Drew, because I won't cause a rift between you and your daughter. I'd leave Camden because of that, but I don't like the idea of being fired."

For a moment Drew sat in silence. Then he said, "I should put you on the train, by force if necessary."

"When Merle posted that notice, you asked me to stay and said we'd fight together."

"There's a difference between fighting words and something like rigging a bookcase to fall on you."

"I agree, but it should still be my choice."

"Ruthann, I can't go back on my decision."

"Sending me home isn't going to solve the problem."

"Not for me, certainly. I'll miss you."

"What about me?"

"You'll be safe. I'll visit you, and…"

"Just seeing you occasionally would make it harder on both of us."

He closed his eyes. "Have you told your parents what happened?"

"No. But I'll do what Chief Edmondson told me about not going out alone or staying late at school again."

"I think you should tell them."

"I'm not going to tell them anything. They gave me the choice of coming back after Christmas, but Daddy would come pack me up and take me home, and you'd let him."

"We don't have a future if someone finally kills you."

"Kills me? You really think…"

"I don't know what to think anymore."

"When I said once I didn't want to fight anymore, I was wrong. You're worth fighting for. The two of us together are worth fighting for." She leaned her forehead against his. "Please, Drew, don't do this."

His lips skimmed her cheek and moved down. "I'm afraid of losing you. If you stay, and something worse happens, I'd never get over it. If you go home, time and distance could tear us apart." He kissed her, a gentle kiss hinting at more than his physical weariness. "Merle is going to get what's coming to her someday."

"We usually do reap what we sow." With the tips of her fingers, she smoothed the lines from his forehead. "Are you sure you shouldn't just go home and get a good night's sleep?"

"I want to take you to dinner. I want to spend every possible moment with you, even if I know I shouldn't."

She tried not to see the pain in his eyes as he got to his feet. "I could drive," she suggested as they reached the car.

Drew scooted over to let Ruthann take the wheel while he stretched his leg as far as he could in the small space along the floorboard. "I'll admit this is better."

"I knew it would be."

"Well, my life is in your hands." He guided her hand to the dashboard. "This is the ignition, and…"

"Oh, stop it!" She slapped his hand away. "I've been driving since I was fourteen."

She put in the clutch and started the car. "Where are we going?"

"The steakhouse in Hodding Corner. Straight down Main and turn left at the light onto Highway 19."

When the town disappeared behind them, Drew said, "Ground rules for tonight. We'll enjoy our dinner and won't talk about Merle Fulton or what's happened. How does a nice ribeye sound?"

"Heavenly."

\*\*\*\*

The headlights of the car had just illuminated the faded green sign reading "Camden, Texas pop. 10,366" when a sharp pop followed by the crack of breaking glass caused Ruthann to brake without putting in the clutch. The car stalled and died. Drew threw open the door and pushed himself off the seat. "What..."

Ruthann abandoned the driver's seat and skirted the car, bringing his cane with her. He grabbed it but didn't let go of the door.

"There's a flashlight in the glove compartment. Check the tires."

Ruthann did as he said but stopped short at the sight of the shattered back window. "Drew, look at that."

"A tire must've thrown up a rock."

"A back tire? How could it hit the window from that angle?"

"Get Nathan Wolfe to explain the physics of it, because I can't. I'll drive from here."

Ruthann got in on the passenger side. "I'm sorry about your window."

"It can be replaced." He stopped with his hand on the ignition. "But you can't." He drove a few yards and pulled into a rest area. When he held out his arms, Ruthann slid into them without a word.

He smoothed her hair and cupped her face in his hands. "I can't explain the difference you've made in my life. I feel new somehow. I can't remember when I last felt whole the way I do now."

"Are you very sure I'm what you want, Drew? What you need?"

"Everything." His mouth caressed hers. "Everything, precious girl."

**\*\*\*\***

A cold damp January slid into a drier February with no more incidents. Mr. Cabrera installed a new lock on the third grade classroom and told Ruthann to secure the door every afternoon. "I'll use my own key to come in and clean. Not that there's much to do. You make the *niños* clean up before they leave."

Harry insisted on a latch inside Ruthann's door at the boarding house and admitted he'd already changed all the outside locks after the incident at Christmas. "Camden's never been a place where we had to worry about locking doors, but I guess we do now."

Rena and Ruthann walked to school together every morning and home again in the afternoons. Once again the faculty quietly rallied around Ruthann. She wondered if she symbolized a rebellion against Merle Fulton, who made her presence known in the various classrooms on a regular basis. She tried not to live on the edge of wondering when the woman would appear next in the third grade.

Ruthann, Rena, and Gwen became a tight-knit group. Sometimes Gwen spent Friday nights at the boarding house on the rollaway Aggie kept in an upstairs closet.

"I always wished for a sibling," Gwen told Ruthann after they'd turned out the lights one night. "I had friends when I was growing up, but I wasn't invited to many things. The girls knew I'd be a wet blanket because I couldn't afford to risk getting into trouble—my father being who he was."

"My sister was eight years older than me. She resented the attention I got as the baby, and later I resented all the attention she got when she had one of her own. We get along better now, though. Sometimes we do, anyway." Ruthann propped herself on one elbow and peered through the darkness. "You never mention Daniel."

"We go out sometimes."

"Why do I get the idea it's not all that serious?"

"Because it's not. I didn't come to the Christmas party with him because he was beginning to get out of line, if you know what I mean. I know he was taught better, but he fancies himself irresistible to the opposite sex."

"I went to school with some boys like that."

"Daniel did it all in high school. Captain of the football team, all kinds of honors in track and field, voted most handsome, and a lot of other things. He dated all the girls. All of them except me. When he came back here at the same time I did, they were either all married or gone. He didn't have much choice."

"Aren't you selling yourself short?"

"Not by his standards."

"Why put on an act if you're not happy about it?"

"Because…because if anyone ever found out…"

Ruthann heard her turn over. "Gwen?"

"Goodnight, Ruthann."

****

Just before the weekend of Valentine's Day, Gwen stopped by to tell Ruthann she'd taken a modeling job in Dallas.

"You'll miss the dance at the hotel."

Gwen shrugged. "Daniel will find someone else to haul along, or make himself obnoxious to the other girls' dates. What about you and Daddy?"

"He mentioned a concert in Kerrville. It's a long way just for that, but maybe he'll let me do the driving. I'm still hoping for a chance to bring up the specialist Dr. Leeson wants him to see, but after I convinced him to let me stay, I didn't want to muddy the waters."

"Nothing else has happened, has it? Maybe Merle's backed off. Accepted the inevitable."

"Maybe. Call me when you get home, all right?"

****

Drew brought a dozen roses and a box of candy when he arrived on Saturday night. They held hands through the concert. "Would you rather have gone to the dance?" he asked as they crossed the parking lot behind the auditorium.

"Only with Fred Astaire."

He laughed. "First I lose out to Paul Henreid's suave persona and now to the fleet feet of Fred Astaire."

"To tell you the truth, I wasn't even invited to my senior prom."

"Someone missed a golden opportunity then."

"I told you I was a wallflower."

"I'd say you were a late bloomer, but you're blooming now."

Ruthann noticed Drew stop abruptly and seem to struggle for balance. His limp, when he began to walk again, was more pronounced than earlier in the evening. "Would you like for me to drive home?"

"That might be a good idea," he said almost too quickly.

After a few silent miles Ruthann said, "Your leg's much worse."

"It comes and goes."

"I think it stays."

"You and Gwen have become thick as thieves—not that I disapprove—so I'm sure she's told you what Dr. Leeson said during the holidays."

"Yes."

"I've managed all these years. I can manage a little longer."

Ruthann steeled herself and plunged ahead. "One of the first things you told me about yourself was you were going to lose that leg sooner or later. So how much longer is a little longer?"

"A while."

"An infection could cost your life."

He didn't reply.

"Your leg isn't you. Losing it won't change your value to Camden Schools. Are you afraid it will make a difference in how I feel about you?"

"Would it?" The blunt question seemed out of character.

"No. Gwen asked me straight out how I'd feel about seeing it, and I told her I wouldn't know until it happened. But I know it won't make any difference in how I feel about you."

"I wonder if you've thought it through. You're very young and inexperienced, Ruthann."

"Inexperienced as in a physical relationship?"

"Yes, it…"

"I told you I wouldn't come between you and your

daughter, and that worked out," she interrupted. "I won't come between you and your health, either. If you're trying to keep that leg because of me, you're risking everything we could have together."

Again, he didn't reply.

"Promise me you'll make that appointment, Drew."

He reached for her hand and squeezed it, but he didn't promise.

****

As March began, she'd learned to live with locks and with Rena as her shadow, but now Drew's health loomed larger than her own safety. Though there had been no more classroom visits, she had to wonder if it was just the calm before the storm.

The faculty buzzed quietly about how Drew didn't seem to get out of his office often. His regular brief visits to their classrooms became fewer and fewer, and the teachers as well as the students missed his encouraging presence and predictable bags of peppermints and day-old cookies from the local bakery.

He let Ruthann do most of the driving when they went out on Saturday nights. Sometimes they didn't go out at all and ate at the boardinghouse with the others, who then gave them the privacy of the parlor. Gwen confided to Ruthann that Dr. Leeson had prescribed something for Drew's increasing pain. "But I'm not sure he's taking it. Or if he is, it isn't doing much good."

If Drew lay awake in pain, Ruthann tossed restlessly in dread. On several occasions, she tried to bring up the visit to the specialist in San Antonio, but Drew changed the subject or simply cut her off. Her heart broke every time she saw him wince

185

involuntarily. When they were alone together, he often held her in silence as if willing them into a place where dread and pain couldn't accompany them. She lay down every night with his face before hers and a yearning to have the rest of him with her, too.

Chapter Eighteen

On the first mild Saturday in March, they took a picnic to his hidden refuge at the lake. Ruthann refrained from mentioning his difficulty navigating the path from the car. She spread the blanket and settled down to read while he painted. After a couple of hours, he called her to join him on the shore.

"This is for us," he said, gesturing toward the canvas. "I'm not much of a portrait painter, but I take my cue from the impressionists." He chuckled. "I give the *impression* of folks."

She rested her chin on his shoulder and gazed at the freshly created painting of two somewhat gauzy figures in the very spot where she'd set up their picnic. "It's us, isn't it?"

"It's our present. I wish our future were clearer."

"The year's almost over."

"Then what, precious girl?"

"Then I'll go home for the summer, I suppose. That's what I'd have done if none of this had happened. Maybe I won't be offered another contract anyway. Merle Fulton's been quiet, but she's still on the school board."

"She can't get you fired without a majority, and you haven't given any reason for non-renewal."

"Aren't the contracts due next month?"

"First week of April."

"We'll see then, won't we? Are you ready to eat?"

"Did Aggie pack our lunch?"

"Should I feel insulted you always ask that?" Ruthann tucked her hand through his arm. "Yes, she did. She doesn't trust me to feed you. She says you're too thin."

"Julia's a good cook. We eat well."

"I'm a good cook, too. I told you I learned early." She matched her pace to his slow, laborious one on the slope leading up from the lake.

"I hope I'll find out for myself."

"Maybe you will."

He braced himself against the tree and slid down onto the blanket. Ruthann unpacked the wicker basket and served his plate.

"What do superintendents do during the summer?"

"Go to meetings. Do paperwork. Plan for the coming year." He settled himself against the tree. "Did you know I got the superintendent's job because they couldn't find anyone else?"

She handed him his plate. "No, I didn't."

"I was young for the position—thirty-two. They'd had a bad situation here for a long time, and most of the faculty was fed up. Oh, they weren't threatening to quit, but morale was low, and the students felt it. John Clifton was on the verge of leaving, though. He had a small inheritance from his grandmother which could have carried him a while, but the Depression had a stranglehold on everyone by then. The teachers needed to hang onto their jobs no matter what. Anyway, the board interviewed several more experienced men, but they got wind of the impending revolt and wouldn't touch it with a ten-foot pole. I wanted to leave east

Texas, so I jumped on the offer. I was too green to know better."

"Was Merle on the school board then?"

"No. She was still married to Norman Wolfe and playing the society *grande dame*."

"Did you ever regret taking the job?"

He smiled around a large bite of chicken salad. "Every day and every night for a year. But I couldn't afford to move on, and I'd found a staunch ally in John Clifton. I called all the teachers in one at a time, asked about their particular beefs with the system, discussed everything with John, and then called a general meeting where the two of us outlined a new regimen. So long as a person was doing his or her job, we'd back them to the hilt. And our doors would always be open. After that, things started to get better, and you see what we are today."

Ruthann didn't miss the pride shining in his eyes. "I see very well, and I'm proud to be part of the Camden Schools."

He reached for her hand. "Sometimes I think about how it might be if you'd never come here."

"Maybe it was meant to be."

"What will you do at home?"

"I haven't thought about it. Mother's involved in half a dozen clubs and organizations. I'm sure she'll expect me to volunteer for this and that."

"What about your social life?"

"Most of my friends from high school are married or have moved away. My situation is much like Gwen's."

"She's gone a lot these days."

"Modeling must be exciting for her."

Drew crunched a carrot stick and swallowed before he answered. "I'm not sure that's what she's doing."

"What?"

"It's just a feeling I have. Call it parental instinct. And she and Daniel Clifton aren't close these days."

"Would you like my opinion of Daniel Clifton?"

The corners of his mouth turned down. "I didn't know you had one."

"He's always been courteous to me, but he carries himself with a certain arrogance."

"He's a good young man. Proficient at his job. A devoted son, especially since they lost David."

"He can be all that and arrogant, too. Maybe I'm being unfair. I haven't had much interaction with him, but he seems a little too sure of himself. Bernie says he hasn't moved past being the star in high school."

"He's young."

"So is Gwen. So am I."

He looked at her over the edge of his cup. "Touché."

"Is your lunch good?"

"Very tasty. Aggie's a true culinary genius."

"I think a couple of my skirts are tighter after eating at her table all year."

"You're just right." He reached over to pinch her cheek. "I like some meat on my bones."

"Your bones could use some meat."

He helped himself to a second sandwich. "I'm still a growing boy."

"I'd cook for you if you came to the VA Hospital in San Antonio this summer."

"Trying to bribe me?"

She took a deep breath. "You can't keep on like

this, Drew. You're having more and more trouble walking, and you're in a lot of pain almost all the time. I can tell."

"I'm just not ready to give some sawbones my leg. Not yet anyway."

"If you don't do something, you may give some mortician your body." Her face flamed. "I'm sorry. I shouldn't have said that."

He held out his arms. "Come here."

She didn't need urging. "I don't care about your leg. I care about you."

"Have you thought about what life would be like with an amputee? They're not going to just trim the thing—they're going to chop it off at the hip. The leg's a mess."

"Is that what this is all about?"

"I'll have to learn to walk again and manage without the ability to bend at the knee—unless they've improved on peg-legs since the first time I saw one. I won't be able to drive. I might not be able to…"

She put her hand over his mouth. "You started all of this, remember?"

"Maybe I shouldn't have."

"Then why are we here together like this?"

His stroked her back. "It's crossed my mind I won't be a whole man anymore."

"You'll be what you've always been. And you'll be alive."

"Alive."

"I'm afraid I'm going to lose you if you let things go much longer."

His arms fell away from her. "Surgery is risky, too."

"So is life."

His forced smile kindled a deep sadness in her. "You're beginning to sound too much like me."

When he stretched out after lunch, she produced a pillow for him. "You looked so uncomfortable the last time we came." She tucked it under his head. "How's that?"

"It would be perfect if you'd share it with me."

"Is that a good idea?"

"Probably not, but I'd like for you to."

She moved the remains of their lunch and lay down beside him.

"That's nice," he murmured. "Very nice."

In a few minutes, the even tenor of his breathing told her he'd fallen asleep.

*This is what it would be like married to him. Falling asleep beside him every night and waking in the morning. I never really thought about that with Jack. He was almost larger than life to me in his uniform. The hero going out to slay dragons and returning to his fair maiden. Except he didn't come back, and I'm not sure I would've wanted to spend my life as his fair maiden. What would our marriage—if we hadn't changed our minds—have been like?*

*But Drew's different. He's real. He's here. He loves me, and more than that, he needs me. I feel a connection to him like I've never felt to another human being.*

"Ruthann?"

"I'm here."

"I dozed off."

"Another catnap."

He pulled her closer. "You feel so good."

She savored the warmth of his body. "So do you."

In a few minutes, she knew he'd fallen asleep again.

She woke him before the sun began to set. "We don't want to cause a scandal," she said.

"I'd like to." He pulled her down beside him again.

Against her better judgment, she snuggled against him. "What if Merle is out with her camera again?"

He caressed her back and put his lips against her throat at the V of her blouse. "Let's make it worth her while."

"I don't think so." She felt his hands moving over her shoulders and down, stopping just short of where they shouldn't go.

"When I gave up on Marlene being a real wife to me, I started sleeping in the spare bedroom. Lying in the bed beside her...smelling the talcum powder she favored...hearing her breathe...after a while I couldn't do it anymore."

Ruthann closed her eyes against the image of his torment with a wife who wasn't a wife.

"Then she got sick, and toward the end, I slept on a cot next to the bed in case she needed something for the pain. It was easier when I knew it was going to finally be over. Does that shock you?"

She buried her face against his chest and felt his heart beating beneath her cheek. "It was an unnatural situation, to say the least."

"You and Jack..."

"We were never together. Not like that. When I think back, the whole relationship had a superficial feel to it. We were playing our parts in the middle of a war."

"I think everyone was."

"It's as if we couldn't think about tomorrow because it might not come."

"Look at me, Ruthann."

She lifted her face.

"Tomorrow is here, precious girl. At least my tomorrow. But sometimes when I look at you like this, I wonder what I'm thinking. How can I ask you to tie yourself to a man old enough to be your father...and perhaps, eventually, not even a whole one."

Ruthann tried to bury her face against him again, but the unanswered question held her at bay. She moved away from him and sat up. "You've got to do something soon. You can't live on pain pills and..."

His jaw tightened. "Gwen told you about those, too, did she?"

His gaze made her uncomfortable, but she didn't back down. "Maybe you should've told me first."

He struggled to bring himself upright. "We'd better be getting back to town. Like you said, we don't want to cause a scandal."

****

On the third of April, Ruthann found a new contract in her school mailbox. "What are you going to do?" asked Rena, coming up behind her.

"I don't know."

"Is there trouble in paradise?"

"You've noticed."

"Mr. Mallory hasn't been around much these past two weeks."

"We didn't quarrel, if that's what you mean. But he's having second thoughts."

"Why?"

"His age. His leg."

194

"Are you having second thoughts?"

"No. I'm not the same person I was a few months ago. Knowing him has changed me. I look at life differently. I look at him and…" Her voice trailed off. "Anyway, I haven't changed my mind." She tucked the contract into her leather case. "Let's go home."

They found Gwen waiting on the front steps of the boarding house. "I've got to talk to you," she said. "Both of you."

As soon as Ruthann closed the door of her room behind them, Gwen blurted, "I'm married."

Ruthann sank down on the bed. "Obviously not to Daniel. So who?"

"Tomás."

"Tomás!" Rena's hand flew to her throat. "But he's…"

"A Mexican. Right. We were good friends all through high school. Both of us were outsiders—me because of who my father was and him because of his race. Oh, there wasn't any overt discrimination, but he wasn't really accepted. Daddy liked him, though, and didn't object when we'd study together in the evenings. I was hopeless at math, but it was easy for him. We couldn't go out, so sometimes we'd meet at the park at night. That's what Chief Edmondson has on me. He caught us there one Friday night when all the other kids had gone to the football game. We weren't doing anything wrong, but…"

"But in his opinion, just being there together was wrong." Bitterness tinged Rena's voice.

Gwen nodded. "Then Tomás got a scholarship to UT, and I went to Mary Hardin Baylor. We wrote letters, and sometimes he'd hitch a ride to Belton. By going to school in the summers, he had enough credits to finish a year early. By then the war had started, and he enlisted right after graduation."

"Did he get overseas?"

"Just in time for D-Day, although he went in a week after the main invasion. I was working in Dallas then, so it was easier to keep things quiet."

"Are you sure your father and your aunt don't know?"

"I'm positive. I didn't want to come back to Camden because I knew it would make things harder for us to see each other, but the store said they needed me to do the buying when they bought out Clyde's. Tomás got out of the Army last summer and worked as an off-the-cuff clerk for a law firm in Austin before starting back to school in January, and I…"

"Lied about all those weekend modeling assignments in Dallas," Ruthann interrupted. "I wondered. Actually, I didn't, but your father said he thought something wasn't right."

Gwen worked a thin chain holding a narrow gold band from beneath her blouse. "While Tomás was here at Christmas, we decided not to wait any longer, so in February we went to the courthouse in Austin and got married."

"Why are you telling us this now?" Rena asked.

"Because of this." Gwen took a single folded sheet of paper from her purse and held it out.

Ruthann unfolded it. *I saw you. I know the truth. Everyone in Camden will know soon.* "How did you get it?"

"It was on my desk when I went into the store this morning. I've been frantic all day, trying to decide what to do. Tomás has midterms soon, and I don't want to worry him."

"So you came to us," Rena said. She folded her legs under her at the foot of the bed. "Well, honey, you came to the right place."

The others stared at her.

"Did you ever wonder why I'm fluent in Spanish?"

"You studied it in college," Ruthann said.

"Did I tell you that?"

"I...no, I suppose I just assumed it."

"It was my first language. Catarina Guadalupe Aguilero Gilbert. I'm exactly one-quarter Mexican, and while that's not as suspect in the outrageously bigoted public eye as being under the one-drop-of-black-blood-makes-you-black rule, a south-of-the-border heritage is still unacceptable in some places." She shook her hair over her face before repinning it with a barrette. Her eyes fixed on Gwen. "Close your mouth," she said.

Gwen startled. "You just surprised me, that's all."

"Yes, well, I'm surprising myself by coming clean, but I think it's the right time. And the right place, so long as it doesn't go out of this room."

"You know it won't," Ruthann said. "Tell us about your family."

"It's an ugly story, and right now Gwen's situation is more important. Suffice it to say my grandfather died when a bunch of greedy *gringos* attacked his ranch and tried to run off his workers. Even though it happened long before I was born, it affected my grandmother's life until she died, and my mother still harbors a lot of bitterness. I can't blame her, either."

Ruthann chewed her lip. "Oh, Rena, I'm sorry."

"That was a long time ago, and Gwen's dealing

with her situation now. I guess you couldn't take the note to Chief Edmondson?"

"He's the last person I'd take it to. Besides, there's more. She fished in her purse again and came up with a handful of similarly written notes. "They say terrible things about you, Ruthann. About younger women and older men. I guess I believed them because I felt so guilty about my own situation that I was ready to think the worst of you, too. These are why I fought you tooth and toenail over my father."

Rena snatched the notes from Gwen's hand and scanned them. "These are…and look at this one! *Your father sacrificed his whole life for you in ways you can't imagine, so it's up to you to save him from that little tart.* Little tart indeed!" She jumped up and began to pace, waving the papers wildly around her head.

The words *in ways you can't imagine* echoed in Ruthann's brain. Someone knew. Whoever wrote those notes, be it Merle Fulton or someone else, knew the details of Gwen's birth.

Gwen caught up with Rena. "Give me those." She put them back in her purse. "I hated myself for deceiving Daddy. Maybe it was easier to blame Ruthann for how I felt, even though she had nothing to do with it."

"You have to tell your father before he hears it from the person who wrote the note," Rena said.

"I know who wrote it," Gwen said. "I just don't know how she found out."

"I agree you have to tell him," Ruthann said. "You said you were always protective of his position when you were growing up. This could be worse than any adolescent mischief you might've gotten into. The war has changed things a little. The men on the front lines didn't care about the race of the soldier fighting next to them."

"Unfortunately, it hasn't changed things enough," Rena muttered. "Dear old Ed, my erstwhile beau, used to talk about all the *wetbacks* in Texas. Obviously, he didn't know he was dating one."

Ruthann threw Rena a sympathetic glance. "He isn't worth thinking about." Turning to Gwen she said, "Your father has a lot of respect for Tomás's father, and also he loves you. He'll understand." *But will he tell you the truth, and if he does, what will you do with it?*

"Will you come with me to tell him?"

"I think I've interfered enough by nagging him to see the doctor. He hasn't exactly avoided me lately, but he doesn't look for excuses to see me during the school day, and when we're together on weekends, I can feel the issue hanging between us."

"He's not mad at you, just worried about everything that's happened. He's worried about whether or not he should've gotten you involved with him, all things considered. I told him once he was having a middle-aged fling, and even though I've apologized more than once and said I was wrong, he's thinking about it now and wondering if I was right. Oh, he loves you, but…"

Ruthann sighed. "I don't know, Gwen. But if you really need me with you, I'll come."

They arranged dinner at the boarding house for Drew, with Gwen to arrive later. At the last minute, she backed out. "I can't do it, not now. I'll talk to Tomás when I go to Austin this weekend, and then we'll see."

"I think I understand how she feels, but she's put

me in a bad spot," Ruthann told Rena after Gwen had gone. "I don't like hiding things from Drew, especially about his own daughter."

"You didn't ask her to tell you her secrets, and he can't expect you to be an informer."

"I don't know what he expects. I don't know what I expect of myself."

"Do you wish you'd never come to Camden? Never met him?"

Ruthann sank down on the edge of her bed and tried to focus. "I had my moments after that horrible notice in the faculty lounge. I thought about Jack and how I was certain I loved him enough to marry him. After he died, I acted like a grieving widow until my mother and my sister pointed out how unattractive it was—not to mention dishonest. And then I began to reflect and wonder about the whole thing. Who he really was. If I loved him enough for a lifetime."

"What about Drew Mallory?"

"Do I love him enough for a lifetime, however long or short that may be? Yes. Oh, yes, I love him enough."

"Then it's all right."

"Is it? Someone doesn't think so."

"After he saved me from making a terrible mistake with that weasel Edwin, I wondered if my father would have been like him if he hadn't died in the first war. You know, looking after me and protecting me. Making sure I didn't get myself in too deep. Mamma says he was a good man, and Mr. Mallory is a good man, too. The two of you are right for each other. Even Gwen thinks so now." Rena patted Ruthann's shoulder. "I get the shower first tonight, for giving you an ear and all this sage advice."

Chapter Nineteen

On Sunday, Drew called and asked Ruthann to meet him at the hotel coffee shop. It was empty, and Buck closed the blinds and turned the sign on the door to read Closed. Then he made himself scarce.

"I'm worried about Gwen," Drew said as soon as she sat down.

A knot of dread formed in Ruthann's chest. "Why?"

"She's off again this weekend for another *modeling gig*, as she puts it."

She considered her words. "It's good money, isn't it?"

"I don't know what it is. Has she— No, I'm not going to ask if she's told you anything. If she'd wanted me to know, she'd have told me."

Ruthann felt frozen. *I can't lie to him, but I can't betray Gwen's confidence, either.* "She's a grown woman, after all," she said carefully and knew he'd noted the deliberateness of her words.

"I know. But Julia's acting strangely, too, these days, and when I ask her if anything's bothering her, she says no. I don't want to push her. She has a temper. She flew into a two-month-long rage over her husband's affair with Merle Fulton. I thought... Well, it wasn't pretty."

"She doesn't seem like a person who's prone to

that kind of anger."

"You weren't here when she found out about Len's…indiscretion."

"I heard about that. The affair, I mean, not her reaction to it."

"Len died very shortly afterwards. Otherwise, I think Julia might have killed him. Merle, too."

"You don't mean that."

"Oh, not literally, no." His mouth formed a twisted smile. "If she had, it would've saved me the trouble of wanting to do it now."

"You shouldn't say things like that."

"I don't suppose you're going to repeat them." He lifted his eyebrows. "I won't hang for wanting her gone, but if she ended up that way, it wouldn't look good."

Ruthann wrinkled her nose at him. "You're downright wicked sometimes."

"Not as often as I'd like to be." He ran the tip of one finger from her palm to her wrist and laughed when she shivered. "For a while Julia talked about going back to Commerce, but she stayed when the county offered her a job. She loved the community choir and didn't want to leave it."

"How old was Gwen?"

"Twelve. We could've managed on our own."

"I suppose if anyone knew she wasn't really your sister, it would create a stir."

"More than a stir. I've always wondered if she knows I'm not Gwen's biological father."

Ruthann's mouth went dry, but she forced herself to say, "Have you ever considered Gwen has a right to know the truth?"

"Why? My name is on her birth certificate. I raised her. Blood means nothing."

Ruthann nodded. "I just asked the question."

"Now I have a question for you. Are you going to sign your new contract?"

"I'd like to."

"I want you here in Camden with me, but if anything happened to you, I couldn't live with myself."

"So you don't want me to sign it."

"I don't know what I want, precious girl. Except I want you forever. If nothing else happens between now and the end of school, maybe we're home safe."

"You asked a question, so I get one. Are you going to see the doctor about your leg?"

"I told you I would."

"You said eventually. That's not soon enough, Drew. It's getting worse by the day."

"I can't give you the answer you want."

"Why?"

"I'd have to recover from the surgery, then go through rehabilitation. I couldn't do my job."

"You don't think they'd keep it open for you?"

"I couldn't ask them to do that."

"I think they'd insist on it, after all you've done for them."

"If they didn't, I probably couldn't get another position, at least not as an administrator. I'd have to go back to the classroom."

"Would that be so bad?"

"Sometimes I miss teaching, but the money wouldn't be as good. Not that I'm paid a fortune, but at least I can save something."

"If I kept teaching, we'd have twice as much."

"What about that little boy you've talked about?"

"Women work and raise their children, too, these days."

"Is that what you want to do?"

"I want to do whatever's best for us."

"I feel like I'm running out of time, Ruthann. I felt old and dried up, like every day would be the same as the one before it, and I'd just plod through until I died. But then you came along. You're all I want, but for some twisted reason, everything that's happened to you comes back to me."

Ruthann touched his arm. "Rena asked me last night if I was sorry I'd come to Camden and met you. I can't imagine what life might've been like if I hadn't. I don't even want to try. Don't die, Drew. Don't die because you think I wouldn't love you if you didn't have your leg or a job that made a certain amount of money. I don't want you to live with this constant pain. It breaks my heart to see you struggle."

"You're asking me to do something that would change our life together before it got started." He reached for her hands across the table.

Ruthann held them tightly. "Either way, both our lives are going to change."

\*\*\*\*

That week, Merle Fulton paid a visit to Ruthann's classroom during a hands-on science lesson in which the children participated with noisy enthusiasm. Afterwards she let it be known Miss Cooper had no discipline and allowed the children to handle dangerous chemicals.

"Baking soda and vinegar," Ruthann exploded when John Clifton reluctantly questioned her. "How dangerous can those be?"

"I'm not asking except to be able to say I did," he said, raising his hands in a gesture of surrender. "She's kept a low profile since everything that happened in January, but now she's getting her second wind. Just do your best to ignore her. You've got your contract. She can't rescind it." He glanced approvingly around the cheerful room. "But you haven't signed it yet."

"I have until May fifteenth, don't I?"

"Yes. Yes, you do. Personally, I hope you'll come back, Miss Cooper. Nothing that's happened has been your fault."

"It wouldn't have happened at all if I hadn't been here."

He rubbed the bridge of his nose with two fingers. "Well, if there hadn't been a war my son wouldn't be dead, but the war wasn't his fault either, was it?"

\*\*\*\*

As the final month of the school year began, Drew didn't press Ruthann for an answer to his question, but when she signed her contract, she told him, "My parents aren't happy about it. I can't blame them."

"I'm not either." He took her face in his hands and kissed her. "But I want you here."

They'd driven out to the lake but opted to stay in the car because of the dark clouds looming overhead. He maneuvered the car into a grove of trees so they were hidden from the road and tried to stretch his leg into a more comfortable position.

"Put your leg across the seat," Ruthann said. She didn't wait for him to do it on his own before she lifted the limb across her lap, untied his shoe, and began to rub his foot. As she worked her way toward his knee, she could feel the rough, pitted texture of scant flesh beneath his lightweight khaki trousers.

He leaned his head on the window and closed his eyes. "Nice," he murmured. Then he opened them. "But you need to know it looks much worse than what you're feeling."

"I'm sure it does," she said, aware he was watching her reaction.

"I'm moving my office downstairs. The mimeograph room and supply shelves are going up."

"Whose idea was that?"

"Why wouldn't it be mine?"

"Because you don't give over easily."

He put his head back against the door. "Well, I did this time. I almost fell the other day. I didn't, but I realized it was more than a possibility. If I break the bum leg, it won't heal, and if I break the good one, I'll be a lot worse off than I am now."

"When is this happening? I can help move things, and Rena will, too. You know she's never forgotten what you did for her."

"Did for her?"

"Warned her off that married soldier."

"Oh, right, I remember. She deserved better, and he didn't deserve her at all. I recognized his type the first time I saw them out together. Anyway, the move is all arranged. Luís is painting this weekend, and Coach Billings is organizing some of the high school boys to bring everything down on Monday or Tuesday. The telephone company has to run a line in, but they'll get around to it when they're ready. Meanwhile, Mrs. Leland will stay upstairs so she can answer the phone."

"I'm glad you made the decision."

"I am, too, I guess. What's in Aggie's basket?"

"I don't know. See if you can reach over the seat and get into it."

They ate chicken salad and deviled eggs to the sound of rain spattering the top of the car and skidding across the windshield. When they'd finished and transferred the basket again, Ruthann moved across the seat, careful to keep Drew's leg level, and leaned back in his arms.

He scattered soft kisses on her neck and cheeks and buried his face in her hair. "I love you, precious girl." He slid his hands down her arms to her hands. "Someday—someday soon, I hope—I'll lead you up a mountain, and then we'll take the last few steps together and fling ourselves into the abyss."

"That's almost like poetry."

"Does it need interpreting?"

"I don't think so. No, it doesn't."

His warm breath on her neck stirred feelings Ruthann savored rather than shrank from. His breath came faster. "You make me hope again. To remember what it means to be young and in love."

"Maybe those two things don't really go together."

"Why not?"

"I suppose you can be both, but maybe one doesn't appreciate the other."

He laughed softly. "I've rubbed off on you."

She turned in his arms. "You have a beautiful soul. I want to deserve it."

"You will. You do." His hands drifted up to her shoulders. "Marry me, Ruthann." His eyes searched hers as they'd done the first day she'd met him. "Marry me soon. I love you…need you…want you."

"Yes," she whispered. "Yes."

****

On Monday, Ruthann arrived at school to find her room in disarray. Books littered the floor in the reading circle area, the children's supplies had been pulled from their desks and lay scattered in the aisles, and every drawer in Ruthann's desk had been taken out and overturned. "I locked the door on Friday," she told John Clifton when he arrived after Rena flew out of the room before Ruthann could stop her.

"I checked it behind her," Rena said beginning to pick up books and put them back on the shelves.

Luís Cabrera stormed in brandishing a feather duster like a club. "I cleaned this room first and locked it behind me," he said. Ruthann thought he resembled a fire-breathing dragon as he snorted his way through the mess.

"And you keep the spare key where?" the principal asked.

The man reached into his pocket and produced a single key. "It goes home with me at night. All the keys do. But I keep this one separate."

Ruthann and Rena exchanged glances. "I leave my key in a dresser drawer on weekends," Ruthann said.

"Well, someone got in here with something. A key, a lock-pick, who knows?" John Clifton started out but poked his head back inside. "Mr. Cabrera, let the ladies do the cleaning up. I want you to check for booby traps."

"Booby traps?" Ruthann's eyes widened. "Oh, surely…"

The custodian nodded. "I'll check, all right." He headed for the closet and jerked open the door. A stack of empty boxes waiting for returned textbooks pitched forward and scattered. He muttered something in English and something else in Spanish. Rena giggled.

"I'll pretend I didn't hear that," the principal said, his mouth twitching. "Just keep looking, and make sure things are safe." He turned to Ruthann. "Are you all right?"

"I think so," she said. "But enough is enough. I'm ready to snatch someone bald-headed, as my grandmother used to say. It's one thing to go after me, but the children don't deserve this."

"I agree. I'm going to divert the third grade students to Miss Gilbert's room until this one is cleaned up. I'll send my wife to monitor the whole bunch so you can help in here, Miss Gilbert. Let's just keep this in the family for the present, shall we?"

Mr. Cabrera didn't find anything else amiss, but Ruthann couldn't help being both amused and touched at his growing fury as he walked the room wall to wall, keeping Rena laughing over his Spanish invectives uttered freely now that the principal had gone. When he'd declared it safe, Ruthann thanked him and said she and Rena could finish the cleanup. "We'll be fine," she assured him. "Really."

"Lock the door," he ordered.

"I can't keep it locked with the children here. It's against the fire code."

He glared at her and slammed the door on his way out.

Rena began gathering the scattered school supplies from the floor around their desks. "I heard his parents wouldn't let him speak Spanish at home after he started school, but he can cuss like a native." She straightened up. "And he knew I understood every word and didn't care. He was that mad."

"I didn't understand."

Rena tossed her hair out of her face. "You didn't need to."

"I wonder if he only spoke English to Tomás? He doesn't have an accent either."

"Gwen would know, I guess."

"It's too bad he didn't get to finish his education."

"It happened to a lot of kids, especially boys of his generation, but I'll bet he knows more about running the school plant than Mr. Mallory and Mr. Clifton put together. I think the school board pays him well because they know they couldn't replace him."

"They should. He's saved *my* neck at least twice."

"Mr. Mallory isn't going to like this."

"I wish he didn't have to know, but Mr. Clifton will tell him."

"Has he said any more about sending you home?"

"He wouldn't exactly fire me. I don't think he would anyway. But he's worried. I know he's more worried about everything that's happened than I am."

Rena placed a pile of supplies on the last desk. "The children will just have to sort out their stuff themselves." She glanced around. "Did Mr. Cabrera look in the cloak room?"

Ruthann hesitated. "I'm sure he did. I wasn't watching him—just listening and trying not to laugh."

"You wouldn't have laughed at what he said."

"You did."

"Well, I've heard it before, but not from a gentleman like Mr. Cabrera. That's what made it funny."

Rena skirted the science table against the wall and disappeared inside the long narrow room where students hung their coats and lunch pails. Her scream sent Ruthann flying down the aisle from her desk—and close on her heels came Luís Cabrera yelling—in English—he'd forgotten the cloakroom in his zeal to check the obvious.

Ruthann and Rena clutched each other in shock as he grasped the feet of the figure hanging from the light fixture. "It's only the Halloween scarecrow," he called to them. "It's all right, *niñitas.*"

They retreated as he came out carrying the stuffed dummy, trailing straw in its wake. Rena retched silently. "Sit down and put your head between your knees," Ruthann said, but her stomach churned, too. In the shadows, the figure hanging from the ceiling had looked all too human.

Cabrera shook the dummy furiously, showering straw around him like snow. "Everything's stored in my basement," he said between clenched teeth. "*My* basement! I put it away myself. If I find out who's been down there…" His words switched to Spanish, but this time Rena didn't laugh. Then he threw down the scarecrow. "I'm going for Mr. Clifton."

The two men seemed to be back before the first ever left. "Are you ladies all right?"

"We're okay." Ruthann kept her hand on Rena's neck. "I think we are, anyway."

The principal tore away a paper pinned to the scarecrow's overalls. "Something worse is going to happen to you. You won't see it coming, but it will happen," he read aloud. "This is a direct threat. I'm going to call the police."

"No, you're not." Drew Mallory stood in the door, leaning heavily on his cane and panting with the effort of walking the long corridor from his office.

"Drew, it's a threat. I don't have a choice."

"I know what it is." His angry, clipped words made him a stranger. He grabbed the paper from the principal's hand. "So was the acid before Christmas, and the closet, and the bookcase. Edmondson didn't find the perpetrator then, and he won't find who did this." He crossed the room to Ruthann and fastened cold, steely eyes on hers. "I'm tearing up your contract. You're going home."

"You don't mean that!"

Without another word, he limped back through the door and kept going.

Chapter Twenty

By mid-morning, order had been restored. Rena left, and John Clifton escorted the third-graders down the hall to Ruthann. "I've explained we had a little accident in here which needed repairing," he said clearly as the children filed in. "Also that they'll need to be responsible for organizing their own things."

"Thank you, Mr. Clifton."

"Shall I stay a while?"

"No, sir, we'll be just fine." She turned to the small sea of confused faces. "I know you'll each be able to pick out your own belongings and exchange if you have something belonging to someone else. Then we'll have reading circle as we usually do first thing in the morning. I'll let the class vote on what you don't want to do today, since we've gotten a late start."

"What happened, Miss Cooper?" Ronnie Peters' freckles stood out on his pale face.

"I'm not sure, Ronnie. Something got into the room and made a mess. But you can see it's all cleaned up now."

"A wild animal?" he asked.

"Maybe a cougar," Karen said.

"No cougars around here," Ronnie pronounced. "Maybe a mad dog."

*That's apt*, Ruthann thought. Aloud, she said, "I'm giving you fifteen minutes on the timer, boys and girls, so get busy!"

With the promise of choosing a subject to skip for the day, the children asked no more questions about the disruption of the morning routine. Even when Merle Fulton appeared after lunch, a malicious smile playing around her bright red lips, they ignored her and continued to do their math, which had survived the vote between that subject and cursive writing.

"I hear you had a little problem in here this morning," she said.

Ruthann paused beside a child she'd just reminded about keeping his numbers lined up when subtracting, and faced the woman. "Yes, we did, but everything's all right now. And this isn't a good day for a classroom visit because we're a bit behind."

Merle narrowed her eyes. "Yes, well, another day then," she said.

Ruthann didn't reply, nor did she watch the woman leave. But she let out her breath in relief when she heard the door close.

"You're glad she's gone, aren't you, Miss Cooper?" Ronnie asked.

She smoothed his perpetual cowlick. "Mind your business, Ronnie Peters. And you forgot to borrow from ten's place right here."

He grinned, and some of her tension begin to dissolve.

****

After school she told Rena to go on alone. "I've got to talk to Drew."

"From the look on his face, I don't think it'll do any good."

"I've got to try."

Rena hugged her. "Good luck, then."

Without even glancing up Drew seemed to know she was standing in the always-open door of his office. "You and Miss Gilbert go home," he said.

"She's already gone."

"Then I'll have to drive you, because you're not going out alone."

She closed the door. "We have to talk about this. I'm not one of your students you can expel from school."

"I've never expelled anyone in my life. But you're one of my teachers, and I can fire you."

"For what? And doesn't the school board have to…"

"They'll do what I ask them to do."

Ruthann circled the desk to stand beside his chair. "Look at me, Drew."

"I should never have looked at you in the first place."

"Two days ago you asked me to marry you as soon as possible."

He slammed his palm on the desk, making his open fountain pen bounce and leave a splatter of ink. "Leave it alone, Ruthann!" He jerked open a drawer and grabbed what she recognized as her signed contract. Without hesitation, he ripped it into four pieces and dropped them in the metal trashcan beside his desk. "It's finished. You're going home and forget you ever came to Camden."

"How am I supposed to forget I love you?"

"At this point, it doesn't matter. I want you out of Camden by the weekend. I'll fill in with a substitute for the next three weeks."

"Out of… Drew, no. Please."

"It's done and over!" He reached back into the open drawer and tossed a small object onto the desk. Then he picked it up, jerked her hand toward him, and slapped the object into her palm. "Look at it!" he ordered.

It took only seconds to realize she held a spent bullet in her hand. "I don't understand."

"That night in the car, remember? I convinced you a rock flew up and broke the back window. Bill Gee knew it wasn't a rock and ended up digging this out of the back of a front seat. The driver's seat. You were driving. He said it looked like it was deflected by a spring. Otherwise it might've killed you."

"And you didn't tell me?"

"I didn't tell anyone, and it's been eating on me ever since. I tried to believe it wasn't intended for us, but I was a fool. I should've sent you home then, but I was too selfish. Now I finally see myself for the idiot I am. I let this go too far. I've behaved like a schoolboy who had to have the girl no matter the cost."

Ruthann realized she'd been holding her breath and gasped for air.

Drew struggled to his feet. "Now I'll drive you home."

She sprinted for the door. "Don't bother."

All but blinded by her tears, she stumbled along the familiar sidewalk. Her chest screamed for air, but she kept going. At some point she realized she was still clutching the bullet in her hand, and it seemed to sear her palm.

In her room, she collapsed on the floor by the bed. She remembered how she'd wept hysterically for Jack, but this loss was too deep for tears. Her chest ached. "Oh, Drew," she whispered. "Oh, Drew."

Rena opened the door. "Ruthann...oh, Ruthann, what happened?" She sat down on the bed and smoothed Ruthann's tangled hair from her face.

Ruthann managed to stumble through the conversation with Drew and showed Rena the bullet. "Someone tried to kill us...kill me...and now..."

Rena took a deep breath. "You have to go home like he said."

"I can't leave him."

"You can't die on his doorstep, either. Go home, Ruthann, and let things settle down."

They were still discussing recent events when Gwen burst in at five o'clock. "I heard what happened."

Ruthann's legs tingled as she stood up. "I watched him tear up my contract. He told me to leave Camden by the weekend."

Gwen paled. "Oh, Ruthann, he couldn't have. That's not my father."

"It's not the man I love with all my heart," Ruthann said. Then she opened her hand, which still held the spent bullet, and repeated the story. "He's kept it in his desk all these months. He never told me."

"Maybe he's right," Gwen said. "Maybe you should go home. At least for a while. But he didn't mean what he said about things being over between the two of you."

Ruthann sat down on the bed. "I know he didn't mean it, but he said it. He's blaming himself for everything that's happened, and I'm blaming myself. It's a vicious circle."

At the sound of the dinner bell, Rena poked her

head in the room. "I'm going to bring up your plate. I'm sure there's enough for you, too, Gwen."

"I'll call home to let Aunt Julia know I won't be there," Gwen said. "I can't leave Ruthann like this. And I can't handle myself with Daddy right now, either."

Rena brought three plates on a tray. They ate in almost total silence. Finally, Gwen said, "You know, I think when Tomás and I made the decision to get married, I really understood for the first time what it means to love in spite of all the barriers. We'll have to deal with the issue of race for the rest of our lives, and so will our children if we have them. You and Daddy have the age difference and the fact he's going to lose his leg. All of us will have to adapt to our circumstances and learn to live with them. Live in spite of them."

"Now you sound wise like Drew."

"I hope I've inherited the best of him."

"Of course you have."

"And it's not over between the two of you. He just wants you safe."

"He won't change his mind. That's one of the things I love about him—his self-confidence when it comes to making decisions."

Gwen moved from the chair to the foot of the bed. "Then you have to make him decide something different."

"How?"

"I don't know. I've got to go. Maybe I can sneak in without Daddy seeing me. I don't know what I'd say to him right now. But tomorrow night, I'll tell him I'm married. It's time to clear the air."

"He loves you. He'll understand."

"He loves both of us—and we've got to stick together." Gwen reached down to hug Ruthann. "It's you and me, kid," she said with a smile. "By the way, I've parted with most of my savings to buy a car. Tomás talked me into it. He says I'm spending a lot more on train fare. Mr. Gee is checking it out at the garage, but I'll pick it up tomorrow and come by, all right?"

****

Rena carried the tray back to the kitchen. When she came back, she said, "Mr. Wolfe is in the hall. He wants to talk to you."

"What about?"

"After dinner I…I told him about the bullet."

"Why did you do that?"

"I'm not sure. He's not going to spread it around, but he said there's something you should know."

Ruthann stood up and straightened her dress, then sat down on the stool in front of the dressing table. "I've heard enough today to last a lifetime, but all right. Tell him to come in."

Rena sat down on the foot of the bed, and Nathan took the chair. "First of all, I'm very sorry for what's happened," he said. He held up the bullet Rena had given him. "I'm not an expert on firearms, but I'd say this came from a .38 because of the size and configuration. And, yes, it did hit something hard—perhaps the springs in the seat as Bill Gee told Mr. Mallory. But what you should know is that Merle Fulton is an expert marksman, thanks to her father, who collected all kinds of guns. I know this because my brother told me she threatened him with one of them when he argued with her about the divorce."

Nathan Wolfe closed his eyes for a brief moment. Ruthann thought he looked very old. "He knew she could take everything he had. Everything he'd worked for. He tried to reason with her that night, and she pulled a gun out of a drawer in her dressing table and told him she'd kill him if he didn't get out. She fired, and the bullet embedded itself in the wall behind him. But he said he heard it go past his head and knew she'd deliberately missed. It came that close."

"She's...she's..." Ruthann searched her mind for a word to finish her sentence and couldn't find one.

"She's not insane," Nathan said, "but she's twisted, and that makes her even more dangerous. She knows exactly what she's doing and why. She's capable of carrying out any number of diabolical schemes. Miss Cooper, I...all of us regret everything that's happened to you this year. Drew Mallory is a good man. I've watched him when he's with you. It's as if he has a new lease on life. He needs...he deserves more than he's had, at least in his personal life. But maybe you should go home after all, for a while anyway. Miss Gilbert also told me about the note pinned to the scarecrow. You can't live life looking over your shoulder, and neither can Drew. Frankly, I don't think he'll stay here after this, and I can't blame him. No one can."

"Tell her about Mona."

Nathan frowned at Rena. "That has no bearing on..."

"It might. Just tell her."

"After Mona was sent away to school, my brother met and married Merle. Mona came home on holidays, and for the summer. Merle moved her to the third floor so Norman would have more privacy, or so she said, so he didn't see a lot of Mona. She kept to herself upstairs and rarely went out. Then the second year when she came home for the Easter holidays, she and Merle had a terrible row. When Norman asked if he could help, Merle told him to mind his own business, and the next morning she said Mona had gone to visit a school chum. He never saw her again."

"She didn't come home that summer?"

"No, she didn't. In the fall Merle told him she wanted a divorce, and you know what happened after that."

He rose and started for the door. "I'm speaking to you as a father, though I've never been one." He looked down at Rena. "I was the one who put the bug in Drew Mallory's ear about the soldier you were seeing during the war, Miss Gilbert. I'd been in Floresville that year during the Christmas holidays and saw him with a woman who wore a wedding ring. It was plain to me their relationship wasn't platonic. So I went to Drew and told him, and he got in touch with the man's commanding officer and confirmed it."

Rena bit her lip. "Thank you, Mr. Wolfe."

He waved his hand dismissively. "You're a good teacher." He turned back to Ruthann. "What the woman did to my brother...to Lillian...and to Kitty with those filthy rumors...she'll pay for all of it one day. But until then, I don't want anything to happen to anyone else, least of all two young women with their whole lives in front of them."

****

"Do you think Merle killed Mona? Her own sister?" Rena asked when Nathan Wolfe had gone.

"I don't know what to think. People say they've

seen Mona around town, especially after something bad happens, and Lillian swears Mona was driving the car that tried to cut us off after the Christmas party. Is she the ghost in the school bell tower?"

"None of it makes any sense."

"Are you going to school tomorrow?"

"If Mr. Clifton had a substitute for me, wouldn't he have called?"

"I guess so. But please think about what Mr. Wolfe said."

"I may be on the train tomorrow night, but I'm going to school tomorrow morning. I want Merle Fulton to know I'm there. I want her to know she hasn't scared me off."

Rena nodded. "I'll see you at breakfast."

Chapter Twenty-One

She didn't see Drew the rest of the week. John Clifton checked on her daily—sometimes twice—but he didn't mention a substitute. By Wednesday of the following week, Ruthann only wanted the year to end.

That particular day, she couldn't shake the feeling of dread which hung around her like a dark cloud. For reasons she couldn't pinpoint, the children seemed restless. Perhaps it was only anticipation of the fast-approaching summer vacation, she reasoned as she glanced at the clock. Two-thirty. "You may put away your geography books," she announced, closing her own. "Karen, you and Ronnie pass out some manila paper, and we'll spend the rest of the afternoon drawing."

"What will we draw?" Marianne asked.

"Anything you like. Perhaps something you're looking forward to doing this summer."

As the children bent over their desks, busy with crayons and art pencils, Ruthann struggled to contain her tears. *I'm going to miss all of them next year. They'll be moving on, but I was looking forward to a new group.* She picked up her red pencil and tried to focus on the stack of spelling papers. Behind her on the wall, she could hear the clock ticking the seconds while the children worked in silence.

"Miss Cooper."

She glanced up at Ronnie's freckled face. "Miss Cooper, I smell something burning."

Ruthann sniffed the air and smelled it, too. Then she saw a wisp of smoke curling from the cloakroom. She rose from her desk unhurriedly so as not to alarm the children and skirted the desks until she reached the back. Inside, the glow of two small flickering flames made her heart speed up. She reached for the fire extinguisher—but her hand met air. The brackets on the wall were empty. The flames gathered sudden momentum and shot upward.

Backing out of the narrow room, she hoped her voice reflected calm. "Boys and girls, I'd like for you to leave your desks in an orderly way and line up at the door. Stephen, open the door and lead everyone into the hall."

The children, accustomed to obeying, did as Ruthann said, but fear swept over her as she watched Stephen rattle the doorknob. "It's locked, Miss Cooper."

Ruthann was beside him in a second and twisted the knob. It didn't turn. Now several children saw the smoke billowing from the cloakroom. "We're on fire! We're going to burn up!"

Ruthann felt dizzy, but she willed herself to cross the room to the bank of long windows above the radiators. "Of course we're not." She pulled a chair under one of the windows. Then she unlatched the screen, but it didn't budge. "I need the pointer," she said.

When it was in her hand, she began to stab at the screen. Behind her, she heard someone cough. Others began to cry. The children pressed against her as she continued to try to break through the screen. Finally she managed to make a small hole. "Someone get the scissors from my desk!"

She began to cut through the hole, but it was slow going. She heard more coughing and wailing, and the children pressed closer to her. She snatched up a smaller chair and attacked the screen, this time with more success. A hole large enough for a child's body opened up.

"Listen to me! All of you be quiet and listen!"

The wailing stopped, but the smoke rolling from the cloakroom was beginning to take its toll.

"You're going to climb up on this chair one at a time, then onto the windowsill, and then wiggle through the hole. It's not far to the ground. Ronnie, you go first and run around the building to the office and tell them to sound the fire alarm. Karen, you're next. You stand there and make sure everyone gets up and runs to the basketball court."

She grabbed Ronnie, already scrambling onto the chair, and pushed him through the screen. He rolled, then jumped up and took off like he'd been shot. Karen went next, but the smoke was thicker now, almost suffocating despite the open window. It had a thick, oily feel, not the clean smell of wood smoke at a bonfire.

One by one she wrestled the children up to the window. *I've got to count. How many is that so far? Six, I think. Seven. Eight...*

She heard Karen yelling from below. "Run! Run!"

Ruthann fished her handkerchief from her pocket and put it over her nose with one hand while she continued to help the children with the other. *Eleven.*

*Twelve. Thirteen. Sharon's absent today. Only ten more.*

"Don't push!" she managed, then coughed. "You're all going to get out! Don't push!" *Sixteen. Seventeen. Eighteen.* Flames licked the door of the cloakroom and then found fresh fuel in the stack of paper bags she'd brought so the children could take home their supplies on the last day of school.

At the same time, she heard the fire alarm sound and knew Ronnie had completed his mission. *Twenty. Twenty-one.* She recognized the sound of Georgia's asthmatic wheezing and berated herself for not sending her out first. *Twenty-two. One more.* "Stephen? Where are you?"

Through the haze she saw him still standing at the door rattling the knob. "Stephen! Come here now!" A spasm of coughing overtook her. "Stephen, now!"

He turned to look at her with terror-filled eyes. Then she remembered hearing how his father had kept his plane in the air over Belgium, allowing his crew to escape before going down in flames. She sprinted across the room and grabbed him, but he slumped to the floor. She dragged his dead weight toward the window. With the last of her strength, she hefted him onto the windowsill and shoved. Just as she started to climb up and follow him, the back of the room exploded in flames. Their angry glow was the last thing she saw.

When she opened her eyes, a sea of faces surrounded her. "Boy, she whacked that screen!" Ronnie Peters informed the onlookers. "She whacked it good!" Someone moved him away then.

Mr. Cabrera knelt beside her. "You're all right, *niñita.*" A fresh wave of terror swept over her at the sight of his blackened face and hands.

She turned her head and saw Rena on her other side. "He got you out through the window," she murmured. "He didn't dare open the door and let the fire escape into the hall."

"The children," Ruthann rasped. Her chest felt heavy.

"All out," John Clifton said. "The fire's out, too."

Ruthann tried to sit up, searching for Drew's face in the milling crowd. Instead she saw Merle Fulton's gaping mouth. Her face reflected the horror of the moment. *You didn't do this. I know you didn't. Even you aren't a monster who would try to incinerate children. But someone did. Someone tried to burn us all alive.*

"Let me through, let me through." Dr. Leeson stood beside her, clutching his bag. "Get her into the teachers' lounge," he ordered. As four high school boys stepped forward and lifted her, she drifted into unconsciousness again.

When she woke the second time, Dr. Leeson glanced over his shoulder at her. "You got too much smoke," he said, "and whatever stuff was used to start that fire. But you're okay."

Then she saw him working on Luís Cabrera. "What…"

"Burns," Dr. Leeson said. "Minor, thank God."

"I'm so sorry," she whispered.

"No need, *niñita*," the custodian said. "And we're both all right, *gracias a Dios*."

"*Gracias a Dios*," Rena echoed from the foot of the sofa and crossed herself in slow motion.

\*\*\*\*

Ruthann soaked herself in a tub of hot water and shampooed her hair twice, but the faint odor of the oily smoke remained as she crawled wearily into bed. Rena insisted on bringing up her supper, and Gwen followed on her heels. "Daddy's still at the school," she said. "So is Mr. Cabrera."

"He's hurt."

"Dr. Leeson says the burns aren't serious. I called Tomás. He's coming as soon as he finishes exams next week."

"It's my fault."

"No, it's not!" Rena hit the wall with her hand. "We know who's to blame!"

"Rena, she didn't do it," Ruthann said. "I saw her face this afternoon. It was like she couldn't believe what happened. Even Merle couldn't try to burn up a classroom full of children."

Rena slumped to the floor beside the bed. "Then who?"

Gwen rested a comforting hand on Rena's tousled hair. "I hung around long enough to pick up a few things," she said. "The fire started in a pile of oily rags Mr. Cabrera had set outside the basement door in a metal tub for cleaning. That's the first thing he looked for, but they were gone."

"But how did they get into the cloakroom? And who locked my door? How could it have happened without me knowing it?" Ruthann's trembling hand dropped the roll she was trying to butter.

"That's as much as I heard. Daddy saw me and told me to leave. But I do know your door wasn't actually locked. It was jammed with a shim—like the ones used on the bookcase. I heard Mr. Clifton tell Daddy."

Rena stood up. "You've got to go home tomorrow," she told Ruthann. "I'll pack for you tonight."

"Mr. Clifton's notifying all the grammar school parents that classes are cancelled for the rest of the year. It's only two weeks anyway. The high school will finish exams, but they're in a separate wing."

"How is…"

"Daddy's shaken, but he's doing what has to be done."

"He's like that."

Gwen picked up her purse. "I've got to go home. I keep trying to talk to him and tell him about Tomás and me, but he stays late at school. Midnight sometimes. The one time I mentioned you, he told me to mind my own business and leave him alone. He's never talked to me that way before. It's like living with a stranger. He's as miserable as you look, Ruthann. I'm worried about both of you."

Ruthann patted her back. "I'm all right, but he needs you to take care of him."

"He's not sleeping. I hear him up prowling the house in the wee hours, even though his leg pains him more when he's on it. And he hardly eats anything."

"Maybe he'll do better if I'm gone," Ruthann said.

Gwen paused at the door. "Don't go, Ruthann. Daddy needs you. And so do I."

****

Rena and Ruthann walked to the school the next morning, but the doors of the grammar school wing were locked tight. The smell of smoke still hung in the air. They skirted the building and stood looking at the window of the third grade classroom where the ragged screen bore silent witness to Ruthann's frantic assault.

"I'd like to have my leather case," Ruthann said. "My father gave it to me when I graduated from college."

"I heard the room didn't burn completely. Maybe Mr. Cabrera can get it for you."

"Get what?" Luís Cabrera rounded the corner of the building. "You shouldn't be here, *niñitas*."

"How are your hands?" Ruthann said. "I'm so sorry…"

He held them out, encased in work gloves, and flexed the fingers. "They work. You don't have any reason to be sorry."

"If it wasn't for me…" Ruthann stopped and lifted her chin. "Thank you for getting me out, Mr. Cabrera. You saved my life."

He shrugged. "I heard the children crying and saying you were still inside. A couple of the high school boys had come around to see what was going on, so they boosted me up to look in the window, and there you were." He shrugged again. "I got in, picked you up, put you through the screen, and the boys caught you."

"Thank you."

He nodded. "When are you going home?"

"I told her she should go today," Rena said.

"Tomorrow, I guess," Ruthann interrupted. "I wondered if maybe I could get my leather case out of the classroom."

"I'll go in and look for it." He took a ring of keys from his belt. "We'll go through the girls' entrance."

He wouldn't let Ruthann into the classroom, but from the door she could see more than she wanted. The flames had licked their way almost through the middle of the room before the fire department arrived. A few charred desks held together. Only the metal frames remained of others.

She shuddered. "Oh, Rena, my children could've died in there," she whispered.

"They didn't because of you."

"I just reacted."

"You did everything right."

Mr. Cabrera emerged with the leather case. "It's good leather. Take it to a saddle shop when you get home. They'll know how to restore it."

"Thank you, Mr. Cabrera. Thank you for everything. I'm so sorry for all the trouble I've caused." Ruthann's tears spilled over in spite of her efforts to the contrary.

He patted her back. "Just go home and be safe. You didn't make all this happen. The evil was already here. It's been here for a long time." He shook his head as if he knew he'd said too much and walked quickly away.

"What did he mean by that?" Rena asked. "The evil is already here?"

"I'm not sure, but I can't help wondering if…"

"If what?"

"Never mind. Let's go home so I can start packing."

An hour after supper, Aggie appeared at Ruthann's door. "Mr. Mallory is downstairs."

Ruthann straightened from bending over her trunk. "Drew's here?"

Aggie crossed the room and touched her arm. "I've never seen him look like he does tonight, Ruthann. Don't get your hopes up."

Drew leaned against the empty fireplace as Ruthann entered the living room. "You and twenty-three children might have died yesterday."

Ruthann's stomach felt leaden. "I know that."

He held up two thin pieces of wood. "Do you know what these are?"

"No."

"They're shims. They're what were under your bookcase that caused it to tip, and these particular ones jammed your classroom door so it couldn't be opened from the inside."

She wanted to flee from the haggard, gray-faced stranger in front of her, but she couldn't move.

"Aggie told me you were upstairs packing. You should've gone last week instead of coming to school like nothing was wrong."

"I didn't…" Her voice died away.

"I told you to go, and you didn't listen." His eyes—colder than they'd been the day he tore up her contract—repelled her now, where before they'd drawn her into his heart.

"I'm sorry. I didn't think…"

"It doesn't matter what you thought," he interrupted her. "All that matters is that you and your pupils almost died."

She stepped aside as he started laboriously for the door, his leg dragging.

"I didn't ask you to love me, either," she managed to whisper as he came even with her.

He stopped, but this time he didn't look at her. "It was a fling, that's all. A fling, like Gwen said. Go home, Miss Cooper. I want you out of Camden permanently."

When the outside door opened and closed, Ruthann raced to the window and watched him struggle down the walk toward his car. At one point, she thought he was going to fall, but he managed to stay upright.

*Was I really just a fling? All those talks we shared, all those sweet, sweet kisses...were they all lies? Am I really such a fool, believing anyone could love me the way I thought you did? Oh, Drew, why did you let me love you?*

\*\*\*\*

Ruthann wrapped her arms around herself and rocked back and forth on the edge of the bed. Drew's cold words had replayed themselves in her mind until it felt numb and incapable of thought. Her packed trunk stood under the window, locked and ready to be freighted to San Antonio. Only the clothes she would wear tomorrow hung in the half-open closet. The dresser scarf she'd bought at Fall Fest remained on the barren vanity. She'd left it there on purpose because it reminded her of Drew and how his eyes had twinkled as he'd mentioned Sara Teasdale's poem.

She stretched out on the bed and closed her eyes. Well, it would be all over soon. She'd be sleeping in her own bed tomorrow night. Camden and her third-graders and Drew Mallory would be a memory.

## Chapter Twenty-Two

She didn't remember drifting off, but when she woke in the morning, she knew she couldn't leave. *Not like this, banished like a naughty child. Not with things unresolved. Someone thinks they've finally driven me out, but I'm not going. And I can't leave Drew, even if he says he doesn't want me. I told him he was worth fighting for, and he still is. I know he didn't stop loving me just like that.*

She found Aggie in the kitchen. "Oh, you're up. How do you feel?"

"All right, I guess."

"Sit down. I'll fix you some breakfast. Rena's gone to school to close up her classroom for the year."

"I'm sorry about everything, Aggie."

"It's not your fault."

"In a way it is, and when you hear the favor I'm going to ask, you may toss me out the window."

"You want to stay, don't you?"

"How did you know?"

"Ruthann, you're in love with Drew Mallory, and despite everything he's said, he's in love with you. If you're willing to stay and fight for what the two of you deserve, I'll back you up."

Tears welled in Ruthann's eyes. "Thank you, Aggie. And I'll help out around here. I need to stay busy."

"Offer accepted. What's your plan of attack?"

"I want all this finished, and I don't think just getting on the train will end it."

Aggie put a plate of eggs, bacon, and toast in front of her and sat down. "No, it won't."

"Drew's already fired me, but he can't run me out of town."

"He wouldn't do that anyway."

Ruthann picked up her fork. "I'm not so sure."

Aggie sipped her coffee in silence while Ruthann started on the scrambled eggs and toast. "Ruthann, I think all of this started years ago. No one knows the whole story, but I'm going to tell you what I do know."

Ruthann looked up. "Years ago? How?"

"I didn't grow up in Camden, but Harry did, and he told me about the night Elizabeth Greene died."

"The doctor's daughter."

"Yes. If things had been different, Lillian would've married Simon Greene and lived happily ever after. Harry said Elizabeth was a good student but wild outside of school. She and George Baucom were closer than they should've been—if you get my drift. He'd graduated that year, but Elizabeth was only sixteen. She and Mona Fulton were best friends, and they were two of a kind.

"Anyway, that night Elizabeth climbed out her bedroom window when Lillian thought she was asleep and joined the group at the lake: Merle, Mona, George, Horace Leeson, Paul Edmondson—and Harry. It was innocent enough at first. They built a bonfire and passed around the bottle Merle had brought. At some point, Elizabeth left—everyone assumed for a call of nature—but then George left, too."

"I had no idea all those people knew each other before."

"Oh, yes. Harry's folks had moved to Camden a few years earlier, but the others started school together in the same building where you taught."

Ruthann pushed the remaining eggs around with her fork as her appetite dwindled. "And they were all connected with Elizabeth's death."

"All except Harry. He knew he shouldn't be there and decided to go home just about the time George left the group."

"So he didn't know what happened to her?"

"No. The next morning, Luís Cabrera went to the lake to fish and found her body floating near the shore. She also had a wound on the side of her head, not a fatal one, but she was probably unconscious when she went into the water, so she drowned."

"I probably shouldn't ask, but had she been…"

"Well, she wasn't…intact…but it probably hadn't happened that night. Brady Collins was the sheriff then. No police department as such. He knew everything that went on in Camden, so he hauled in the group he knew she ran around with, and they all told the same story—she'd left the bonfire and hadn't come back."

"What about Harry?"

"He went in, too, but his father told Brady that Harry was home just after midnight. He'd been waiting up for him. Then Harry told Brady that George Baucom had also left the bonfire, but he and everyone else denied it. Later, George's father—who was president of the only bank Camden had then—told Harry's father he'd call in the loan on his barbershop if Harry stuck to his story."

"Did he?"

"He sure did, and Mr. Baucom backed down, but that was the end of it. Five people said the same thing, and Harry was the only one who didn't. George went away to the university in Austin, and Harry graduated the next year and went to Baylor. When they both came home, neither of them ever mentioned it again. Harry and George both ended up working at the bank."

"So there's no bad feelings between them?"

"Harry says George might've slept with Elizabeth, but he didn't kill her. But Harry wasn't going to lie about what happened that night, either."

"So her death just went down as a drowning?"

"Eventually. However, some people in town wanted to blame Luís. Fortunately he'd been driving the wagon for Father Callaway that night. He was new and didn't know the county, so when he had to go to a sick or dying parishioner, especially in the middle of the night, Luís drove for him."

"I can't believe anyone tried to blame him."

"He's Mexican, Ruthann. You know what that means in south Texas."

Gwen and Tomás filled Ruthann's mind. "The evil was already here," she murmured.

"What?"

"Mr. Cabrera said that yesterday when Rena and I walked up to the school to see if I could get the leather case my father gave me. He said, 'The evil was already here. It's been here for a long time.' But I didn't understand. I still don't, not really."

"There's more to the story. Franklin Fulton sent Mona away to school in San Antonio, and Merle, who'd already graduated, made her society debut. Then

Nathan and Norman Wolfe came here. You know they were half-brothers. Nathan was younger, but they were very close. Anyway, Norman opened a hardware store, and Nathan started teaching. And the next thing anyone knew, Norman and Merle were married. After two or three years, her father died, and she filed for divorce from Norman—and you know the rest of that story."

"What happened to Mona?"

"The story is that Elizabeth's death unhinged her. It's a carefully guarded secret she spent some time in a sanitarium, but after her father died, Merle brought her home. She was seen around town from time to time, but she wasn't really right. And then she disappeared again for a while."

"But she came back, didn't she?"

Aggie shrugged. "I think she's around."

"So you think she's behind all the things that have happened to me?"

"I don't know. But Merle didn't try to roast you and twenty-three children alive. Even she couldn't do that."

"She didn't. I saw her the day of the fire. The look on her face… Well, it convinced me she had nothing to do with it. But why would Mona go after me?"

"Maybe so Merle would get the blame?"

"What good would that do?"

Aggie rose from the table. "Harry thinks it's all connected somehow, and he's not far wrong very often."

"If he's right, she'll keep on even if I leave. There's something she wants to do. I was just the trigger—or the opportunity."

"Maybe."

238

"Drew had heard about Elizabeth Greene, because when I told him what Lillian said, he filled in a few missing details—but nothing that you told me."

"He knows it all now. Harry went to see him the night after the fire."

"And Drew came to see me the next morning and told me I was just a fling and to leave Camden."

"He's terrified for you, Ruthann. It might be better for you if you did leave, but I'll support your decision to stay."

"Oh, Aggie, I don't know what to do now. I really don't!"

"Like I said, if you want to stay and fight for Drew Mallory…"

"I love him so much…"

"I know you do, and he needs you."

Ruthann carried her plate and silverware to the sink and washed them. "My trunk is packed."

Aggie nodded. "Do you want me to call the freight company?"

Ruthann leaned against the counter. "No."

"All right. Come down around four and peel some potatoes for me."

"I will. Meanwhile, I'll see if I can peel away some of the layers of this tangled mess I've gotten myself into." She paused in the door. "While I unpack."

**** 

When Rena came in after school, she found Ruthann in the kitchen. "You're not going home, are you?"

"Not today. Grab a knife."

Rena did. "Everyone's closed ranks again at the school. Nobody's talking, even to each other." She slashed a large potato with more force than necessary. "The fire chief has been there with someone from Kerrville. An arson specialist."

"We know it was arson."

"The fire started in a pile of oily rags someone swiped from outside the basement door."

"Gwen said that. But how did they get into the cloakroom, and how did someone start the fire and get out again?"

"I heard Mr. Cabrera thinks he knows. He talked to the fire chief and the other man, but nobody's saying anything."

"Did you…"

"See Mr. Mallory? He stayed holed up in his office all day, I guess. He hasn't been around."

Aggie came through the door. "Ruthann, leave what you're doing. You're wanted in the parlor."

The knife spun from Ruthann's fingers into the sink.

"It's not Drew. I'm sorry."

John Clifton and Luís Cabrera stood as she walked into the parlor. "How are you, Miss Cooper?" the principal asked.

"I'm all right."

"We have some information for you." He gestured toward a chair. "Sit down."

She folded her hands tightly in her lap to still their shaking.

"Luís asked me about the original blueprints for the building. It took some doing, but we located them in the basement of the courthouse, and now we know how someone was getting in and out of your room."

She hadn't noticed the thick roll of paper beside

Luís Cabrera until he tapped it with his fingers. "It's all here. The original school built in 1881 was only the wing where the grammar school is. The basement was just one large room, and that was walled off before I came. I only use the rooms under the newer wing built around 1900. I should have thought of it sooner."

John shook his head. "None of us thought about it, but we found the entrance just about where the first-grade room is. It's behind some shrubs and was probably buried for a while, but once we got through the bushes, we could see it. When we went down, it was easy to spot the trap doors opening into each of the cloakrooms."

"Trap doors?"

"About three-foot square, right at the back. They fit so tightly into the subflooring that no one ever noticed them."

"But someone knew."

"Someone knew." Luís's face hardened. "And I should have known, too."

"You thought of the blueprints," John said.

"What were they used for? The trap doors, I mean."

"Only the builders knew," Luís said.

"So it was easy enough to stuff those rags up through the trap door, light a match, and leave." Ruthann closed her eyes against the image of the flames licking closer to the children pressing around her at the window.

"One good thing has come from all of this," John Clifton said. "We're going to change all the window screens in that wing to make them easier to open."

"And I've asked to have the basement door paved

over," Luís added.

"What about my…about the third grade room?"

"It will need a new floor, but that's easy enough. And some paint. It's not a total loss. Thank God the fire didn't spread."

"My children could've died," Ruthann whispered. "Drew says it would've been my fault."

"He didn't mean it, Miss Cooper. I think it would've happened whether you'd been there or not," John said, "and I'm not going to say more right now. When are you going home?"

Ruthann lifted her chin. "I'm not. Not until it's over."

Luís leaned forward. "It's over for you, *niñita*. You didn't start this."

"Miss Cooper, I know you don't want to leave with things like this between you and Drew Mallory, but…"

"I can't leave him," Ruthann whispered. "I can't. He told me once we all fight a personal war over something—but if it's worth fighting for, we don't quit."

****

No one reacted to seeing Ruthann at the dinner table. No one mentioned her leaving, and no one brought up the fire. As Rena had said, they'd closed ranks against the evil of which Luís Cabrera had spoken.

"Trap doors," Rena said as she and Ruthann washed the dishes. "I never heard of such a thing except in attics."

"I guess whoever designed the original building had a reason for putting them there," Ruthann said.

"They didn't count on the Fulton girls…"

"You said you didn't think Merle started the fire."

"She didn't."

"But Mona did."

Ruthann shrugged. "Aggie says she's still around."

Rena hung up her dishcloth. "Lock your door tonight, Ruthann."

"I plan to."

Chapter Twenty-Three

Ruthann spent the next morning helping Aggie in the kitchen. Just before noon, Gwen called. "Meet me at the employee entrance of the store. I have to talk to you."

"Give me ten minutes," Ruthann said.

Gwen hustled her up the back stairs into the room where she processed new shipments of clothes. "I heard what Harry Pollard told Daddy."

"Do you know about the trap doors?"

"Daddy told me last night."

"What did you want to tell me?"

Gwen pushed aside a mound of tissue paper and flopped down in a chair. "Just this. Daddy's quitting."

"He can't do that!"

"He wrote his letter of resignation last night. The board doesn't meet until after graduation next week, but he took it by the bank to George Baucom this morning."

"Oh, Gwen, he loves his work here. What is he going to do?"

"I don't know. But since things were in such a mess anyway, I told him about Tomás and me. He said he'd already figured it out."

"How?"

"I don't know. But at that point I gave him the letters, and he took them to his room and closed the door. He left before I got up this morning."

Ruthann put her head down on the table in front of her. "It just gets worse and worse."

"The point is, between what Harry Pollard told him and what Mr. Cabrera found out, he knows it hasn't been all about you. About the two of you."

"He told me I was a fling."

Gwen winced. "I could have bitten my tongue as soon as I said that back in the fall."

"So what now?"

"I wish I knew, but at least you're staying in Camden."

"I can only stay so long. Does Drew know?"

"Probably."

Ruthann picked up her purse. "Thanks for all the information. I'll go back to the boarding house and think about it."

"I'll call you tomorrow or come by." Gwen held out her arms. "I'm so glad you're still here," she murmured as she hugged Ruthann. "For Daddy and for me, too."

****

Aggie met Ruthann in the hall. "John Clifton came by while you were out," she said, handing Ruthann an envelope. "He said he'd written you a glowing reference."

"He's been very good to me in spite of all the trouble I've caused."

"That's the good news."

"What now?"

"Your father called. He heard about the fire—don't ask me how. And he's not happy you're not already home."

"I suppose I should call him."

"Oh, he insists you do. And so do I. The way he sounded over the phone makes me think I don't want him turning up on my doorstep."

Ruthann nodded. "I'll reverse the charges." She sat down on the stool beside the phone. "Aggie…"

"You'd better call, Ruthann. He's your father, and he's worried."

\*\*\*\*

"When did you plan to tell your mother and me about the fire, Emily Ruthann?"

*When he calls me by my full name, I'm in trouble.* She took a deep breath. "Did Drew call you?"

"He wants you out of town today, and so do I."

"No."

"No? What do you mean, no?"

"I mean I can't come home now. He tore up my contract and told me to leave Camden, but he needs me more than ever right now"

"He needs to know you're out of harm's way."

"I love him. He's worth fighting for, and I'm going to do it."

"You've tried, Ruthann, but…"

"I'm staying, Dad. I know you and Mother are worried. I love you both very much, but somewhere, somehow, I've got to finish the war."

"Your war's over, Ruthie."

"No. You were right at Christmas. My war began when I came to Camden and met Drew and fell in love with him…and found out I was a woman who could stand on her own two feet. I'm not coming home. Not now. Not until I finally have to hoist the white flag in surrender, and that's not a consideration at this point."

Her father's silence unsettled her.

"Daddy? Are you still there?"

"Yes. All right, Ruthie, you've won this skirmish, but I haven't surrendered either."

"I know."

"Be careful."

"I will. I promise."

\*\*\*\*

The sound of someone beating on the front door, followed by Harry bellowing, "Do you know what time it is?" and hurried footsteps on the stairs made Ruthann sit straight up in bed with the sheet clutched around her. Then the pounding began on her own door. "Ruthann, let me in! Let me in!"

A near-hysterical Gwen all but fell through the door when Ruthann unlocked it. In her hand she clutched some crumpled papers. Her words tumbled over each other in an garbled cacophony as she collapsed at the foot of the bed.

"Gwen, what? Is it Drew? Tomás?"

Gwen's slight body heaved with sobs. Ruthann pried the papers out of her hands. "These are the letters you gave your father."

"Look at them! Look at them!"

"What am I supposed to see?"

Rena poked her head in. "Can I do anything?"

"I'm trying to find out what's going on."

"I'll be in my room if you need me." The door closed with a soft click.

"Gwen, try to stop crying. I can't make heads or tails of what you're saying."

"I can't…I'm not…"

Ruthann froze. *She knows. Somehow she's found*

*out she's not Drew's biological child.* She sat down and put her arms around Gwen. "This is about your father and you, isn't it?"

Gwen's head snapped back. "You knew?"

"He shouldn't have told me and kept you in the dark. I'm so sorry, Gwen."

Gwen scrubbed her wet face with the end of the sheet and struggled for control.

"How did you find out?"

"Aunt Julia. But she's not my aunt, either."

"*She* told you? Why now?"

"Daddy told her about Tomás and me, and she just went crazy. It was almost like when she found out about Uncle Len and Merle Fulton."

"So she hit back."

"Not really at me. Not exactly. Look at the letters." Gwen reached for them and spread them out on the bed. "Take a good look. What do you notice about all of them?"

Ruthann scanned the sheets. "I don't…do you mean how the 'w' drops a little?"

"That's what I mean. Now look at these." She shuffled the papers and brought out two more from beneath the others.

Ruthann recognized one as the vicious notice posted in the teachers' lounge early in the school year—the infamous accusations of her unsavory activities during the war, as well as the one pinned to the scarecrow hanging in the cloakroom. It only took a moment to see the 'w' remained in line with the other letters.

"How did you get these?"

"Daddy had all of them together."

"So they were written on separate machines."

"Yes. All but the last two came from the typewriter in Daddy's office. Not the one Mrs. Leland uses, but the smaller one he keeps for his personal use. It pops out of a specially made drawer in the desk."

"I don't understand."

"Aunt Julia uses it, too. She takes it to the community center to type up programs for the choir performances."

Ruthann's mouth went dry. "She wrote these?"

Gwen nodded.

"You're saying she wanted to put you between your father and me?"

"I don't know what she was trying to do except maybe point the finger at Merle, because they didn't start until after that first note on the bulletin board in the teachers' lounge. It was natural to assume Merle wrote these, too."

"How can you be sure Julia wrote them?"

"Daddy had them all spread out on the kitchen table when I came in from work. She was there, too, and apparently I walked in about the time he confronted her with what he'd figured out. Talk about bad timing."

"Did she deny it?"

"No, but then she…" Tears began to stream down Gwen's cheeks again. "She told me the truth about myself. Daddy jumped up and went for her, but she ran into her room and locked the door. I think he'd have killed her if…"

"Oh, Gwen."

"I understand why Daddy didn't tell me. I'm not mad at him. He was doing what he thought was best for me. That's what fathers do."

"A lot of men would've walked out."

"But he didn't. I wanted to tell him it was all right, but he left too. I don't know where he went. I've been driving around for hours looking for him. I couldn't go home, not with her there, so I came here."

"You did the right thing."

"Ruthann, we've got to find Daddy. He's been walking around like a dead man since the thing with the scarecrow. Or dragging around. His leg's even worse all of a sudden, and…" She broke down again.

"Did you look for his car at the school?"

"That's the first place I looked, but that was about six-thirty. And I even drove out to Sorrells Woods, where he likes to go to paint. His car wasn't there either." Gwen looked at her watch. "It's after eleven now."

"I'll get dressed and come with you if you want to keep looking."

"Maybe he's gone home. We'll check there first, and if he's still gone, well, we'll keep looking."

"I'm sure he's all right, Gwen." *But I'm not. Julia Schaeffer betrayed him in a way far worse than Gwen's mother. And worst of all, his life's work here in Camden is crumbling in front of his eyes.*

Chapter Twenty-Four

Drew's car wasn't in the driveway or the garage, and neither was Julia's. "I can't imagine where she'd go at this hour," Gwen said.

"Why do you think she wrote those notes to you?"

"No idea. She hates Merle Fulton. Maybe she thought she'd get the blame, considering everything that's happened to you."

"Merle didn't start the fire, and I have an odd feeling she didn't write the threatening note pinned to that scarecrow, either."

"Then who did?"

"I intend to find out before I leave Camden."

"Good luck."

Gwen turned down Oak Street toward the school. Her father's car sat just outside the side entrance to the high school wing. "I've got a key," she said. "Daddy gave it to me when I came home to work. He was putting in some pretty long hours during the war, and I used to take him supper sometimes."

"It's awfully dark up there," Ruthann murmured. "Do you want me to go in with you?"

"There's strength in numbers."

They mounted the steps to the single side door, which Gwen unlocked. Inside, the entrance hall lay bathed in shadows thrown by the dim light from a single bulb above the stairwell leading to the main hall.

A light shone from beneath the door of the former mimeograph room Drew had taken over as his office. "He's going to kill both of us," Gwen whispered.

"Me, maybe. I'm supposed to be long gone from Camden."

Gwen took a deep breath and put her hand on the doorknob. "Daddy?"

"What are you doing here?" The defeat in Drew's voice pierced Ruthann's heart.

"I've been looking everywhere for you."

"You shouldn't be out alone this late."

"I'm not. Ruthann's with me."

"She shouldn't be here either."

Ruthann moved even with Gwen. "But I am. I can't leave with things like this."

"They're not going to change." His voice, less defeated and more angry, made her take a step back.

"You really want me to go?"

"For your own good. But I shouldn't have said those things to you the other day. I'm sorry."

"You were angry—and I knew you didn't mean any of it."

"I'm not angry with you, only myself. And scared to death of what I've set in motion."

"Daddy, you didn't make any of this happen. I understand why you never told me the truth about myself. I guess I needed to know eventually, but I'm sorry it happened this way. I'm sorry Aunt Julia hurt you."

"You have every right to feel betrayed, Gwennie, but for what it's worth, I did think I was doing the best thing for you."

"I understand why you did it. You're my father,

and I'll always love you. Ruthann loves you, too."

Ruthann focused on his blue eyes reflecting both physical and emotional pain. "Everything you said, all the dreams that included me… They can't be over just like that."

He fell back into his chair, and his cane clattered to the floor. Ruthann crossed the small office and stooped to pick it up, then hung it on the corner of his desk. She heard the door close and knew Gwen had left them alone. Kneeling beside Drew's chair, she put her head against his leg. In a moment, she felt his hand on her hair and closed her eyes to savor the hopeful moment.

"Don't you understand this is for the best, precious girl? *Your* best."

"Whatever we do has to be for *our* best. Mr. Cabrera said there was an evil here, but we can fight it."

"No. No, we can't. And if this leg is going to kill me, better sooner than later." He withdrew his hand from her head. "You're making it very hard for me. I love you enough to send you away. Love me enough to go."

"Drew, please don't do this."

"It's all I have left to do. Get Gwen to take you back to the boarding house, Ruthann. Please go now."

She stood up. "I'm not leaving Camden."

"I can't throw you on the train." He began to shuffle through a stack of papers in front of him.

"Gwen said you'd written a letter of resignation."

"I can't do my job anymore."

"You could if…"

"Ruthann." He spoke her name as if pronouncing judgment. "There are a lot of *ifs*. If you hadn't come to Camden to begin with. If I hadn't gone against my better judgment and started a relationship with you. If I'd refused to let you come back after Christmas." He swiped a thin hand across his eyes. "If I hadn't been such a fool as to believe life could be different after so many years alone."

"But it can be, don't you see?"

"No. It's over, Ruthann. If you won't go home, at least get out of my office."

Tears blurred her path to the door. In the corridor, she leaned against the wall and fought the impulse to turn and beat on it with both fists. Then she looked around for Gwen. "Gwen?"

Only silence answered her.

"Gwen, where are you?" She started for the short flight of stairs leading to the entrance and noticed the bulb which lighted it had gone out. *The evil is already here.* "Gwen, answer me!"

The faint sound of footsteps on the staircase leading to the second floor made her back up. She recognized the painful poke in her back as the barrel of a gun and stumbled with terror. "Not a word. Up the stairs." She didn't recognize the voice, but she knew to whom it belonged.

"Mona?" she whispered. "Where's Gwen?"

"Shut up."

As she put her foot on the first step, Ruthann considered throwing herself back against the woman but rejected the idea. She kept climbing. No one waited on the landing, but she could hear voices coming from somewhere. Mona nudged her again, this time toward a narrower flight of stairs leading to the bell tower. "Up."

"Who's up there? Is Gwen there?"

An unpleasant, guttural laugh assaulted her ears.

"Not for long. Hurry up." At the top of the short climb, her arm snaked around Ruthann and turned the key sticking out of the lock.

In the cramped, dimly lit space outside the door leading to the actual bell and clock works, Merle Fulton and Gwen huddled together in a corner. George Baucom stood inches away. Ruthann reached for Gwen's outstretched hand and clasped it tightly. Then she turned to face a slightly younger version of Merle Fulton.

Mona wore the same black cocktail dress her sister had sported at the Christmas party. A sleek blonde bob framed her expertly made-up face. She might have stepped from the pages of a fashion magazine except for her glittering eyes, which spoke of madness, not *haute couture*.

Ruthann glanced at Merle. Her haughty expression had been replaced with one of stark terror. "Mona, please let the others go," she murmured.

"I'd be glad to, but they were just at the wrong place at the wrong time, weren't they? I've waited a lifetime for this."

George Baucom seemed to shrink farther back against the wall, but he didn't speak.

"It wouldn't have come to this if you'd all told the truth," Mona went on. "But you didn't, and when I threatened to go to Brady Collins, Father had me locked up."

"I brought you home after he died," Merle said in a softer voice than Ruthann had ever heard from her.

"You sent me back, too. You divorced Norman Wolfe to get the money to do it, since Father hadn't left anything but bad debts."

"I couldn't think of anything else to do. You needed help."

"You helped Norman to an early grave, and he didn't deserve it. It's time for the truth to come out."

"I didn't mean for him to…" Merle's voice, choked with unshed tears, trailed off.

"I dream about Elizabeth every night, you know. All these years she's been begging for justice, and tonight she's going to get it."

"Mona, I didn't…" George began.

"Of course you did. She told me how you'd promised to meet her that night so the two of you could run away and be together. But you changed your mind and killed her."

"I didn't! I told her I thought we should wait, and she got hysterical. When I tried to leave, she wouldn't let go of me, and I pushed her away. I guess…I guess she fell and hit her head and went into the lake, but I didn't know it. I swear I didn't know she was going to drown!"

"But she did, and you were responsible, and I was the one who got punished by being put into that hell-hole, Hampton Hills. Do you know what it was like to be locked up for twenty out of twenty-four hours? To have nothing to do but sit on my cot and stare at the walls? To wear the same gray dress day after day? I wasn't crazy when Father put me there, but it didn't take long to get that way."

"Let Gwen and Ruthann go," Merle said again. "They haven't done anything to you."

"But they would if I let them go. I'm not going back to Hampton Hills."

"I told you when I brought you home just before

the war that I wouldn't send you back if you'd…"

"Stay out of sight. And I did—for a while. Then I saw my chance."

"I didn't try to hurt you, Ruthann," Merle said, her voice thick with anguish. "I didn't do any of it, not even the notice in the teachers' lounge. Mona got the idea when I told her about you and Drew."

Mona's red lips parted in a sneer. "You always did talk too much, Merle, except when it came to telling the truth."

Merle straightened. "I knew Norman's death was my fault," she said to no one in particular. "I loved him, and I caused his death. So I went off the deep end trying to make everyone around me as miserable as I was. I did go after your father, Gwen, but he reminded me a little of Norman. A good, quiet, responsible man. I thought…I thought I could change for him, but he didn't want me. When he wanted you, Ruthann, I hated you, and I tried to harass you in your classroom, but I didn't write the note or throw the acid or any of the other things." Her face creased with pain. "I was young and pretty once…like you…I was in love with Norman Wolfe like you love Drew. I'm so sorry…so sorry."

Mona smiled. "I'm not sorry. I knew how to get in and out of the school. George had discovered the basement door and the trap doors to all the cloakrooms, and one night he took Elizabeth and me down there and showed us, too. I had no idea the knowledge would come in so handy someday."

"I'll tell the truth," George said, desperation evident in his words. "I'll resign from the bank and leave Camden."

"It's too late for that." Mona's voice became a purr

of satisfaction. "You're going to tell the truth, all right. You'll have a belated attack of conscience and throw yourself out of the bell tower. The typed note your secretary will find on your desk tomorrow morning will explain everything."

"No!" He tried to lunge past her, but she brought up the gun and fired. He yelped.

"You're not hit," she said. "It's not going to be that easy for you." In slow motion she fixed her attention on Merle. "And you'll go with him, of course. The note on your dresser will explain how the two of you have carried on a long affair, and you couldn't bear to live without him."

"No one will believe that," Merle said.

"You've slept with half the men in Camden, Merle. Of course they'll believe it."

Merle covered her face with her hands.

"It's too late for shame now, and I doubt you really have any regrets." Mona moved toward Gwen and Ruthann. "As for the two of you, you'll go in the lake like Elizabeth. She never grew up. At least the two of you did, even if neither of you will ever grow old." She pointed the gun at George again. "Get over there."

Ruthann watched the man edge toward the opening in the wall, but as Mona got closer to him, he threw his shoulder against her. The gun clattered to the floor. He grabbed her arms and pushed her toward the opening beyond the bell. She stumbled, then plunged through it. Her scream as she fell was drowned out when George grabbed the rope to set the bell in motion.

Ruthann jerked Gwen toward the stairwell door. "Run," she breathed. "Run!"

A dark shapeless shadow passed them on the stairs,

but they didn't stop. Behind them, a gunshot punctuated the bell's strident tones. Then, as they sprinted across the landing toward the stairs leading to the first floor, the shadow passed them again with Merle fleeing in front of it. They watched in horror as the shadow lifted a large object and brought it down on Merle's head. The sounds of shattering bone and her body bouncing on the stairs made Ruthann retch. It was Gwen who steadied her as they slid down the wall to the floor and crouched there.

Sirens split the air as they huddled together afraid to move. Loud footsteps and the shouts of what Ruthann thought must be an army drifted through the corridor below and up the stairs. Only the sound of Drew's frantic voice calling their names gave them strength enough to stand and pick their way down the blood-spattered stairs. But even the warmth of his arms couldn't dispel the shock now freezing their emotions.

****

Ruthann looked straight at Paul Edmonson. "You were there at the lake that night. You know what happened to Elizabeth Greene."

His mouth fell open.

"That's what it was all about," she went on. "Gwen and I were just collateral damage."

He closed his eyes. "Call the state police headquarters," he said to Drew. "I can't ethically do this investigation."

****

The state police swarmed the building, with a captain finally finding his way to the lounge where Gwen and Ruthann still shivered together as Drew held their hands in silence. He wasted no time relaying the story of the old tragedy. Then the captain, an older man who seemed almost fatherly, interviewed Ruthann and Gwen separately before telling them they could go home. John and Kay Clifton led them out the main entrance, but not before they glimpsed Merle's crumpled body at the foot of the stairs. "I can drive," Gwen said.

"Are you sure? Kay will be glad to…"

"Just go back and take care of Daddy," Gwen said. "Tell him I'll be at the boarding house with Ruthann."

"Why did Mona grab you?" Ruthann asked as she slid into the car.

"I saw her when I came out of Daddy's office."

"And when I came out, I called for you."

Gwen shrugged.

"Mr. Cabrera was right. Evil was already here. I didn't bring it, and Drew didn't cause it. Mona wanted revenge."

"I wonder if she really got it."

Ruthann bit her lip. "I wonder if the old saying 'Rest in peace' really applies here. Three souls took a lot with them."

"Like my mother. You know she never told Daddy who my father was. Maybe she didn't know."

"You're who you are, Gwen. Whatever happens, we'll always be sisters."

****

Alerted by Kay Clifton, Rena had set up the rollaway in Ruthann's room, put out a pair of clean pajamas for Gwen, and disappeared. After showering, the young women fell into bed and slept until Aggie roused them just before five in the afternoon. "Drew Mallory is downstairs. No need to dress. I brought a robe for Gwen."

Drew didn't try to stand as they came in, but he held out his arms and embraced them tightly. "Thank God for protecting the two of you," he murmured. "I love you both so very much."

Aggie rolled in a tea cart with hot food. Ruthann and Gwen fell on it ravenously while Drew filled in some details about the night before. "It's obvious how Mona died. George apparently shot himself with her gun after realizing what he'd done. But Merle...both of you said you saw someone on the stairs. The police want to talk to you more about that."

"It was just a figure," Ruthann said. "Man, woman...ghost...I don't know."

"But you know what *it* did."

Gwen reached for a second biscuit. "You do know Merle wasn't behind anything that happened to Ruthann this year?"

"Yes. It was easy to blame her, God rest her tortured soul. I keep thinking I should've been the one to investigate another entrance, but I assumed Merle had a key. And I'd heard about Mona being seen from time to time, but I thought she was harmless. I felt sure she was in the bell tower that night Carter Hodges thought he'd seen a ghost up there."

"What will happen to Chief Edmondson and Dr. Leeson?" Ruthann asked. "You know they kept the secret about Elizabeth Greene all these years, too."

"They've lived with it this long," Drew said. "Both of them are decent men who made a terrible mistake when they were nothing more than boys. Elizabeth Greene's death was technically an accident, so there's nothing to charge them with even if someone wanted to." He turned to Gwen. "I brought you some things, if you want to stay here a while."

"I don't think I can face Aunt Julia…Julia."

"She's gone."

"Gone?" Ruthann and Gwen spoke at the same time.

"When I finally got home this morning, all her things were gone. She'd cleared out."

"Then I'll get dressed and come home with you, Daddy."

He patted her hand. "Good. I'm glad."

As soon as Gwen went upstairs to dress, Drew gathered Ruthann in his arms. "I'm so sorry, precious girl. Forgive me."

"There's nothing to forgive. You were trying to keep me safe."

He took her face in his hands and kissed her. "Can we start again?"

"Only if you make an honest woman of me."

"What?"

"I'm sitting here in my pajamas with you. That could look very bad." She struggled not to laugh at his chagrin.

"I see what you mean."

"So you'll do it?"

"I can't wait, precious girl. I can't wait."

Chapter Twenty-Five

Though school had officially ended, Drew said graduation would go on as planned at the end of the following week. John Clifton called all the teachers together and asked them to attend as a show of support for the students and to demonstrate their solidarity to the community. "Between the town grapevine, the newspaper, and a few leaks from law enforcement insiders, you all know what happened and why. It's been a rough year, but we've gotten through it, and we'll start again in the fall.

"Some of you will be leaving Camden for the summer, and others of you have been asked to stay a little longer as the state police wind up their investigation. Mr. Wolfe is retiring, of course. Miss Cooper's plans aren't finalized, but we hope to have her back in one capacity or another."

Ruthann's face flamed as applause swept the room.

"If your rooms need closing up for the summer, take care of that before graduation, and don't forget to turn in your book count and your keys. Mr. Cabrera asked me to announce to any of you who might have investigated the trap doors in your cloakrooms that they've been permanently sealed from below, as has the outside door to the grammar school basement. He also asked me to remind you that you're not welcome in *his* basement. Put your maintenance requests in writing and leave them in his box."

"He says that every year," Bernie muttered.

"And you know he means it," the principal snapped back. "No exceptions. He caught me looking for a screw for my desk the other day and ran me out."

"With a broom or a hammer?" Kitty asked.

The principal lifted his eyebrows. "I didn't wait to find out."

Ruthann leaned back in her chair as a sense of belonging enveloped her. It was over. The evil had gone. And a lifetime with Drew Mallory no longer seemed only a dream.

\*\*\*\*

On the morning following graduation, Nathan Wolfe didn't come to breakfast. Aggie went to check on him and came down with the information he'd gone, leaving nothing behind but a towel-wrapped bundle on the floor of his closet. The state police captain arrived within an hour. Within a few minutes, he joined the rest of the boarders in the parlor. "A large wrench," he said without preamble. "And I expect the dried blood and hair will turn out to belong to Merle Fulton." He looked around. "Anybody want to tell me anything?"

"What can we tell you?" Bernie asked. "You already know how he felt about Merle Fulton, but I don't think murder was in his syllabus."

Kitty and Lillian nodded in agreement.

He turned to Ruthann. "Could he have been who or what you saw on the stairs?"

"I don't know. I only glimpsed what seemed like a shadow. It just looked very large and frightening to Gwen and me."

"Nothing familiar in the way it moved?"

"I just wanted to get away. Get downstairs."

"Does anyone know where he might have gone?"

"He talked about living on a tropical island," Kitty said. "Whether or not he was serious, I don't know."

"He didn't talk about his plans for retirement?"

"He was always saying he was going to retire," Lillian said. "We didn't know he'd actually done it until the faculty meeting before graduation. When we asked him about his plans at dinner that night, he just smiled."

"Julia Schaeffer disappeared the night of the murder," Aggie said. "She hated Merle because of her affair with her husband."

"We're looking for her, too," the captain said. "I understand the faculty is particularly tight-knit, even clannish. But I have to remind you this is a murder investigation, so if anyone remembers anything, you're obligated to let me know."

"Does this mean the rest of us are free to leave for the summer?" Bernie asked.

The man looked around at them one more time. "Just leave contact information at the school."

"We'll all be back in the fall," Kitty said. "We need our paychecks."

"It would be like Nathan to leave that thing behind," Kitty observed when the police captain left. "Sort of a tacit admission of guilt, and a taunt."

"A taunt?" Rena asked.

"That the police will never find him."

"He always impressed me as a gentle person," Ruthann said. "I haven't known him as long as the rest of you, but I can't see him killing Merle, especially that way. It was...brutal."

"Maybe we never gave enough credibility to his

feelings about his brother," Aggie observed. "Maybe none of us know what someone's capable of doing under the right circumstances."

"For what it's worth, I hope they don't find him," Rena said. "I'm not condoning murder, but he was a good man."

\*\*\*\*

Ruthann repeated the conversation to Drew when they drove to Sorrells Woods later. "Someone killed Merle, probably either Julia or Nathan. Something tells me we'll never know." He pulled the car into the grove of trees but made no move to get out. "I didn't bring my supplies. I can't walk down to the lake anyway."

Ruthann lifted his leg across her lap as she'd done before and began to knead the ruined flesh beneath his khaki pants.

"I made an appointment with the orthopedist for June."

"I'm glad."

"George refused to accept my letter of resignation when I took it by his office the day before he died."

"I'm glad about that, too."

"John says he'll step in as interim superintendent while I'm in the hospital and getting rehab, if the board will finally give him an assistant principal."

"Will they?"

"I expect so."

"Gwen said she'd interviewed for a job in Austin."

"Luís Cabrera isn't happy about the marriage, but he'll feel better once Father Louis marries them in the Catholic church."

"Surely he doesn't dislike Gwen."

"No, but he knows what they're going to face in a

mixed marriage." Drew leaned his head back. "We're going to face our own hurdles, Ruthann."

"They aren't important, not in the long run."

"We've still got a fight on our hands. At least, I do. Surgery. Learning to walk again. I won't lie and say I don't dread it."

"I dread it for you, but I'll be right there with you. So will Gwen."

He caught her hand. "You've become a formidable woman, precious girl. I guess the two of us together will survive, just like Gwen and Tomás."

"Isn't that what life is all about? Surviving?"

"A little more than that, I think."

She moved his leg gently and scooted over into his waiting arms.

\*\*\*\*

Ruthann accompanied Drew to his appointment in June. The doctor didn't mince words. "It should've come off at least a year ago, Mr. Mallory. I suspect you've been navigating on sheer force of will rather than on what doesn't even resemble muscle and bone anymore. I wish I could save the knee for you. It would make things easier. But I'll leave as much of the upper leg as I can."

"I just want him alive," Ruthann blurted.

The doctor nodded. "We'll have to clear up the infection first, and that could take four to six weeks. As soon as it's gone, I'll schedule the surgery."

\*\*\*\*

"John Clifton wants you back next year," Drew said over dinner later. "Aggie's holding your room."

Ruthann drew back. "I'll go back to work, but not this year. Being married to you will be a full-time job for a while."

"We'll get married when everything is over."

She shook her head. "No. If we're not married, they won't let me be with you in the hospital."

"It's not going to be pretty, precious girl. It might be better if you weren't there."

"I want to be with you."

"You're stubborn like Gwen."

"We're very much alike."

He shook his head. "The doctor said six weeks, no more. Is that long enough to plan a wedding, get married, and have any kind of honeymoon?"

"We'll make it long enough. My parents have a cabin at Lake Travis, so we can get away by ourselves. Rest. Swim. Forget everything but each other."

"Are you sure the idea of what's ahead—the surgery—won't spoil things for you?"

"I won't let it."

He added cream to his coffee. "I don't mind losing the leg, but I'd have minded losing you."

"I came to Camden last fall to make a new start. I knew I couldn't do it in San Antonio. But I brought the war with me, in a way. You're the one who made me know I had to move on. You made me want to get out of the sort of limbo I'd lived in for three years."

"You've thought all this through very carefully?"

"It doesn't matter how much I think about it. I'll never be sure what will happen tomorrow or next week or even next year." She leaned closer across the table. "All I'm certain of is loving you now and forever."

\*\*\*\*

While Ruthann planned their wedding, Drew spent the summer turning over his office—temporarily—to

John Clifton, who'd finally gotten his assistant principal. "The board basically told both of us we could do what we wanted to do and have whatever we asked for," Drew wrote. "I offered again to resign, but I'm glad they didn't let me. Just knowing I have something to come back to will go a long way toward a faster recovery. I put down a deposit on one of the new duplexes just past the football stadium. It will do until we're back here permanently and can find what we want. Gwen took her bedroom furniture for the apartment in Austin. But I have mine, and..." The leering face he'd sketched in the margin made Ruthann laugh.

A few nights before the wedding, Drew came to San Antonio. Over dinner, he filled her in on the latest Camden gossip. The police weren't any closer to finding Nathan Wolfe than they'd been in the spring. No one expected him to be found. Julia also seemed to have disappeared off the face of the earth.

"So who did kill Merle Fulton? Nathan Wolfe? Or did Julia do it and plant the wrench in his room?"

"At this point, I don't think anyone really cares."

"So the town will just have to live with all the unanswered questions."

He winked at her. "Just don't forget to answer the minister's question when he says, *Do you take this man.*"

Unexpected tears filled her eyes. "To love and to cherish forever."

"I hope our forever will be a long, long time, precious girl."

\*\*\*\*

One too-warm morning at the end of August,

Ruthann took her father's arm and fixed her eyes on Drew's as she floated down the ivy-bordered path toward the backyard arbor. Drew handed John Clifton his cane and folded her hand into his.

\*\*\*\*

They arrived at the cabin just before dusk. "I loved to come here in the summer," Ruthann said as they unpacked. "I used to sneak off just about this time of day and go swimming."

"Then let's do it. I think my leg could use a cold soak anyway."

"You did a lot of standing and walking today."

She knew she'd never forget the first raw sight of his mangled leg as she emerged from the bathroom in her swimsuit and found him sitting on the bed wearing his trunks. With hardly enough flesh to cover the blood vessels pulsing unevenly on its pitted surface, the almost unrecognizable limb was a collage of colors and textures, from fiery red to near-blackened bruising to smooth, ghostly white scar tissue. He met her eyes with an apology in his own. She knelt on the floor and laid her face against his knee without speaking.

"I know it's bad," he said, "but you had to see it sooner or later."

"How have you lived with it all these years?"

"At this point, I honestly don't know."

"It might have killed you long before this."

"I had to live long enough to love you. That's all that matters now."

\*\*\*\*

In the rippling water, as the moonlight played over their bodies, Ruthann clung to him and considered how he'd just made love to her with the gentleness that characterized his soul as well as with the passion for living which had carried him through too many lonely years. "If this were a fairy tale, we'd simply float away and live happily ever after," Drew murmured as his lips moved over her neck and shoulders.

"We're going to be happy forever." She took his face in her hands and traced the deeply etched lines across his forehead and his jaw. They hadn't been there in September. "You said once I had a calm face. You have a kind one."

His soft laugh drifted out over the water. "Men want to have strong, masculine countenances."

"Your kindness is your strength."

He smiled. "Well."

"A man who's worried about his masculinity—or lack of it—doesn't attract people the way you do. The children see you for who you really are. I noticed how after you'd visited the classroom the children seemed less restless and more thoughtful. You're a role model."

"That's a heavy responsibility."

"Which you've carried for a long time without having anyone to lean on."

"Now I have you."

She rested her head against his shoulder. "I meant what I said about being on equal footing, Drew. I'm your wife, not your daughter, and you'll have to remember the difference about how to look after us." The moon, drifting out from behind the cloud where it had taken a brief refuge, seemed to spotlight them in the water. She lifted her face and studied his again, recoiling inwardly at the constant pain reflected in his eyes. His cheeks, after a long day, were no longer clean-shaven, and a gray-white stubble glistened along his damp jaw line.

"If things hadn't worked out for us, I could never have loved anyone again, not the way I love you."

"I would've wanted you to be happy no matter what."

"And now I am, always and forever."

They left the water and stretched out on one of the quilts Ruthann had brought along. With the other she covered them both. "Now you can have one of your catnaps," she said.

He pulled her close to him. "I have other things in mind." His hands slid over her bare shoulders. "I believe you enjoyed our first journey up the mountain together."

"You know I did. And I like the view from the pinnacle."

"What do you see?"

"You and me. A snug little house with a yard for Peter Andrew to play in."

"Peter Andrew Mallory." Drew spoke the name with soft satisfaction. "What else?"

"I see the two of us traveling the Lake District in England. I'll read poetry aloud while you sketch."

"You see all that, do you?"

"And much, much more. Oh, Drew, always love me…need me…want me."

"Forever." His mouth came down hungrily on hers. "Precious girl," he whispered. "Precious girl."

**\*\*\*\***

On their last night, they swam again and then stretched out together on a quilt in a grove of chinquapin oaks. The moonlight flickered through the leaves, dappling their wet bodies with bright and dark patches. A chilly breeze blew across the water lapping at the bank. Ruthann covered Drew's legs with an extra quilt, tucking it firmly around what she knew could turn into a torturous mass of nearly unbearable agony at the least provocation. Then she stretched out close to him. "It's as if we shut out the world for a while," she murmured against his shoulder.

"You're my world."

"In a way, I wish Dr. Rath had been less blunt about the pain."

"He said it can be managed. Besides, I've lived with pain for a long time."

"I'll try not to be a coward next week."

"You'll be all right."

"I'll make you think so anyway."

He stroked her hair. "But I'll know the truth."

\*\*\*\*

When she arrived at the hospital on the day of the surgery, Dr. Rath met her in the hall outside Drew's room. "He's going to be fine," he said.

"I want to believe you, but I feel so cold inside. It's almost like a premonition or something. Not that I believe in them, you understand, but I woke up terrified this morning. I couldn't stand to lose him."

The doctor rested his hand on her shoulder. "Of course you're afraid. You love your husband."

"We've only had two weeks, you know. I wouldn't let him put off the wedding until everything was over, because I wanted to be with him."

"And that's going to make the difference."

"How?"

"He's going to lose part of himself, but he'll have you."

Ruthann fought back the tears she'd sworn not to cry. "He's such a good, good man," she whispered.

"The two of you are going to have a good life. Trust me on that."

Drew recognized the fear in her eyes as she approached the bed. "Whatever happens, Ruthann, I wouldn't have missed loving you." He grasped her hands tightly. "We've had two perfect weeks."

"Dr. Rath says we're going to have a lot more."

"I'm counting on that."

She leaned over to meet his lips. "Gwen and my parents are down the hall."

"We had a good talk last night. I didn't realize how strong she is."

"You gave her all the best of yourself."

"Do you know what day this is?"

She shook her head.

"It's the second of September. The war officially ended one year ago today. I don't know why I thought of it, but maybe it means something."

"I'll figure it out while I wait." She looked up as a nurse came in. "Is it time already?"

"Almost." The woman took a syringe from the covered tray she carried. "Five minutes after I shoot you up with this, you won't care if Patton's Third Army marches over you."

The doctor allowed Ruthann to accompany the gurney as far as the doors of the operating room. Drew, already drowsy from the medication, opened his eyes with difficulty. "Precious girl," he murmured thickly.

"I'm right here," Ruthann whispered in his ear. "I'll be right here when you come back. I'll be here forever." She pressed her lips against his forehead. "I love you so much." He smiled and closed his eyes again. Their twined fingers slipped apart as an orderly rolled him through the double doors.

For a moment, Ruthann stood motionless, still feeling Drew's hand in hers, and breathed in the antiseptic smell of the hospital. What they'd known all along was inevitable, what had nibbled at the fringes of her happiness these past two weeks, had become reality.

*The war ended a year ago today.* She reflected on his words as she moved down the empty corridor to where Gwen and her parents waited to get through the hours with her. The war was over, all right, but there were still battles to be fought. Drew's greatest one had only begun.

She turned the wide gold wedding band on her finger. *But it's mine, too, isn't it? My battle, as well as his, and we'll fight it together.* She lifted her chin and lengthened her stride. *And we'll win. We'll win.*

Epilogue

Tomás Cabrera eventually formed his own successful law firm, which employed young men and women of various ethnicities. He and Gwen had two sons and two daughters, all of whom followed in their father's professional footsteps. They were married happily for fifty-five years.

Luís Cabrera continued with the Camden School District until he retired and moved to Austin to be near his grandchildren.

Rena Gilbert married Robert Kelley, the new assistant principal John Clifton had lobbied for. Both continued in the field of education. Their daughter earned her Ph.D. in history and became a college professor.

John and Kay Clifton remained in Camden after he retired. Their son Daniel went on to an outstanding coaching career in several large Texas high schools.

When Drew Mallory retired after thirty years as superintendent of the Camden Schools, he and Ruthann made their long-awaited trip to the Lake District of England. The sketches and watercolors he completed there were exhibited in the new Camden Art Gallery (formerly the Fulton house). Some were auctioned off for charitable causes. He and Ruthann were blessed with thirty-one years together.

Peter Andrew Mallory, born three years after his

parents' marriage, became a physical therapist, married, and had five children.

Nathan Wolfe's whereabouts were never discovered, nor was anything heard of Julia Schaeffer until she was identified as the victim of a one-car accident in Oklahoma some twenty years after she disappeared from Camden.

The story of the haunted school bell tower endures, but few people remember what happened there in May of 1946.

**A word about the author...**

Judy is a retired teacher who has written stories and poems since she could hold a pencil. Grandparents and older friends instilled a passionate interest in history and genealogical research from which she draws many of her characters and plot ideas.

Widowed for many years, she has two grown sons and five wonderful grandchildren. And, she is having her adolescent rebellion fifty-plus years late.

Thank you for purchasing
this publication of The Wild Rose Press, Inc.

If you enjoyed the story, we would appreciate your
letting others know by leaving a review.

For other wonderful stories,
please visit our on-line bookstore at
www.thewildrosepress.com.

For questions or more information
contact us at
info@thewildrosepress.com.

The Wild Rose Press, Inc.
www.thewildrosepress.com

Stay current with The Wild Rose Press, Inc.

Like us on Facebook

https://www.facebook.com/TheWildRosePress

And Follow us on Twitter
https://twitter.com/WildRosePress